Argentine

BY THE SAME AUTHOR

The Miller of Carnac
The Song of the Skylark

Antoine-Louis Duclaux,
Comte de L'Estoille
writing as "A. de L'Estoille"

Argentine
and Other Stories

translated, annotated and introduced by
Brian Stableford

A Black Coat Press Book

Acknowledgments: Thanks to Marie Duclaux de L'Estoille, Thierry Fraysse, Christine Luce and Jean-Marc Lofficier.

English adaptation and introduction Copyright © 2020 by Brian Stableford.
Cover illustration Copyright © 2020 Michel Borderie.

Visit our website at www.blackcoatpress.com

ISBN 978-1-64932-022-3. First Printing. December 2020. Published by Black Coat Press, an imprint of Hollywood Comics.com, LLC, P.O. Box 17270, Encino, CA 91416. Printed in the United States of America.

TABLE OF CONTENTS

Introduction

This is the third volume of a set of translations of the
works of Antoine-Louis Duclaux, Comte de L'Estoille (1835-
1894), works that were published in two distinct phases. In the
first sequence of his publications, which extended from 1864-
1869, he employed the pseudonym Louis de Lyvron, the sur-
name being borrowed from his maternal grandmother, and
work from that phase was sampled in the first volume of the
present set, *The Miller of Carnac and Other Works*.[1] In the
second phase, which extended from 1880 to his death, he employed the signature "A. de L'Estoille," Antoine de L'Estoille
being the name he employed in common usage. The second
volume of the present set is constituted by a translation of *La
Chanson de l'alouette* (Lemerre, 1880), his longest individual
work, as *The Song of the Skylark*.[2] This third volume is a collection of subsequent works from the second phase, originally
published in two volumes: *Les Amoureuses* (Ollendorff, 1883)
and *Contes du Nord* (Sauvaitre, 1892; tr. as *Tales of the
North*).

The work signed "A. de L'Estoille" recycled a good deal
of material originally published under the Louis de Lyvron
pseudonym, and although it was revised for republication,
some of the revised versions are sufficiently similar to the
originals to be omitted them from the present collection in
favor of the translations included in *The Miller of Carnac*. The
stories omitted from *Les Amoureuses* are "Lia" (a version of
the story earlier published in the 1867 *Poèmes en prose* as
"Rachel et Lia"; tr. as "Rachel and Lia") and "Hildewige" (a

---

[1] Black Coat Press, ISBN 978-1-64932-007-0.
[2] Black Coat Press, ISBN 978-1-64932-017-9.

version of the prose poem originally published in 1866 as *Les Runes d'Attila* and subsequently reprinted in *Contes du Nord* as "Attila, conte danois"; tr. as "Attila: a Danish Tale"). Three of the stories from *Les Amoureuses* that are translated in the present volume—"Balkis," "Hélène" and "Meyrin"—are also derived from material first published in works signed Louis de Lyvron, but they are sufficiently transfigured for the new versions to be considered as independent works.

Because of his continual revision of his materials, L'Estoille's bibliography is inordinately complicated, and its investigation is made more difficult because, in spite of the recycling, no one in the 1880s and 1890s appears to have noticed that his two signatures belonged to the same individual. It took some time for the cataloguers of the Bibliothèque Nationale to realize that fact, and to ascertain the author's real name. His works are still catalogued there under the heading "Louis de Lyvron," with a note registering the attribution as "erroneous." Although the identity is now firmly established, there does not appear to be any critical work previous to the introductions of these three collections of translations surveying and comparing the publications of the two phases and attempting to analyze and evaluate L'Estoille's work as a whole.

The introduction to the first volume of the present set includes a synoptic account of L'Estoille's early life and career, which is as complete as presently recoverable information permits, but it can be further compacted here. He was a native of Renaison, in the Monts de la Madeleine, where he also spent the latter part of his life, although he was an enthusiastic traveler and he revisited many regions that he had visited in his youth as a tourist or as a soldier, including Algeria, Syria, Italy and Scandinavia. He always remained an "Arvernian" at heart, and that sense of identity is very obvious in his work, even when its immediate subject-matter derives from his exploits in Algeria or his love of Scandinavian mythology.

L'Estoille attended the military academy of Saint-Cyr, then located in Yvelines, and then joined a cavalry regiment of the kind known as spahis, in which French officers supervised native recruits from North Africa; he spent his early adult life, during the late 1850s, involved in colonial adventures in the region south of Algiers, before his regiment was dispatched to Italy in December 1858 to fight, temporarily, in Napoléon III's campaign against the rival Austrian imperium. When he launched the first phase of his literary career, in 1862, he based most of the material that he published on his experiences in North Africa, and the remainder on his lifelong interest in the ancient history and legendry of his homeland, following a recent tide in the fashionability of interest in the ancient history of "Gaul" and its supposed folklore and legends, particularly legends associated with Bretagne.

It is necessary to say "supposed folklore" because much of the material published by folklorists and historians associated with the French Romantic Movement was greatly embroidered and often invented wholesale, thus producing material sometimes described nowadays as "fakelore." L'Estoille took license from several significant examples of that eccentric creativity and he became a prolific and highly imaginative "fakelorist." He was particularly inspired by Elias Lönnrot's attempt to synthesize a national epic, *Kalevala*, for his native Finland from folkloristic material collected in the 1820s and 1830s. In his longest work, *La Chanson de l'alouette*, L'Estoille attempted to do something similar for France, but with much greater imaginative license, and toward the end of his career he returned more directly to that particular source of his inspiration in the two *Contes du Nord* translated in the present volume.

Because the 1880 version of *La Chanson de l'alouette* is now reproduced on *gallica*, and has been made commercially available as a set of print-on-demand books, it is easily accessible, but the same cannot be said of the other works that Duclaux signed "A. de L'Estoille," which are phenomenally rare; *Contes du Nord* (1896) is not in the Bibliothèque Nationale at all, let alone on *gallica*. It appears that by the time of his reincarnation, "Louis de Lyvron" had been almost forgotten, his significance as a precursor of the Symbolist

Movement being noted only in a single article by Anatole France published in *Le Temps* in 1888, in which France remembered having met the dashing spahi in his the bookshop owned by his father, Noel Thibault, when he was young. That reference is slightly puzzling, the spahi having presumably identified himself to Thibault and his son by his pseudonym, either without mentioning his real name, or doing so in such a fashion that the son was unable to remember it a quarter of a century later. At any rate, France failed to observe that the author he knew as Louis de Lyvron was, in fact, still an active and fairly prolific contributor to the Symbolist Movement, and had been even before that name was popularized in 1883. None of the subsequent historians of the movement deigned to recognize A. de L'Estoille's contribution to it, or even his existence.

The near-absence of contemporary attention paid to the works of "A. de L'Estoille" partly reflects the fact that he was living and working a long way from Paris. He does not seem to have retained any of the literary associations that he had formed during his incarnation as Louis de Lyvron, which might have been slight even then. Although his publications as A. de L'Estoille were mostly issued in Paris, by reputable publishers, they seem to have remained relatively obscure, and most, if not all of them, were probably financed by the author. There was no clear distinction in the 1880s between what would later become known as "vanity publications" and the routine productions of commercial publishers, the latter routinely requiring "unknown" authors to pay for the publication of their works.

It may be significant that Alphonse Lemerre, the publisher of *La Chanson de l'alouette*, as well as several books signed Louis de Lyvron, was favored by *avant garde* writers, especially those associated with the Symbolist Movement, because he did not ask for cash up front when taking on commercially risky projects, but only required the author to promise to purchase a certain number of copies of the printed book. It is not improbable that he and other publishers employing the same stratagem only printed as many copies of some of their more esoteric publications as they had required the author to purchase. The unusual scarcity of many of "A. de L'Estoille's" publications might well result from the fact that they were only distributed privately, with no copies sent for review or marketed through bookshops. Whereas Parisian authors usually distributed their compulsorily-purchased copies to friends in the literary community—copies that, notoriously, routinely ended being hawked by the *bouquinistes* of the left bank of the Seine and thus circulated within the said community—most of L'Estoille's privately distributed copies presumably remained outside Paris.

The prefatory material of *Contes du Nord* reveals that only two hundred copies were printed, and the fact that no copy was sent to the Bibliothèque Nationale suggests strongly that the book was commissioned by the author, probably intended for private circulation, as was the case with a subsequent publication prepared after the author's death by his widow, the lavishly illustrated *Les Mois* (Lemerre, 1896). Several of the later books and pamphlets that are contained in the Bibliothèque Nationale, are even rarer, notably *Au Soleil* (1887), published in Lyon by A. Stock, who also issued an 1895 edition of *La Chanson de l'alouette*, which might be revised.

L'Estoille's status as a literary outsider was further ensured by the fact that within his favored genre, the "*poème en prose*," he plowed a lone furrow. Although his early publications appeared in Auguste Villiers de l'Isle-Adam's *Revue des lettres et des arts* in 1867, alongside the early prose poems of Stéphane Mallarmé and a reprint of *Gaspard de la Nuit* (1842)[3]—signed "Louis Bertrand," although the author had preferred to styled himself Aloysius—he was clearly hesitant with regard to the label, which Villiers played a key role in popularizing, and devised his own within the pages of the periodical, some of his works being gathered there under the

---

[3] Black Coat Press, ISBN 978-0-9740711-2-1.

heading *Fusains*, likening them metaphorically to charcoal sketches rather than poems. He accepted the label in his own collection of *Poèmes en prose* (1867), but the items it contains are mostly much longer than the exemplars previously provided by Bertrand, Charles Baudelaire and Mallarmé, bearing a much closer resemblance to works that rendered foreign poetry into prose in French translation, such as Louis Léouzon Le Duc's version of the *Kalevala*, various alleged translations of Breton legends, and the books of the Old Testament.

Les Amoureuses recycled numerous short prose poems (or *fusains*) originally published under the Louis de Lyvron pseudonym, but it is noticeable that the new versions often bear a closer resemblance to short stories, following a trend established in Baudelaire's works and continued by many of the writers working under his influence in the 1880s. The most substantial of the new works added to the collection are, however, framed as dramas, all apparently composed with possible stageability in mind.[4] The longest of them, "Gyptis," is a relatively orthodox tragedy set within the context of L'Estoille's pseudohistory of Gaul, whereas "Marthe" and "Rosalie" are both resentful responses to the French defeat in the Franco-Prussian War, as is the long prose poem "Alsa." As with *La Chanson de l'alouette*, whose first part appears to have been composed before July 1870, some of the early inclusions in *Les Amoureuses* probably antedate the Franco-Prussian War, but it is notable that their downbeat world-view is only intensified, and not actually transformed, by the intense bitterness consequent on the French defeat in that war manifested by items composed thereafter.

By the 1890s, when the original materials in *Contes du Nord* were presumably written, time had apparently soothed that bitterness to some extent, and "Argentine" is markedly

---

[4] The playwright Claude de L'Estoille or L'Estoile (1597-1652) might have been an ancestor; even if he was not, Antoine de L'Estoille would probably have been aware of the coincidence.

more upbeat in its conclusion, although that conclusion is hard-won. "Argentine" and "Lemmi Kainen" are both reflective of a burst of interest in Scandinavian mythology among French neo-Romantic writers, several of whom borrowed motifs from Hans Christian Andersen in the vague fashion of "Argentine." It is not impossible that L'Estoille's work had some influence on other writers who did that, especially Catulle Mendès, much of whose early work has appeared alongside Louis de Lyvron's in the *Revue des lettres et des arts*, although Jean Lorrain and Gaston Danville probably had more direct influences, and the writer whose fakeloristic tales resemble "Argentine" most closely, Maurice Magre—especially "La Fleur de Jeunesse" (1902; tr. a "The Flower of Youth")—is unlikely to have read his work, although he would surely have appreciated it if he had.

Such similarities do serve to illustrate the fact that L'Estoille's work was not so very far from the spirit of his time as his apparent isolation implies. His erotic prose poems are as "Decadent" in their stylistic affections and thematic obsessions as anything else produced in the *fin-de-siècle* period, and, as Anatole France observed, "Louis de Lyvron" was a Decadent Symbolist *avant la lettre*, a trifle ahead of his time and a little too extravagant in his stylistic experimentation to win widespread approval. As an eccentric representative of the literary *avant garde* he was always a colonial spahi, leading the charge from the front, perhaps too flamboyantly for his own good, but never quite convincing as the glad wielder of a bloody saber, always giving the impression that he was a pacifist at heart.[5] He was always a slightly paradoxical writer, but

---

[5] It is interesting to contrast L'Estoille's work with that of another soldier-poet more explicitly associated with the Decadent Movement, "Georges de Lys" (Georges Fontaine de Bonnerive, 1855-1931), whose work is often more aggressively bellicose—but Fontaine only enlisted in 1874, never served in the colonies, and spent his entire military service in

that is not a bad thing in a true Decadent artist, because an ironic paradoxicality lies at the very heart of the Decadent world-view. He was a maverick even within the motley maverick herd, but for connoisseurs of the unusual, that serves to make him even more interesting as a writer and as a man.

The translations from *Les Amoureuses* were made from the copy of the Ollendorff text reproduced on *gallica*. The translations from *Contes du nord* were made from a pdf of a scan of the Sauvaitre edition kindly supplied by Christine Luce, Thierry Fraysse and Jean-Marc Lofficier.

Brian Stableford

---

the interim between the major conflicts of 1870-71 and 1914-18)

LES AMOUREUSES

One morning I went past the tent of Ahmed, the lieutenant of spahis.

"Where are you going, *mon capitaine*?" he said to me.

"To shoot a few partridges in the esparto grass. The days are so long."

"Do as I do; tell the beads of your chaplet and the days will seem short to you."

His gandoura open, his feet bare, a morocco leather cushion under his elbow, the old soldier was sitting cross-legged on a thick caret, telling the amber beads of a long chaplet and smiling.

"Have a cup of coffee, *mon capitaine*; it will be too hot for hunting today; a viper might bite you and you'll get sunstroke."

We had been running the plain together for a long time; we were friends. I sat down beside him on the yellow and black carpet.

"I'm not a believer, Ahmed; I have no chaplet."

"I'm not a marabout, *capitaine*; I pray to saber cuts. If you knew it, you could tell my chaplet as well as me. You find the days long because there is nothing but our tents for as far as a horse can run. In the land of the sun, it's necessary to dream by day and live by night; the days are long for you because the nights have no stars."

"And yours?"

"Oh mine!" he said, passing his hand over his gray beard. "They're no longer anything but the blue jewel-case from which the rubies and the pearls have escaped; but the case had kept the sweet perfume of bracelets and warm necklaces; when it opens, I close my eyes and I think I can still see the rubies scintillating and the pearls strung out.

"I'm no longer anything but an old miser, the mere sight of my treasure is sufficient for me. But you're forever curious; as soon as the smoke of the incense rises, you search for the cassolette. So, when the angel of the sand brings you on his wing the perfume of the oasis, you say: 'The oasis is too far away!' and you close your eyes, in order not to hear the hours chiming in your empty tent.

"That's why you wake up anxious. That's why, like a jackal on a chain circling its stake, you circle the camp while the sun burns. The oasis is too far away, *mon capitaine*, so don't think about the oasis any more. Dream by night of the paradise of Allah and tell your beads in the shade by day."

"Give me yours."

"If the sultan said to me: 'In exchange for your chaplet I'll give you my harem.' I'd reply to the sultan: 'Your roses will fade; I'll keep my chaplet."

"I no longer understand."

"For thirty years I've had no other house than my tent, and I've never fastened its door—camel-drivers had picked me up from beside my dead mother and I've grown up all over the place, without a family or a homeland. I'm only a soldier and I've only possessed what I could take, but I've made some fine raids, *mon capitaine!* I've stripped brunette clusters of grapes, I've picked blonde peaches. Amour gilded the grapes and desire sugared the peaches; I wasn't a jealous gardener, I was a gluttonous hornet.

"When I saw my beard whitening I said to myself: "What you have done others will do if you buy a garden. You only love amour; buy a chaplet."

"I comprehend less and less."

"Never be a gardener, *mon capitaine*; like the others you would say: 'Today's roses no longer have any perfume.' To see heaven in those bright mirrors in which we love to gaze at ourselves, it is necessary that amour illuminates them; if it is duty or ennui, they are as dull as ashes.

"You can still climb over a garden hedge; peaches will be sugared for you and grapes still gilded; but autumn turns to winter—think about winter, *mon capitaine*. Since the garden is too far away today, begin to tell your chaplet, in order to know it when you can no longer climb over the flowery hedge."

"You're mocking me, Ahmed."

"Without you, my head would no longer be on my shoulders; listen and we'll be quits; what is the point of life when the heart is no longer anything but a desiccated leaf."

The spahi brought under his fingers the coral bead that closed his chaplet; then, making the amber beads slowly slide, he said while gazing at me: "Aïcha, Fatma, Aïchouna, Meyrin...do you understand? When I tell these beads, each of which has a name, I see again the days when I loved. How quickly the days pass! Every time the beads return to my fingers, I find one beauty more in those who were beautiful; on to the tears that have dried I let another tear fall; over the drops of blood that have blackened I shake my saber before wiping them, and if I feel a little soot on my lips when I kiss a bead I saddle my horse and the sun burns it.

"There is nothing true but amour; at your age is called desire, and at mine memory. Desire burns like gunpowder; memory intoxicates like the smoke of combat. Think about winter, *mon capitaine*, and before your hand trembles, pass over the golden thread the amber beads that, in days without sunlight, will warm your icy hands again. Don't let forgetfulness tarnish them. While they're still bright and warm, as amour has given them to you, put them on your chaplet.

"Today, you're alone; today, you're like the man gone astray in the desert, whose thirst shows him sapphire lakes under diamond cascades. Regard your dream, and of that unrealizable dream make the coral bead that will seal your chaplet, in order that, until you are dead, you can rediscover amour between your first desire and your last kiss."

I followed Ahmed's advice; while the sun burned my tent, I sculpted the pink bead of the caressed dream; then I gathered together the amber beads that amour had left me.

How far reality is from the dream! Next to the pink bead, how small the amber beads are!

Like the old spahi, I was only a soldier. I had had other houses than my tent, but the veils that parted before the proud cavalier in the red burnoose were crusaders before the infidel. How short it was, my chaplet!

To occupy a single evening, the same beads returned to my fingers ten times over; they were worn away very quickly. And the winter was imminent—the autumn nights were cool and they would soon be white with frost—and I wanted to be able, like Ahmed, to revive on sunless days the days of the past.

I said to myself then that if I put a cameo—a brilliant pebble or an old medallion—between each pair of amber beads, it would take the place of one and extend my chaplet.

If life had permitted it, I would have been a lover of old things, a collector of debris, a lover of trinkets. In traveling the world I have picked some up here and there, and accumulated my finds, pell-mell with my pipes and my clothes, in the pack-saddles of my mule.

My pack-saddles were too small for large items; all my riches, bound with braid detached from my sleeve and mingled with my amber beads, would not make a long chaplet...

Today, winter has come, its breath has folded up my tent, and since I left Ahmed under the distant palm trees, amour has given me no more amber beads.

By dint of passing my meager chaplet between my chilly fingers, the little beads had been worn away. There is nothing left now but a necklace of cameos, pebbles and medallions, which stop at a coral bead: the unfinished dream.

Tomorrow I am departing for an unknown country. I cannot even take with me what my pack-saddles once held; it is necessary to throw the cameos, pebbles and medallions I have picked up back into the dust where I found them. I can only conserve the coral bead—the unfinished dream.

In order to detach my dream, it would be necessary to break the thread, but if the beads were tiny, they were nevertheless amber, and the necklace has retained a vague perfume; it pains me to break it.

The coral bead comes from a profound bay in which no one fishes any longer; it is a strange color; one could mount it on a pin in order to fasten a shawl. The rest have no great value.

I am giving it to you. If a morsel pleases you, take it, and throw away the others.

RHODOPE

In the land of Egypt, on the bank of the Nile, there is a city as white as a swan called Naucratis. Our merchants go there to purchase flute-players and dancing girls.

The eyes of those flute-players are so long that their hair hide a third of them; the feet of the dancers are so small that their slippers are tailored in a lizard skin.

In the time of Darius, when Amasis was Pharaoh, the most beautiful of the dancers of Naucratis had, so sailors said, blue eyes spangled with gold; between themselves they called her Rhodope, her cheeks having the color of roses.[6]

The stairway of her house went down as far as the Nile, and iron rings were sealed into the last step, in order that boats could be moored there. A green silken tent glazed with silver shaded it.

Three dancers, their arms enlaced, were painted above the door. Their colors were so bright that they stood out from the wall by night and seemed to be floating on the silvery mist of the river.

All rich foreigners moored their boats to Rhodope's staircase at least once.

---

[6] The hetaera Rhodope (Rhodopis in the original) is mentioned in Herodotus as a fellow slave of Aesop, who was taken to Naucratis, presumably in the sixth century B.C., by one Xanthes, where she met and fell in love with the visiting merchant Charaxus, brother of the poet Sappho, who ransomed her and was ridiculed by his sister in consequence. The story was repeated and embroidered by other Classical authors and also featured in a satirical pamphlet by the Comtesse de Murat, one of the most significant writers of *contes de fées*, in 1694.

Rhodope danced before them by the light of the stars on the terrace sanded with mica. She allowed her amber shoulders and her delicate ivory-ringed ankles to be admired, but she fled as soon as desire extended a hand toward her.

Not one merchant had bought a kiss from Rhodope; she loved the handsome pilot Caraxos, the brother of Sappho the Lesbian.

Twice every year, when the wheat inclined and the chrysanthemums opened their golden eyes, Caraxos dropped anchor in the port of Naucratis.

He only brought Rhodope vermilion lips, but his lips were better received than a necklace of rubies.

In each voyage the pilot spent a week with his friend, and during that week, her door no longer opened to strangers. During that week, Rhodope danced every night, and in the moonlight, her bronze torso ached so graciously that the storks took flight in order to gaze at her. During that week, the swallows that nested in the windows of the yellow and black room fell silent in order to listen.

As soon as the wheat inclined and the chrysanthemums opened their golden eyes, Rhodope went up on to the terrace and searched in the crimson of the sunset for Caraxos' blue sail.

As soon as she perceived it, she descended to light the cassolettes and put jasmine flowers in her hair.

One evening, when she was waiting and she saw nothing on the Nile but fishing boats, she started to weep' Caraxos ought to have been in Naucratis a week ago. She wept, and as her tears prevented her from seeing, she sat down on her balustrade, her knee in her hand.

Then she thought that perhaps Caraxos had forgotten her next to a woman of Moetilis, and in a movement of anger, she kicked off her green slipper. An eagle that was hunting mistook it for a lizard, seized it and carried it away.

But it was only the skin of a lizard; the eagle opened its claws and the green slipper fell on the knees of Amasis, who was settling accounts with his farmers.

Pharaoh picked it up in his royal hand, and as he had never seen such a small slipper, he declared that he would marry the woman who could put it on.[7]

But the slipper had fallen from the sky; where could the dainty foot be found?

Amasis dreamed about that foot, and the next day, he summoned all the women of Naucratis to his palace.

Only Rhodope's foot was able to enter the green slipper.

The Pharaoh, inflamed by the dancer's beauty, declared that he would marry her that very evening, and she was taken to an immense hall, the ceiling of which was sustained by a hundred stone warriors ten cubits tall. A golden viper was placed around her head, incense was burned and, the people having knelt down, couriers were sent to tell the cities of Egypt that the Son of Ammon had a companion.

At sunset, the queen was taken to a chamber paneled with cedar-wood.

The window of that chamber overlooked the Nile; Rhodope leaned on it and began to weep. She said: "I shall no longer read in your eyes; I shall no longer kiss the curls on your head.

"When you furl your blue sail, you will no longer see my scarf fluttering. When you climb the steps, you will no longer

---

[7] This anecdote, originated by Strabo, is widely, but ludicrously, cited as the "origin" of the story of Cinderella. The motif was actually appropriated by Perrault from a story by the Comtesse de Murat's great rival Madame d'Aulnoy, but as Murat's pamphlet featuring Rhodope is unobtainable there is no way of judging whether d'Aulnoy might have borrowed it from Murat.

find me under the porch and my companions will say to you: She is the wife of Amasis, she no longer loves you."

While Rhodope was weeping, a boat glided over the Nile. The boat stopped under the window of the palace and a sad song rose up as far as the beautiful queen. The song said:

"Immortal Aphrodite of the scintillating throne, daughter of Jupiter savant in artifices, I implore you! Do not heap my soul with disgust and ennui, O Goddess!"

"It's him!" cried Rhodope, and in order to show that she had recognized him, she sang:

"O Goddess, come to me again today! Deliver me from my cruel troubles! All that my heart burns to see accomplished, accomplish, and be my ally yourself."

A cry of joy rose from the river.

Pharaoh came into the hall paneled with cedar-wood. He said: "Your voice, my queen, is too vibrant for such an insipid song."

"That insipid song," replied Rhodope, smiling, "reminds me of the past; that is why, son of the sun. I repeated it this evening, when I am commencing a new life; it was made for me by Sappho the Lesbian. I was a dancer then...

"O my royal husband, permit me to dance once again by the light of the stars."

Amasis consented, and went up to the terrace of the palace with Rhodope.

The boat from Lesbos, with its blue sail, was floating like a lotus on the scintillating river.

"O Goddess," sang Rhodope, in a clear voice, "What my heart desires, accomplish! Amour is burning my veins! I am as green as the grass, and like the turtle-dove that falls with open wings, I am falling arms extended on the steps of your altar."

She tears the golden viper from her forehead, unties her hair, lets her tunic slide, and spins slowly, gazing at the sky...

...For a long time, a very long time, she dances. Her eyes moist, her breast breathless, she stops; the Pharaoh, intoxicated by amour, opens his arms; she puts her two hands to her lips and hurls herself into the Nile.

GYPTIS

I. THE GOLDEN CUP[8]

An immense gallery sustained by wooden pillars, over-looking the bay of Massalia. One climbs up to it by three steps.

In the middle, a long table charged with golden vessels, pitchers and fruits. To their left, the door to the royal hall, closed by a double curtain of leather, lifted by two Gauls with naked swords in hand. To the right, two smaller doors, also closed by leather curtains; the one at the back leads to the kitchens, the other to Gyptis' apartments. On the walls, panoplies and hunting trophies.

Chiefs traverse the gallery and enter the royal hall. Maidservants come and go, supervised by Darthula. A slave, a prisoner of war, is leaning on a column.

---

[8] The legend of the cup of Gyptis relates to the founding of the Greek colony of Massalia, which subsequently became Marseille, by a sailor named in various sources, as Protis or Euxenes. He was invited to a banquet held by the chief of a local Ligurian tribe for suitors seeking the hand of his daughter Gyptis. She presented a symbolic cup to Protis/Euxenes to indicate her choice, and the couple founded the colony, which subsequently had to repel an attack by the natives. L'Estoille, unsurprisingly, adapts the legend to his idiosyncratic "history" of Gaul. A woodcut print of "Gyptis presenting the Goblet to Euxenes," credited to Alphonse de Neuville, which L'Estoille surely saw, was popular in the early 1880s and is still available.

Glentinat, Siffada, maidservants, Malthos, Cathmor, Darthula, and then young women of the clan of Nann.

GLENTINAT, *considering the table.*
Gyptis smiled at me yesterday.

(*He counts on his fingers.*)

MALTHOS, *aside.*
My daughter will be sixteen years old tomorrow; but she is the daughter of a vanquished man; no table has been set up in Malthos' house, and while Gyptis will choose a husband, the daughter of the vanquished man will go hungry.

(*Cathmor enters, stops under the first pillars and passes his hand over his forehead.*)

CATHMOR
I've sung at the wedding of her grandfather, I've sung at the wedding of her father; I shall weep at hers.

SIFFADA, *clapping Glentinat on the shoulder.*
The vessel is very heavy, the girl is very pretty, but all this is not for you.

(*He heads toward the royal hall.*)

GLENTINAT
Let's wager that it is.

SIFFADA, *turning round.*
My necklace against your horse?

GLENTINAT
Done.

(They go into the hall; the Gauls let the curtain falls back and remain immobile, leaning on their swords.)

CATHMOR
People have paid for my verses what they were worth; I have silver ewers and golden shields; let them leave me Gyptis and I will give them everything.

(He steers slowly toward the royal hall, then stops and goes to sit down at the end of the table.)

DARTHULA, *to Malthos*
It's not worth the trouble of watching flies swarm. (*As he goes away.*) All the cowards are idle.

MALTHOS
Gyptis has always had soft words for the slave; may God give her a husband who will not be vanquished.

CATHMOR
In days of joy, as in days of proof, a bard's place is beside his chief, but today, my heart will speak more loudly than my lips.

(A maidservant arrives, running.)

THE MAIDSERVANT
Here they come! Here they come! They all have branches of box in their hands. Come quickly!

(All the maidservants gather at the entrance to the gallery.)

DARTHULA
She will have a beautiful wedding, my daughter, a wedding about which people will talk for a long time.

(*She goes into Gyptis' room.*)

CATHMOR

Tomorrow, in the evening, she will no longer let her forehead fall on to my shoulder in the middle of a poem. Tomorrow she will no longer say, while raising her heavy eyelid: "Why are you stopping, Cathmor? I closed my eyes in order to hear better." Gyptis, Gyptis, will the husband to whom you will listen tomorrow, beside another hearth, love you as much as you love your old bard?

THE MAIDSERVANTS, *clapping their hands.*
Here they are! Here they are!

CATHMOR

King Nann, you have often repented of not having listened to the companion of your youth; you will mourn the cheerful sparrow whom you are pushing into the hunter's trap. (*To Malthos.*) Why aren't you going with the others?

MALTHOS

They ought to be weeping instead of laughing; tomorrow she'll be taken from us.

CATHMOR

What is he saying? The vanquished has nothing but his shame. Shut up. (*Aside.*) I only have smiles for her, and she has them for everyone. (*Letting himself fall on to the bench.*) Bard, you're nothing but an old blind dog to whom a bone is thrown out of pity.

THE YOUNG WOMEN, *who cannot be seen as yet.*
Betrothal! Betrothal!

CATHMOR

I have sung to her what the men of old were; where is the fiancé who resembles them? Their eyes shine, their teeth

29

gleam and woman is only a skylark, have you forgotten that, bard?

(*The troop of young women enters from the rear, to the left, and stops. A maidservant is detached from the group and addresses a young woman who is in front of the others.*)

THE MAIDSERVANT
In the almond tree in your grounds a turtle-dove is singing; have you come to listen to it?

THE YOUNG WOMAN
In the apple tree of our field a hawk is building his nest, and it's to give her to him that we've come to seek your turtle-dove.

THE MAIDSERVANT
It's not for a hawk but for a handsome wood pigeon that our turtle-dove is singing. Go on your way, beauties.

THE YOUNG WOMEN
No, no, we're coming in. Betrothal! Betrothal!

(*The maidservants, laughing, go to bar their path.*)

CATHMOR
I believed that the old willow was no longer anything but bark.

(*He hides his head in his hands. Gyptis appears on the threshold of her room with Katheline; she is holding a mirror.*)

The Same. Gyptis, Katheline.
Then young men of the clan and a chief.

KATHELINE
They won't be the stronger.

GYPTIS
What if I helped them?

KATHELINE
Would you like to shut up? (*Indicating Cathmor.*) Look
at Cathmor; he's searching for the verses of your nuptial song.

GYPTIS, *heading slowly toward him.*
I don't think so.

THE MAIDSERVANTS, *who have repelled the young
woman.*
Victory! Victory!

KATHELINE, *running to them and picking up a branch
of box.*
To the wolf! To the wolf!

(*She pursues the young women; the maidservants follow
her.*)

GYPTIS, *going past Malthos.*
Malthos, cry "Betrothal, betrothal!" like the others. For
my sixteenth birthday I've requested your liberty.

MALTHOS
Free! I've become a man again, Let me embrace you,
Gyptis, my daughter will also be sixteen tomorrow.

(*Cathmor gets up abruptly.*)

GYPTIS, *offering Malthos her forehead.*

Ask anything from me that you wish, and may the future enable you to forget the past. (*To Cathmor.*) You're only jealous. (*To Malthos.*) Adieu, don't forget Gyptis. (*To Cathmor.*) What are you doing there all alone. Look how beautiful I am.

CATHMOR
You're too beautiful.

GYPTIS, *indicating the royal hall, in which laughter can be heard.*

I've done my best to see that they don't tell such terrible lies. (*She sits down next to Cathmor and takes his hand.*) Why are you sad?

CATHMOR
Because I love you too much.

GYPTIS
When someone says "I love you too much," it's as if they were saying: "I no longer love you." (*Putting her hand over his mouth.*) Shut up, I don't love you too much, I simply love you. Sit down while I scold you.

(*She speaks to him in a whisper.*)

(*The maidservants, preceded by Katheline, re-enter from the left; a troop of young men appears to the right.*)

THE YOUNG MEN
Betrothal! Betrothal

KATHELINE
A hawk wants, we're told, to carry away our turtle-dove; you're bold hunters, pick up your bows and arrows.

(*A chief enters.*)

THE CHIEF
The hawk will take her.

THE MAIDSERVANTS
No! No!

KATHELINE
She is no longer in the almond tree; we have hidden her.

THE CHIEF
The hawk has good eyes.

A YOUNG MAN
In order not to blacken her wing, have you hidden her under the lid of the bread-bin?

GYPTIS, *standing up*
Isn't the bin the first place the suitor looks?

THE CHIEF
When the bride is ugly. (*Throwing a bearskin down at Gyptis' feet.*) I arrived last because I didn't want to arrive with empty hands. I rode my white horse, the best of my six horses.

GYPTIS
You aren't the last. You could have ridden your gray horse.

THE CHIEF
I've trained it to walk slowly, as a queen's horse ought to walk. (*Pointing at the fur.*) In order not to stain the fur, I choked the beast with my arms.

CATHMOR
It has very thick fur, and we're scarcely entering autumn.

THE CHIEF, *pretending not to have heard.*
I'll have the claws gilded.

GYPTIS
You've done better than all the others; go tell them that.

(*The Chief goes in, a hurrah greets him.*)

GYPTIS, *to Cathmor, pushing the fur away with her foot.*
You aren't proud to see so many suitors for your daughter? (*Cathmor shakes his head.*) Have you se Oedh?

CATHMOR
No.

GYPTIS
Another jealous wretch.

CATHMOR
Why would he be jealous, since you love him?

GYPTIS
You're very jealous! (*To the maidservants.*) Would you like to come, idlers! (*To Cathmor.*) I love you more than you think. (*To the maidservants.*) Why isn't that plate shining? (*Arranging a basket of fruits.*) Why have they hidden the best plums (*To Cathmor, laughing.*) Do you know that, you who know everything?

KATHELINE, *changing the place of a cup.*
It's necessary to put the two highest seats and the two largest cups to the left and right of the king.

GYPTIS, *tapping her on the cheek.*
Two might come, naughty!

KATHELINE
Let a chief and his squire come, and we won't be parted, Mistress.

GYPTIS, *to Cathmor, handing him the mirror.*
What do you see in there?

CATHMOR
An old man who is chagrined.

GYPTIS, *drawing him to the front of the stage.*
No, a jealous one. It's a mirror. To celebrate my sixteen years, my father gave it to me this morning. Why are you chagrined? Think about what I've said to you. (To maidservants bringing pitchers.) Take that away; one only drinks hydromel at betrothal feasts. Isn't that so, Cathmor?

CATHMOR
I no longer know what people drink today; once, it was with blood that they drank to fiancés.

GYPTIS, *laughing*
The men of today aren't worth as much as those of old, but the daughters haven't changed. (*She makes a tour of the table.*) What about the baskets of nuts? Darthula! Darthula!

CATHMOR, *sadly*
There's no need for nuts.

GYPTIS
One can't send suitors away with empty hands; they have a right to a wife or a nut. In your time it was said, it seems to me, that the wise ones took the nuts!

CATHMOR, *pointing to the royal hall*
The one you want to love isn't there, then?

GYPTIS

Oh, no... I've done what I could; I've listened to their genealogies, the story of their hunts and their combats. I've looked at them with all my eyes; I don't like them, and I'm sure that I never will.

CATHMOR
Oedh isn't with King Nann, then?"

GYPTIS
Oedh is my brother, as you know very well. He would have liked me to love him differently, but I couldn't; However, he's handsome, brave and good.

CATHMOR, *running to her*.
So it's true: you want to remain with us? I would have taken in hatred the man who led you away.

GYPTIS
Don't say that. Don't say that, friend; for you see, I can't remain a girl forever. I want to have a house with a broad hearth, a house one can enter with the head held high, and which one can leave with peace in the heart and a smile on the lips; but for that it's necessary that I love my master. It's necessary that I love him like the women you sing about who die of love. It's necessary to love, Cathmor, the man who will take me away; I shall love him so much! You're weeping? You think that I'll no longer love you then? Don't worry; I'll love you more. Isn't amour the sun that causes to germinate in daughters the good grain that their fathers have sown there?

CATHMOR
He'll be very fortunate!

GYPTIS
Yes, if he loves me as I shall love him. Don't repeat that to anyone, though.

It's for you alone that I've spoken, you hear? I saw that you were so sad.

CATHMOR
Amour surprises, like lightning; it runs like flame through a field of furze.

GYPTIS
Perhaps.

A YOUNG WOMAN, *outside*
The bees have given us a golden honeycomb; with the dew we have mingled with it, the cup will be sweet to the lips.

A YOUNG MAN, *outside*
We've been thirsty for sixteen years!

GYPTIS, *laughing*
They're as thirsty as that! Darthula! Darthula!

(*Darthula enters, a necklace in her hand. Oedh appears on the threshold.*)

The Same. Oedh. Darthula.

DARTHULA
What do you want?

GYPTIS, *running to Oedh*
You've arrived last. (*Pointing at the bear-skin.*) The one who arrived before you brought me that. What will you give me?

OEDH
Nothing.

GYPTIS
Well, I'll be more generous. (*Holding out her cheek.*)
Brother, to celebrate my sixteen years.

OEDH, *recoiling.*
No.

GYPTIS
Why, is the wolf going to show his teeth?

DARTHULA, *to Oedh*
You're quarreling again?

GYPTIS
He's so nasty.

DARTHULA, *to Gyptis*
What did you want with me?

GYPTIS
You've forgotten the nuts.

DARTHULA
There are no more nuts in the house; the rats have eaten
them all.

GYPTIS
It's necessary to find some, nurse.

OEDH, *drawing nearer to Gyptis.*
Will there be enough for everyone?

GYPTIS
I told you that yesterday. You're like Cathmor; once you
get an idea into your head, it isn't easy to get it out... But I'm
not talking to you; we've fallen out.

OEDH, *taking her hand.*
Oh! No!

GYPTIS
If I had a little pride. (*To Darthula, who is trying to put the necklace on her.*) Take that away; they'd have too much chagrin.

DARTHULA
You don't want people to find you beautiful, then?

GYPTIS
I don't want that today.

(*Darthula moves away and is stopped by Cathmor, who speaks to her in a whisper.*)

OEDH
Since you don't love anyone else, why don't you want me to love you?

GYPTIS
We ought not to talk about that any longer.

OEDH
But I want to talk about it.

GYPTIS
A lover never says: "I want." You aren't a lover; embrace me, brother.

OEDH
I don't want to be your brother!

(*He leaves abruptly.*)

GYPTIS
He's disagreeable. (*Going to the threshold and calling out.*) Oedh! Oedh!

CATHMOR, *to Darthula*
He's violent, like his father, and if I had a daughter...

DARTHULA
You don't have a daughter. These bards put all their spirit into their songs. What you're doing isn't good, Cathmor; instead of reasoning with Gyptis you support her. The king is old; she needs someone to defend her.

CATHMOR
What about me?

DARTHULA
Do you expect to live for a hundred years?

CATHMOR
No, Darthula, I can feel my soul vacillating like the flame of a lamp; the wind of the imminent winter will extinguish it, but I can keep Gyptis to myself for a few more months; no one will be able to love her as much as I love her.

DARTHULA
Men only think of themselves.

CATHMOR
The veil of a bride stops with a thorn and the heart of a mother trembles incessantly, like the feather of a reed. She's only sixteen and I'm so old; she can easily wait for one more year.

(*Gyptis comes back with Oedh.*)

DARTHULA

It's your fault. Without you, without your sighs and all those sentences you never finish, those children would already love one another.

CATHMOR

You believe that they'll love one another?

(*Darthula leaves, shrugging her shoulders.*)

The Same, minus Darthula.

GYPTIS

Jealous wretch, you know full well that I don't love anyone as much as you.

CATHMOR, *sitting down and hiding his face in his hands.*

Children are ingrate.

OEDH

You loved me more than others yesterday, but tomorrow...?

GYPTIS

Tomorrow! Tomorrow! We're not yet at tomorrow. And what if, tomorrow, you no longer love me?

OEDH

Gyptis!

GYPTIS

As you believe you love me today.

OEDH

I don't know how to speak, I only know how to kill. I'm only an ax a little heavier than the others; but if you wanted, that ax would fell everything that you told it to fell. Why don't you want that?

GYPTIS
Because you're a very disagreeable handsome wolf. (*Holding out her hand to him.*) Who has never bitten this hand. Because I've loved you for too long. Because I've told you all my secrets. Because I've told you all my dreams. Because...because I want a brother, do you hear?

OEDH, *in a slow voice.*
One sometimes needs a brother.

GYPTIS
One always needs a brother, because one always needs a little help, a little consolation, a little forgiveness. One needs a brother when one wants to be loved in spite of everything, and always.

CATHMOR, *aside.*
Brothers are sometimes brutal.

OEDH
Why shouldn't she have a brother?

GYPTIS, *throwing her arms around him.*
I have one! (*The two Gauls lift the curtain. King Nann appears. Gyptis looks at him, smiling, over Oedh's shoulder, whom she then kisses on both cheeks, saying:*) They'll be desolate!

OEDH, *sadly*
Oh! No!

(*Gyptis runs away in the direction of the kitchens.*)

*Nann, Oedh, Cathmor, Chiefs. Then Gyptis, maidservants,
young men and women.*

NANN, *aside, on the threshold.*

Why don't they love one another? (*Aloud, advancing toward the table.*) We were waiting for you, Oedh; you're late,
my son. In your absence we've made a grave determination,
but you're a docile nephew and a devoted friend, you'll obey
the king and you'll do what your companions ask. Yesterday
the Segobriges had only one chief, today they have two; the
sword that they gave me sixty years ago has become too heavy
for my hand; today they'll give it to you. I'll be your adviser,
you'll be my equal. Do you want that?

OEDH
I do.

THE CHIEFS
Long life to Nann! Long may Oedh reign!
(*Gyptis enters carrying a large silver tray on her head.
Maidservants carrying resin torches follow her.*)

GYPTIS
Long may my brother the king reign.

(*She sets the tray down in front of Nann.*)

NANN, *to Gyptis*
Those whose life will be long need a beloved guide.

GYPTIS
The bee always goes to the flower that has honey.

(*She leaves.*)

NANN, *after a pause*
The seats are all equal; sit down, friends.

(The chiefs sit down, Oedh facing Nann. Cries are heard outside: "Long may Oedh reign! Battle! Battle!")

NANN
Do you hear, Oedh? Their fathers were bold soldiers and they're beginning to think that King Nann was a good old king. You can lead them over the Rhône, my son, and bring them back to me with fine scars on the forehead.

(The young men gather on the steps to the right, the young women to the left.)

NANN
Cathmor, my old companion, we're no longer anything but toothless boars, but we had tusks in our time. Tell the young men what we did when we were their age.

(Cathmor gets to his feet.)

A YOUNG WOMAN
In order to save her from the hawk, we wanted to hide our turtle-dove; she has flown away.

A YOUNG MAN
And the hawk has caught her!

CATHMOR
Amour doesn't take, it gives.

A CHIEF, *raising his cup*
To the man whom Gyptis chooses! When she's chosen, we'll forget our dream and her husband will be our friend.

(Euxenes and Philo appear between the two groups.)

A MAIDSERVANT
Enter, your place is empty.

The same, Philo, Euxenes

EUXENES
Greetings, master of the house!

NANN, *indicating the two empty seats.*
You were awaited.

(*Euxenes and Philo sit down. During the chorus, Euxenes converses with Nann; Philo listens.*)

A YOUNG MAN
Has the hawk caught her?

THE YOUNG WOMEN
Alas! Alas!

(*They run down the steps.*)

NANN, *to Euxenes, indicating the Gauls*
They're chiefs; their fathers were the companions of my youth. Speak without dread; their ears can keep a secret.

OEDH, *raising his cup*
And the cups that they hold out can be emptied; when intoxication goes to sleep there, amity wakes up. To our guests!

EUXENES
I am Euxenes, son of Thireus, my friend is Philo, son of Euxis. We come from far away; we are Greeks from Phocea. We are seeking to learn by visiting distant lands and we only have weapons in order to defend ourselves. My galley is anchored in the gulf over there. May the gods give long days to King Nann!

(The young women come back with torches; the young men follow them.)

A YOUNG WOMAN
The hawk has caught her! If she had been caressed by its wing, we would not be in so much pain.

A YOUNG MAN
I passed under the hawk's nest just now and I heard your white turtle-dove singing.

A YOUNG WOMAN
And we're forgotten!

THE YOUNG WOMEN
Alas! Alas!

(They extinguish their torches and flee.)

EUXENES
I have no goal, and no master. I stop where the beach is sure and where the guest is welcome.

NANN
My gulf is blue, and my table is long, while your galley is on the sand. I'll show you my land, and you can tell me about yours. It's said that our ancestors slept in the same cradle.

EUXENES, *pointing at Oedh*
Is that your son?

NANN
I don't have one any longer. What about you?

EUXENES
I'm only a bird of passage, I have no nest.

NANN
Our daughters are beautiful, they're valiant and they're gentle. Repose with us.

(*Gyptis enter the dark part of the hall, slowly.*)

EUXENES
There are too many handsome wood pigeons fluttering around your doves for them to look at a passing crow.

(*Nann darts a glance at the guests and shakes his head.*)

GYPTIS, *aside*
Amour surprises like a thunderbolt.

NANN, *to Philo*
What about you, would you like to stay with us?

PHILO
I'm only a wren, and the nest I shall build would be too small for two.

OEDH
The nest of a wren is softer than that of a crow. You raise your head as proudly as the brave bird you've taken for an emblem, and your gaze is as mild and frank. Would you like me for a friend?

PHILO, *cheerfully*
We're in the land of gold here, one gives without counting. (*Holding out his hand to Oedh.*) Let's be friends, Gaul.

GYPTIS, *aside*
Amour runs like a flame in a field of broom.

(She stops in the light. On seeing her, Euxenes rises to his feet. Immobile, Gyptis looks at him.)

PHILO
By Hercules, that's a beautiful child!

NANN
That's my daughter.

EUXENES
King, your daughter is very beautiful. (*Nann smiles. Oedh looks at Gyptis; she lowers her head and draws away slowly.*) She's more beautiful than the great goddess who dreams out there in the olive groves, as if the immortal artist who sculpted her charming body and animated her proud face had taken for a model the most beautiful women of Greece.

NANN
And the man who picks the vermilion apple will not find a worm at its heart. She'll be sixteen years old tomorrow and I hope that she will choose a husband today, among those at this table.

(Katheline traverses the gallery, speaking in a low voice to the maidservants.)

CATHMOR
King Nann, it is snowing on your head and you want to close your heart to the cheerful sunlight?

NANN
We're too old, Cathmor, still to be thinking of ourselves.

PHILO
It's true, then, that your daughters choose their husbands freely? (*Turning to Euxenes.*) It's not like that in our land, and

48

sometimes, a husband and wife have no reason to be pleased with that fashion of doing things.

NANN
He who sows ivy at the foot of an oak or clematis under an elm unites hands that seek one another.

(*The young men and the young women enter, holding hands, and fill the back of the stage, the young women to the left and the young men to the right.*)

The Same, minus Gyptis, Katheline

A YOUNG MAN, *separating from the group with a distaff changed with flax*
We've brought flax for the bride, which will make the solitary hours seem less long.

A YOUNG WOMAN, *separating from the group with a bunch of violets in her hand*
We've brought flowers for the bride, which will remind her of the sweet perfume of home during distant voyages

CATHMOR, *aside*
Amour surprises like a thunderbolt; I no longer have a daughter!

OEDH, *aside, looking at Euxenes*
He isn't even a Gaul.

(*Maidservants preceded by Katheline enter carrying a cradle.*)

KATHELINE
We've brought, to put in the corner of the hearth, a soft nest in which to hide tears and smiles, oaths and regrets, life and the dream.

PHILO, *lifting his cup*
Évohé!

(*The maidservants withdraw to the right at the front of the stage. The young man and the young woman deposit the distaff and the bouquet in the cradle.*)

NANN, *aside*
The guests have been sent by God.

OEDH, *standing up*
It's necessary, however, that Gyptis knows that the man she has chosen has red blood.

(*Everyone stands up.*)

EUXENES
Do you want us to show her ours? King Nann will say when the swords ought to return to their scabbards. In our homeland, we shake hands before the contest and embrace afterwards. Do you want to?

(*He holds out his hand to Oedh, who pretends not to see it.*)

NANN
We did that in the days of my youth, to honor guests, but we crossed swords without hatred and we returned them to the scabbard without chagrin. King Oedh, you are the bright shield in which men ought to mirror themselves; show that your heart is as large as your blood is red.

(*Oedh takes Euxenes's hand. The two men draw their swords. Cathmor gets up.*)

CATHMOR
Sing of the blue blade that loves flesh! Sing of the blue blade!

(*The two men cross swords.*)

NANN, *severely*
That isn't a wedding song, bard.

CATHMOR, after a momentary pause
The rosy lip of the bride is sweet, but a hundred times sweeter is the red lip of the sword; its kiss causes the kiss refused by the woman one loves to be forgotten.

(*Oedh is slightly wounded in the breast. Euxenes lowers his sword. Gyptis, followed by Darthula, carrying a wheatcake and a basket of apples, stops in front of the maidservants.*)

A CHIEF
Oedh, you're wounded, give me your place.

OEDH
My revenge!

NANN
Embrace, friends; it only requires one drop of blood on a bride's veil.

(*Oedh shakes his head.*)

EUXENES, *to Nann*
Our blood is red too; I would like your daughter to know that.

(*Gyptis steps between the two men and parts them gently with her hand.*)

The Same. Gyptis

GYPTIS, *to Oedh*
Before my hearth you have told a coral necklace; thank you, brother. Through those vermilion pearls a thread will pass that time will not wear away, and I shall put them around my daughter's neck in order that she be beautiful, and around my son's neck in order that he be strong.

OEDH, *dropping his sword*
One sometimes has need of a brother.

CATHMOR, *aside*
Where are the men of old? (*Gyptis picks up the sword, kisses the blade and holds it out to Oedh.*) I was the first to have armed the king. (Oedh takes the sword and returns to his seat. Nann makes a sign to Euxenes to sit down.

GYPTIS, *to the Gauls*
At the table that I have set there are no empty places; thank you all. (*To the Greeks.*) The Almighty has sent us the awaited guests; may his name be blessed!

(*She goes to lean on Nann's shoulder.*)

THE CHIEFS, *all getting up, cups in hand*
To Gyptis.

NANN, *handing Gyptis a golden cup placed in the middle of the table*
Respond to them, my daughter.

GYPTIS
May your sky always be blue, your swords always be sharp, your hearth always be loved, and your names be added to the great names of the past!

PHILO, *lifting his cup*
Évohé

GYPTIS, *circling the table*
But why are you getting up so quickly? If you don't want to offend me, sit down again, friends. But the plates are empty! Excuse me, I have nothing else but the apples of my garden and his cake that I have kneaded. If the apples are pale it's because they have ripened in the shade. If he cake is bitter it's because, while kneading it, involuntarily, I've wept over it. But today I've had the wall that hid the apple tree from the sun knocked down, and next year's apples will be red and perfumed. Today I have turned my head away from the hearth I loved and, seeing the path bordered by wheat and vervain that leads where I want to go, my eyes have dried up and tomorrow's cake will be sweet to the lips.

(*She kneels down in front of Nann. The maidservants take two steps forward.*)

KATHELINE, *emerging from the group of maidservants*
But like the swallow, mistress, you will guide the joyful brood to the old nest every spring.

THE MAIDSERVANTS
We love you so much.

GYPTIS
Break the cake, father, empty the basket, and may the Almighty give to the daughter that you love sons who will love you.

NANN, *getting up again*
May they render you the happiness that you have given me. (*Clasping her to his heart with one hand and lifting the cup with the other.*) I saw her father die with a smile on his

lips and his breast open; good blood never lies. To the beloved of Gyptis!

EUXENES, *raising his cup*
To the land of oaks! To the land that is envied. To the pleasant land of the Gauls, where the men are strong and the women are beautiful!

(*The young men draw their swords; one of them separates from the group.*)

THE YOUNG MAN
We are the men of your sons, Gyptis, their armor and their shields!

THE YOUNG MEN
We love you so much!

GYPTIS, *to Oedh*
Brother, you are like the ash tree that rises straight into the sky in front of the door of the house, but I am only a clematis, which has need of support; what will you be to the green poplar on which I lean? After my beloved father, you are the chief; brother, do you want me to follow the husband I have chosen?

OEDH
Listen to the voice of your heart. Gyptis is as beautiful as the dawning day, as pure as the spring that emerges from a rock; it is an eglantine that I give you. But in the land that I must defend I want the flowers to open joyfully; if a storm menaces them, my shield will extend over them; if a bramble wounds them, my sword will cut that bramble. Go, Gyptis, into the house you have chosen; your brother will love you, the king will defend you.

THE CHIEFS
We all love her! We will all defend her!

(*The young women advance; one of them separates from the group.*)

THE YOUNG WOMAN
For a year, two years, sixteen years, we have kept you, roe deer, in a small enclosure, behind a thick hedge. In the embalmed meadow, on the mossy rocks, under the florid thickets, toward the sunlit beach, escape, roe deer, the barrier is open.

ALL THE CHORUSES
We love you so much!

GYPTIS, *taking the cup*
For all your good wishes, friends, thank you. Excuse me, the pitchers are empty and I no longer have anything but this cup of beer that I brewed while my heart sang. (*Lifting it to her lips.*) I drink to you all, my friends. May your crops ripen! May the grain be gilded, may the farm be white with it! But the cup is too small to slake everyone's thirst. (*Holding it out to Euxenes.*) Would you like Mater, to empty it with me?

NANN
The guest is the envoy of God.

II. MASSALIA

To the right, a rocky coast. To the left, houses of wood and dry stones. In the background, a sandy beach, and then the sea. Euxenes and Gyptis are heading toward the right, following a path that snakes between the rocks. The stars are still shining.

Euxenes. Gyptis.

EUXENES

Anyone who crossed our path would not say: "Those are two spouses." He would say: "They are two lovers, whom the dawn has taken by surprise."

GYPTIS

And he would be speaking truly; am I not your lover, my Master? When I hold out my lips to you, I tremble as I trembled when I held out the golden cup to you. I'm always afraid that your eyes will turn away from mine; I'm always afraid that you won't find the cup bright enough, the liquor sweet enough.

EUXENES

Every day, my Gyptis, I love you more.

GYPTIS

You're imagining it; there are no degrees in amour; one loves or one doesn't love. I don't love you a little or a lot; I love you.

EUXENES

I believed that I would only find intoxication in the cup that you held out to me; I have also found strength there. Where I only dreamed of amour, I have also found amity.

56

GYPTIS

Amour, nothing but amour. I only ask what I have given; I don't want amity, I only want amour.

EUXENES

Amour has a bandage over the eyes; it needs a guide, while amity marches with a sure step, lamp in hand.

GYPTIS

Amour binds like a bramble; I don't march, you drag me. (*Throwing her arms around him.*) But a bramble has thorns and I have only picked flowers. You have treated me like a spoiled child and rendered me naughty; I'm jealous. I shall always want you all to myself.

EUXENES

Even Aphrodite would be jealous of these tresses; their perfume intoxicates like wine of Chio. I am entirely yours.

GYPTIS

A man ought not to think uniquely of amour. When he argues in the council, when he fights, when he entertains a friend, it's necessary to forget momentarily, and his wife ought to say then, while spinning her wool: "He has not taken me in order to have a chain on his foot, but to have a brilliant necklace around his neck." I would not say what the valiant woman says; I would weep.

EUXENES

Is it Gyptis I am hearing? The Gyptis that newcomers call Minerva, the proud and jealous Gaul who speaks like a sage and makes those obey who have been exiled for not obeying anyone?

GYPTIS

I'm not sage and I'm not calm; I'm jealous.

EUXENES, *putting his arm around her waist*
Of whom?

GYPTIS, *leaning back in his arms*
I don't know... How blue those waves are! How gently
they lull us! You see, I hear other wives sighing: "Oh, when I
was a girl!" When I was a girl, people only had tender words
for me, my caprices were laws to which everyone submitted.
(*She disengages herself from Exusenes' arms.*) When I was no
taller than that, the chief before whom all Gaul had trembled,
trembled if I stamped my foot. When I stammered *more*, the
boards made poems for me. I was beloved and I was queen;
however, it seems to me that I had not begun to live until the
day when you carried me away. For all the others, the bramble
had thorns; for me it only had flowers; that's why I tremble as
soon as you quit me.

EUXENES
But I'm not quitting you. I've come, as I did yesterday,
to see whether I can perceive Philo's galley, and then I'll go to
spend a few hours with King Nann.

GYPTIS
Why did Philo leave the day after our marriage? Why, as
he left, did he say to me: "It's necessary for me to go to
Phocea to tell the story of the Gaulish woman with the golden
cup." You never speak to me like a husband, but like an ex-
cessively feeble father, so I now have all the faults, and I'm
curious.

EUXENES, *embarrassed*
My men wanted to go to fetch their wives, and I feared
that they might not say exactly how things had happened.
Sailors... you know...

\

GYPTIS, *putting a hand over his mouth*

Don't tell me anything; you're the chief and I'm only a child, There are so many things that I don't understand. The breeze is warm; come under the rock...the one that leans over...do you remember?

EUXENES, *taking her hand*
Come... (*They take a few steps.*)

GYPTIS

It's from here that I showed you the gulf...do you remember? How softly the sea sang! We'll see Philo's ship from a distance.

EUXENES, *stopping, aside*
A sail! (*Aloud.*) The stars are already paling.

GYPTIS

Do you think so? I only want to be a necklace around your neck, and a necklace of which you never feel the weight. Pardon, Master, a wife ought to be able to divine. I'll decorate the house for the beloveds of your companions.

EUXENES

There'll be noisy recognitions, reproaches, perhaps quarrels. What if you were to come with me to see King Nann.

GYPTIS

No...I'm saying that word very quietly, so that you don't hear it.

EUXENES
He'd be so glad!

GYPTIS, *throwing her arms around him*

A kiss; the sun's rising. You've habituated me to that kiss; that's why I sing every morning like a skylark. (*Putting *her hands on his shoulders*.) You keep all your promises; that's why I love you so much. I loved you before having heard you speak; if you'd been a liar I would have loved you anyway, but I'd have had a great deal of chagrin. Promise me then you'll never lie... I don't know how to tell you...

EUXENES
It's promised.

GYPTIS
It's promised? I'll never be a chain for your foot; on the day when I impede your march, you must kill me... (*Disengaging herself abruptly*.) Scold your servant, Master; the sun is shining and she isn't yet at work.

(*She blows him a kiss and runs away*.)

EUXENES, *watching her draw away*
She has the eyes of a woman and the deportment of a goddess. She's neither one of those cold matrons that we marry back home, nor one of those madcaps that we loved... I was wrong to send Philo to tell the story of the cup; women are so whimsical. Leda would perhaps have been capable of coming to demand a right that she scarcely cared about when it was hers... In life, a man has only one debt to pay, and I've paid mine... If I were to lose Gyptis I'd be truly chagrined. The men promised not to talk about Leda, but will all the women who are going to disembark hold their tongues? It's better for me to tell King Nann everything; if the need arises, he can reason with Gyptis. Perhaps it isn't Philo's galley...

(*He draws away to the right. Oedh emerges from behind a rock*.)

OEDH
What if I killed him! (*He is walking head bowed; Euxenes does not see him*.) In killing him, I would kill her.

60

(*He hides behind the rocks.*)

EUXENES

It's definitely Philo's galley. He's going to tell me: "Your wife is enchanted by your new marriage, in which, between us, she doesn't believe, and she's going to marry your friend Xantippe..."[9] I say Xantippe as I'd say Lysippus or any other name. It doesn't matter to me... I'm anxious in spite of myself; women are so odd. The wise course is to be ready for anything, not to try to divine the future, not to despair, and to wait—and fate will sort everything out in the end. When I quit Phocea, as a husband ruined by a shrewish and stupid wife, with a few companions as badly off as myself, I didn't say to myself: "Let's go here, or there," I let the waves lull me and the wind push me, and before the prow of my ship I found the most beautiful of gulfs and the daughter of a king for the taking. If, impossibly, Philo brought me Leda, we'd see about getting rid of her. It wasn't my fault; I insisted that Philo tell the story of the cup, because it was necessary to avenge myself a little on those who laughed at me when I left. But if Philo hadn't said anything, would those accompanying him have kept the secret? It isn't probable. By going to talk to Nann before Philo disembarks, I'll ward off all malevolent explanations, and if my first wife arrives, I'll tell her to do as I've done. That will be easy enough; she's beautiful. She's perhaps more conventionally beautiful than Gyptis, and if she didn't have such a bad character... (*He glances briefly at the sea, and smiles.*) Crossings make wines that are too acidic milder; perhaps they have the same effect on women? Even in Gaul, kings have privileges, and am I not one here? We'll see.... Old Nann has a slightly weak head; perhaps it will be possible to sort this out.

---

[9] It is unusual to find Xantippe being employed as the name of a man, because it had become legendary as the name of Socrates allegedly-shrewish wife.

(*He draws away slowly. Oedh appears.*)

OEDH
I'm like a prowling wolf hiding from the shepherd; I'm not a man. (*He lets himself fall on to a stone.*) My chagrin is crushing me; I don't know how to say what I feel. (*He strikes his breast.*) If I had been able to show Gyptis what there is in here, she might have loved me. But I didn't know what to say, and it's finished; she's one of those who only love once, and she'll never love me, down here or up above. I'm only a wolf; she said so. I only know how to bite. (*Getting up, he extends his hand in the direction in which Euxenes has gone.*) That's why I haven't killed him. (*Perceiving Philo's galley, which is nearing the shore.*) Here come more of them. What have they done at home in order to go so far away?

(*Groups of Gauls enter.*)

Oedh. Philo. Sailors. Gauls. Arachne. Laïs.

PHILO, *on the prow of his galley*
I'm a week late, and there isn't even a watcher; I'm not awaited with impatience, but they don't know, I suppose, who I'm bringing. (*To the pilot.*) Don't engage the galley too far in the sand and don't dismantle the rudder; it might be necessary to take to sea again.

OEDH
But it's Philo, the only one of the Greeks who's a man. He's my friend, but he's also Euxenes' friend; I can't extend to him the hand that was raised a little while ago to strike his friend. I'm a wolf, who only knows how to bite.

(*He strides away rapidly along the path that Euxenes followed.*)

PHILO, *looking at the Gauls*
We're entering here as if at home...

OEDH, *stopping*
I'm hiding! I'm nothing but a wolf, nothing but a wolf!
Oh, if I could bite…!

PHILO, *to a group of Gauls*
Greetings friends; how is King Nann?"

THE GAULS
The old oak has flourished again in the spring.

PHILO
And Gyptis?

THE GAULS
The swallow is singing gaily under the porch of the
house she has chosen.

PHILO
Then all is for the best.

ARACHNE, *advancing toward Philo*
What are you waiting for to disembark us?

PHILO
You want to surprise Chrysias? Are you jealous?

ARACHNE
I have a good tongue and good fingernails; I want to see
whether the interiors of these houses are as well-cared-for as
their façades. One would never believe that those who live in
them drink from golden cups.

PHILO
But it was only Euxenes who drank from a golden cup!

ARACHNE
That's not what you said. Each of us was to find a marble palace.

PHILO
Shut up, you old fool.

ARACHNE
Old fool!

(*She launches herself at Philo. Laïs holds her back.*)

LAÏS
Don't disturb your hair. Chrysias might appear at any moment.

ARACHNE
What do I care? I haven't come to laugh, me...

(*She descends into the interior of the galley; Laïs follows her.*)

A GAUL, *to Philo*
Have you brought Greek wine?

PHILO
Yes (*Aside.*) Greek wine? Is the altar to amity so rapidly elevated supported on a wine-skin? (*Looking in the direction of the city.*) Still no one! If, instead of arriving from Phocea, I'd arrived from Carthage they'd wake up with shackles on their feet. What a singular idea, to sleep with one's door open!

(*Greeks appear on the thresholds of houses. On perceiving the galley they raise their arms n the air and run toward the beach.*)

The Same, minus Oedh, Lysippus. Greeks. Greek women.

PHILO
By Hercules! They're awake already! (*To the Greeks.*)
Yes, it's me, Philo, with your inconsolable widows. (*To the
sailors.*) Put out the gangplank.

(*The sailors put out the gangplank. Philo disembarks,
followed by the women. The Greeks flock around them.*)

LAÏS, *leaping on to the beach first.*
Evohé! The sky in blue, the sand is fine. Evohé! And the
men have golden necklaces. Evohé, I'm becoming Gaulish.
(*She touches the necklace of a Gaul, who stands up, stupefied.*)

A GREEK
Hey, that's Laïs!

LAÏS
Yes, it's Laïs! When I saw so many women departing to
join their husbands. I followed them in order to go to find one.
(*She searches the crowd for a familiar face.*)

LYSIPPUS, *to a sailor.*
You said that she's stayed in Cyprus.

THE SAILOR
Yes. We were repairing the rudder; a merchant offered
her a marble palace; she said: "I don't know what's waiting
for me out there..." and she stayed.

LYSIPPUS
She stayed! I already had a bowl full of gold powder.

LAÏS
You have a bowl full of gold powder, and you have no wife? What are you complaining about, Lysippus? Come and show me the city.

(*She takes him by the arm and draws him away.*)

PHILO
Euxenes isn't coming! I dare not go away, and it's necessary that I see him; Leda's galley will be here within the hour.

ARACHNE, *in the crowd*
Chrysias! Where's Chrysias?

A GREEK
He's sleeping off his beer in some corner...

ARACHNE
He drinks beer too! Scoundrel!

(*She runs toward the city, shaking her fist.*)

PHILO
What if I were to go to intercept Leda's galley? Euxenes said to me: "Tell Leda the story of the cup and then she can do whatever she wants." She wanted to follow me, and she has. I ought to have prevented her from departing, but just as I was stupid enough to say what I thought, I was weak enough to believe what I was told: I thought that Euxenes was leaving Leda free to come or not to come. Something tells me now that it was necessary to leave Leda in Phocea. I don't know what Gyptis is worth, I've only seen her twice. I'll clarify the matter. (*To a Greek.*) Where's Euxenes' house?"

THE GREEK
There.

PHILO, *to the sailors*.

Disembark, but don't forget that you're men in my pay; be here in an hour, we're leaving again—and above all, no quarrels; I don't want cripples and men with one arm.

(*The sailors disembark. Philo heads slowly toward Euxenes' house; the crowd parts and Gyptis appears*.)

Gyptis. Philo.

PHILO
Gyptis! And he isn't here! Philo, Philo, it's necessary not to stick a finger between the tree and the bark.

GYPTIS
Greetings, friend; you're very late.

PHILO
I was expected, then?

GYPTIS
Did you doubt it? Our country pleases you, since you're returning to it, and we no longer quit it; Euxenes has been waiting for you impatiently.

PHILO
Ah!

GYPTIS
How many times he has said to me: "If Philo were here he could explain that, he'd build us that, we'd send him to such and such a chief; he has honey on his lips, like your Hercules."

PHILO
Amity blinds.

GYPTIS

We've left room beside us to build a house like ours, and there's a beautiful young woman somewhere, almost a sister, who would gladly come to live next door to Gyptis.

PHILO

Everyone has his own destiny.

GYPTIS

You're speaking like a Druid today. Our house will be yours. For several days, Euxenes has forgotten himself for long hours staring at the sea. I'm afraid that he's regretting his homeland.

PHILO

What if he wants to see it again?

GYPTIS

I'll go with him; am I not his, as he is mine? But I'm only a barbarian, I don't know how to speak the language. Come, friend, I'll learn, in listening to you, all the things I don't know and would so much like to know.

PHILO

Sometimes one has happiness and one lets it escape.

GYPTIS

You're suffering—did someone not want to follow you? We'll cure you; come. See how well we've worked; this picket fence is solid; behind it, the ditch is deep; we could sustain a siege. Euxenes said: "Your father is our friend; let's first build houses and storehouses."

PHILO

He said that! He doesn't suspect anything.

GYPTIS

I recognize that he has a little too much confidence in what you Greeks call destiny. He believes that other men are similar to him, but I'm suspicious. I'm only a wild thrush, but like a thrush, I think about the fox while building my nest. When he said to me: "We have nothing the fear," I replied to him: "Nann is old and the Gauls are fickle. Even if our door were bolted, that wouldn't prevent it from opening to our friends." Does that surprise you? We give ourselves entirely; for us, the fatherland is the hearth.

PHILO

It's necessary that I leave again without delay. Tell Euxenes that I have brought what I have brought.

GYPTIS, *sadly*

I'll tell him that, but he'll be chagrined. Will you not see him again?

PHILO, *staring at Gyptis*

You're adorable, and people ought to love you on their knees. Adieu. (*Aside.*) Too bad! (*Aloud.*) I can't tell Euxenes the name of the woman I love.

GYPTIS, *smiling*

You believe you love her because you don't know her. When you know her better you'll love her differently. Stay, friend; all the Gaulish woman are worth as much as one another; I'll give you the one that I've chosen for you.

PHILO

But I didn't mean what you think (*Perceiving a galley doubling the cape.*) It's too late!

GYPTIS

What I thought I heard is true, then?

PHILO

It wasn't true. Euxenes had a wife in Phocea, but it was to flee her that he left...I loved her.

GYPTIS

You're good. She's on that galley, isn't she?

PHILO

Yes, she loves me. She's followed me, and we're going...

GYPTIS

You don't know how to lie.... My Master is with King Nann; go tell him that his servant begs him to keep his promise; that she would have liked always to be a necklace around his neck, but that she cannot be a shackle for his foot.

PHILO

I swear to you that it isn't him who's recalling her...

GYPTIS

What is done is well done. Go where I ask you to go, friend.

(*She takes the path to her house again.*)

PHILO

I've done what I could, I think, to arrange things, but I fear that I haven't succeeded. I can't see how this unfortunate arrival can be explained, since she didn't want to believe in my amour for Leda. I've been stupid. Is it admissible that I've brought Euxenes' wife to Massalia after having stolen her from him? There's still one more means, which I wouldn't employ if I were in Euxenes' place, but which he might, because he's a practical man, knowing that he had friends of which he can make use. He could say to Gyptis, pointing at me: "You see that man that I called my friend He's a traitor!"

She'd believe it; women generally believe what is said to them when they're betrayed, and if I'm not a traitor, I'm a fool; I'd lower my head sadly "I quit Phocea to flee a woman I abhorred," he'd continue, "but he has brought her back to me."

It isn't common sense, but people generally believe what isn't common sense. Then he'd pretend to be blinded by anger, while allowing himself to be softened by our old amity, and instead of killing me he'd say: "Throw that man and that man in the hold of a galley and go sell them as slaves." And I'd allow myself to be thrown into the hold of a galley, which isn't frightening, but which would desolate me because it would distance me forever from Gaul and my dream of a woman like Gyptis. Once outside the port I'd offer Leda a basket of oranges to calm her down and take her back to Phocea with all the consideration that is due to her. That's what I'd advise Euxenes to do, if I didn't know that a wise man never sticks his finger between the tree and the bark. He has two wives and I have none; that's compensation, as the philosophers say. Let Euxenes arrange things as he wishes; the métier of giving advice is a fool's métier.

Philo. Arachne, Laïs. Lysippus

(*Arachne traverses the beach shouting.*)

ARACHNE
Philo! Where's Philo!

PHILO
What does she want?

ARACHNE
Ah, there you are! Where are the marble houses? Where are the gold ingots? Where are the carbuncles? Liar! I believe you, I quit my homeland, an adored family...

PHILO
Heu! Heu!

ARACHNE
Yes, an adored family. I haven't been rejected by mine, like you. Debauchee! Dissipator!

PHILO, *aside*
And to think that Leda is probably going to treat me the same way!

ARACHNE
I thought I was going to find gold to shift with a shovel, and I only find a drunkard on a heap of straw, in a fox-hole. Liar! Liar! Liar! I want to return to Phocea.

PHILO
Me too.

ARACHNE
Immediately!

PHILO, *pointing at a stone on the water's edge*
Wait there, (*She goes to sit on the stone.*) That galley belongs to me, the sailors are mine. I'm going there.

LAÏS, *arriving followed at a distance by Chrysias*
Are you leaving, Philo? You can take me with you.

PHILO *pointing at Arachne*
Wait there. And that's two. (*Lysippus arrives, out of breath, a package in his hand.*) Why did I let my sailors disembark? I should have departed already. (*He strides back and forth on the beach.*)

72

LAÏS, *to Lysippus*

In staying in Cyprus, my dear friend your wife had an inspiration from the gods! This is too nascent a city, and these Gauls are doves.

LYSIPPUS
Oh! No!

LAÏS
Oh! Yes!

LYSIPPUS
You'll see, when they know that Euxenes is rejecting Gyptis. (*He takes a step toward Philo.*) For you'll take me away, Philo' I'll pay for my passage in advance; I'll go put my package sadly aboard.

PHILO
What tale are you telling me?

LYSIPPUS
You'll see... No, you won't see, fortunately for us, what is going to happen to Euxenes in the hands of those big fellows, who could stun an ox with a blow of the fist.

PHILO
Go and sit down with the other two and shut up. (*Lysippus whispers to the two women. Philo continues aside.*) It's no longer a matter of going away; King Nann's Gauls don't joke!

ARACHNE, *getting up abruptly*
That will be frightful!

PHILO
Shut up, or I'll throw you in the water. (*Lysippus continues whispering, Philo speaking aside,*) I should have thought of that inevitable consequence.

ARACHNE, *hiding her face in her hands.*
Horrible!

PHILO
Will you shut up!

ARACHNE
It's Lysippus, who's explaining how Euxenes will be quartered.

PHILO
There isn't a moment to lose; let's run to the house of King Nann.

(*He strides away rapidly.*)

Lysippus, Arachne, Laïs

ARACHNE, *to Lysippus, who is whispering*
Personally, I'd love that young woman.

LAÏS
Not me; she'd like to have us all massacred.

ARACHNE
She's annoyed; that's her right. You can't understand that, Laïs; you're not a wife; but a wife who sees an intruder arrive one morning saying to her: "Get out of here!" has reason to be annoyed.

LAÏS
She can throw the intruder out, but between throwing the intruder out and having her husband quartered by four giants there are nuances, Arachne, there are nuances.

LYSIPPUS
Myself, I blame Euxenes; everything was going so well. What did he expect that Leda to do? Gyptis is as fresh as a rosebud and Leda is painted like an amphora.

ARACHNE
She's his wife, Lysippus, don't forget that; the other isn't... She's a tasty bit, but, fundamentally, she's nothing but that.

LAÏS, *laughing*
You understand the household, Arachne

ARACHNE
I understand it so well that I can hear in my heart the voice that is speaking to Euxenes. Chrysias isn't lovable and I don't love him; he was so drunk just now that he didn't recognize me, but I threw a bucket of water over his head—with him that's infallible—and, at the risk of my life, I'm going to look for him, because he's my husband.

(*She heads for the city.*)

LYSIPPUS
There's some truth in what she says.

LAÏS
Men always make me laugh...You're forgetting Cyprus, wretch! By Hercules, Greeks are too stupid; let's try Gauls."

(*She gets up and catches up with Arachne, who has stopped to consider Gyptis, emerging from her house.*)

LYSIPPUS, *to Laïs*
I'm departing alone, then?

LAÏS, *turning round*
And you'll stop over in Cyprus. Evohé! I'm becoming Gaulish!

(*Lysippus sits down again, sadly. Leda's galley draws nearer. Gyptis marches without looking where she is going.*)

Gyptis. Glycere

GYPTIS
How warm the breeze is! How blue the sea is! How pleasant it would be to be happy today!

GLYCERE, *standing in the prow of Leda's galley*
Salut, gulf where the pines are mirrored! How gently the azure waves are pushing us all the way to the golden sand of your blonde girdle; fatigued gulls of the sea of the hundred isles, we've come so far!

GYPTIS, *putting her hand on her heart*
Shut up. He has never lied. He didn't tell me that he loved a woman out there, hut he didn't tell me that he didn't love one; he has never lied to me, and he has promised to kill me when I became a hindrance to him. He'll kill me this evening... How slowly the sun is moving today!

(*Leda's galley touches the beach.*)

GLYCERE, *on the galley.*
Salut, land where the thirsty have found, under green shade, a stream of clear water! To the brown swallows of the Oriental land, give a warm place for their nests.

GYPTIS, *waking from her dream on hearing Glycere*
Oh! (*Striking her heart.*) You need to shut up.

76

GLYCERE
Salut, blonde girls! The tempest has chased us from the olive groves where Adonis, expiring, turned the roses crimson with his blood. Open your white arms, sisters, to fearful doves.

GYPTIS
I'm cold. I think that I might be dying, and I still have the taste of his kiss on my lips. Perhaps he doesn't love her. Philo might be right. He hasn't lied to me yet. My soul will fly joyfully to the place where one loves forever.

(*One of Philo's sailors bumps into a Gaul, who does not cede the passage.*)

Gyptis. Laïs, Arachne. Glycere, Lysippus.
Greeks, Greek women, Gauls. Sailors

THE SAILOR
Learn to distinguish a soldier from a merchant.

(*The Gaul draws his word; the sailors surround him.*)

GYPTIS, *without seeing anything*
I shall be like those of whom one sings, who die of amour.

(*Leda appears on the deck of the galley.*)

THE GAUL
To me!

(*The Gauls scattered in the crowd gather together.*)

A VOICE
Close the doors! Close the doors!

77

(People run to the doors, which are closed. The Gauls fight with Philo's sailors. The women run to the shore and hold their arms out to Leda, whose galley draws away.)

LAÏS, *to Lysippus, hanging on to his garments*
Defend me.

LYSIPPUS, *pushing her away*
It's was necessary to remain where you were. (*He runs to Gyptis.*) Daughter of King Nann!

GYPTIS, *without hearing*
My soul is flying away...

LAÏS, *falling at her feet*
Save us!

GYPTIS, *passing her hand over her brow and looking*
Already!

(She runs toward the Gauls.)

A WOMAN, *distraught*
They're murdering us!

ARACHNE
Alas! Alas!

(Gyptis speaks to the Greeks; the swords are lowered.)

A WOMAN
It appears that Euxenes had taken a Gaulish woman for a slave, while awaiting Leda's arrival. Leda has arrived, and he has given the slave to Philo.

LYSIPPUS, *putting his hand over her mouth*
Shut up!

ARACHNE
Close the doors! Close the doors!

(*The Gauls raise their swords again.*)

LYSIPPUS, *closing Arachne's mouth*
Shut up! Gyptis is speaking to them.

LAÏS
They're clasping hands; they're embracing.

LYSIPPUS
Gyptis has spoken to them. As long as she's here, we have nothing to fear.

GYPTIS, *to the women*
It's a misunderstanding. You don't understand our language yet, and you're frightened. The Gauls aren't thinking of attaching, but of defending themselves. Go, and have no fear; I'm the daughter of King Nann.

LAÏS
And Leda is only the daughter of an oil merchant.

LYSIPPUS
We all love you, Gyptis.

GYPTIS
And I love you.

ARACHNE
What if we drown that Leda? Where's Chrysias?

(*She runs to look for him.*)

GYPTIS, *to the women*

Sisters, return to your houses. (*To the sailors.*) They weren't thinking of fighting you, they were admiring your weapons. (*To the Gauls.*) They're my guests, friends.

(*The women crowd around Gyptis. The sailors draw away in one direction, the Gauls in the other. Laïs rejoins a Gaul and puts her hand on his arm. Leda's galley lands.*)

> Gyptis. Leda. Glycere. Leda's followers,
> Greek women. Arachne

GYPTIS

I am the cricket of his hearth, the swallow on his roof-beam; I must cheer up his evenings and salute his guests,

(*She remains immobile, arms folded, facing the gang-plank thrown from the galley.*)

LEDA, *before stepping on to the gangplank, in a non-chalant tone*

What does this tumult signify?

ARACHNE, *coming back*

I'll do without Chrysias.

LEDA

Where is Euxenes?

GYPTIS, *recoiling two or three paces*

Oh! (*Stopping.*) There has been no bargain between the two of us. I've given myself to him entirely.

LEDA, *stamping her foot.*

Where is Euxenes? Answer.

ARACHNE

Not seeing you arrive, chagrin has taken possession of him, and he's gone to look for you. We must have crossed paths with him last night.

LEDA
Is that a joke?

ARACHNE
If you go quickly, you might catch up with him.

GYPTIS, *advancing*
The door is open, the fire is lit, your bench is in the corner of the hearth, the master awaits you.

ARACHNE, *planting herself, arms folded in front of Gyptis*
Do you want to make me pass for a liar?

GYPTIS, *moving her aside gently*
Shut up.

ARACHNE
How stupid women are!

LEDA, *to Glycere*
Is this ridiculous enough?

GYPTIS.
The master is waiting.

ARACHNE
Oh, women are too stupid. But I have no desire to sacrifice myself. Listen Leda, we know one another; it isn't malevolence that brings you; if you set foot on that gangplank, I'll throw you into the water.

GYPTIS
You don't know, then, that when I speak, it's necessary
to shut up.

LEDA, *leaping on to the sand.*
Not when I speak.

ARACHNE, *advancing on Leda*
You will have wanted it.

GYPTIS, *to Arachne, whom she stops with a gesture*
I'm doing my duty.

LEDA
Where is my palace?

GYPTIS, *pointing at the house*
There.

LEDA
In Phocea, I had a marble palace and when I mounted the
steps of the portico, a slave extended a carpet under my feet..

GYPTIS
We've done our best.

(*She totters.*)

ARACHNE, *sustaining her*
I admire you, but you're stupid!

LEDA, *to the pilot*
We're leaving again.

ARACHNE, *to Gyptis*
She's leaving again; she knows full well how Euxenes
will receive her.

GYPTIS
Don't let go of me. My legs are trembling.

LEDA
Philo is a liar, we'll depart again this evening' but before then I want the Gaulish woman who holds a cup so graciously to pour me a drink in my house. Where is she?

GYPTIS, *straightening up*.
Here she is.

III. UNDER THE OAKS BEFORE NANN'S HOUSE

To the right, and oak wood. To the left, Nann's house. In the background, rocks, between which snake the road to Massalia. In the distance, the sea. In the gallery, the weapons of Nann's men are attached to the wall Nann is leaning on an oak beside the road to Massalia.

Nann. Then Euxenes

NANN
I am no longer good for anything down here and I'm needed elsewhere, but I'm waiting for Cathmor; a king ought to die with his head on the knees of his bard. He is coming today; we're the same age and we have thought alike for such long years that we have arrived at almost always having the same thoughts at the same time.

(*Euxenes arrives from the right.*)

EUXENES, *aside*
I thought I had arranged my entire story along the way, but now I no longer know my commencement. I should have waited for Philo to arrive; I might perhaps say futile things. (*He perceives Oedh on the road to Massalia.*) Is he coming from Massalia? Has he been prowling around my house by night? He desired Gyptis, so I'm told, and he's a ferocious brute. But brutes go straight to their goal; why would he prowl around my house by night? I don't want him to be a third party in my conversation with Nann.

(*He hides behind the trees. Oedh arrives close to Nann.*)

Nann. Oedh. Then Darthula

NANN

I was waiting for you.

OEDH, *embarrassed*

The men said that an aurochs had been perceived, and I wanted to see whether they were not mistaken.

NANN

When I was your age aurochs were numerous on the banks of the Rhône, but that was a long time ago. I'm going to quit you, my friends.

OEDH

Have you reason to complain of your children? Where do you want to go?

NANN

I'll bless you all as I leave, but it's necessary that I go. I've finished my task, you're all happy; I have a right to the recompense of those who have worked hard. I have worn away my body during what I believed to be good, my soul has grown in the struggle and it has the right to another body, stronger and more docile. Go fetch Gyptis for me: I've fought bravely and I have the right to die with a smile on my lips in a ray of sunlight. Bring Euxenes; I love him too. (*Oedh makes a movement; Nann looks at him.*) If you want to be happy, my son, only think of the happiness of others. If you want to accumulate, never work for yourself. Give me your hand. (*Oedh holds out his hand.*) It's good to clasp the hand of a loyal soldier, whose soul is as bright as a sword blade. I'm departing tranquil; you will watch over Gyptis, who is only a woman, and Euxenes, who is only a foreigner devoid of friends, and tomorrow I shall tell your father that you are worthy of him. Go fetch Euxenes and Gyptis for me; it might perhaps take a long time to go where I am going, and in order to illuminate my route I want to take with me a smile from my three children. (*To Darthula, who appears on the threshold.*) Darthula, have the table laid, today ought to be a day of feasting. It's in the midst of you all, without any regret or dread, that I want to die, in order to rediscover the fiends of my youth in the valleys of the green isle.

DARTHULA
I'd like to be able to go with you.

NANN
It's necessary to stay, in order to help Gyptis raise her children. Your husband was a worthy man, he warded off many blows destined for me; I shall tell him that you still love him and that he should keep a place for you at his hearth. If Cathmor comes, send him to our oak; he knows which one. From there one can see the road to Massalia and Gyptis' roof.

(*He heads slowly toward the forest, his head bowed. Oedh goes into the house, followed by Darthula.*)

Nann. Euxenes

EUXENES, *watching Oedh draw away*
I'll watch to see that he doesn't prowl around Gyptis. He's no longer here…let's go… When it's necessary to take a bitter remedy, one doesn't let it melt on one's tongue. (*He marches toward Nann.*) I salute you, King Nann.

NANN, *raising his head abruptly*
You were awaited, my son. Gyptis isn't with you?

EUXENES
She has stayed in Massalia to receive my companions' wives, who ought to arrive today.

NANN

And you have come to fetch me, in order that I might welcome them? You had a good idea; I have adopted you as mine, so those who will arrive are mine too. We'll walk slowly; I'm no longer the cavalier whose horse never traveled swiftly enough.

EUXENES

I have a secret to confide to you, King Nann

NANN, *smiling*

I'll no longer be here tomorrow. (*Gravely.*) There are secrets that weigh heavily; if it's one of those, tell me, and I'll carry it away.

EUXENES

When I left Greece, I believed that no one there would ever pronounce my name again; that is why I did not tell you what I ought to have told you.

NANN

I have followed so many paths in my life that I can easily quit ne for another today, so speak clearly, as a beloved son ought to speak to an indulgent father.

EUXENES

I have not confesses to you that I had left a wife in Phocea

NANN

You no longer loved her, since you quit her. It appears that there are men whose heart is similar to the leaf of an aspen, which trembles in every wind; those men are to be pitied, so much to be pitied that one dares not criticize them. You should have told Gyptis that when she held out the cup to you; now it's too late. Look at me. If, one day, you no longer love Gyptis, what will you do?"

EUXENES
I shall always love her.

NANN
How do you know?

EUXENES
I believe it.

NANN
You've just replied to me like a man; you didn't say "I'm sure of it," you said "I believe it," and you spoke in accordance with your conscience; a liar has never looked into the eyes of King Nann. Gyptis will always love you. If you had told her the truth, she would not have thought of the past; women believe the man they love, but they are jealous of secrets. Try to see that she doesn't divine anything.

(*A group of Gauls, in the company of Laïs, appears on the road to Massalia.*)

EUXENES, *aside, looking at them*
They seem very animated... (*Aloud.*) Perhaps the women who have just disembarked will talk.

NANN
They will talk! The straight road is easier to follow than the tortuous one! If I had not become a child again, whom a grain of sand causes to stumble, I would take Gyptis, put her on my horse and say to her: "Come with me. We will go far enough for your companions to lose track of you." But I'm no longer anything but a child, my head is as feeble as my arm, and I don't know what it's necessary to do.

EUXENES, *aside*
Why is that woman with them?

NANN

Gyptis is nothing but amour; a doubt will kill her. You alone can convince her, but what is it necessary for you to say to her?

EUXENES, *aside*

Perhaps Leda has come. (*Aloud.*) I'll go rejoin Gyptis; true love is eloquent.

NANN

But its wounds are mortal. One who does not speak always gives good advice; come, my son, and let us implore the aid of the one who is never mistaken.

(*He goes into the forest; Euxenes follows him, turning round to look and those who are arriving. Oedh and Darthula emerge from the house.*)

Oedh. Darthula

OEDH, *who takes a few steps and then stops*

I can't...I can't go into her house. She would say to me: "Sit down here," and I would see by my side the other's place... That isn't possible.

DARTHULA

Don't shake your head; today you're the chief, but today as yesterday I'll tell you what I think. Don't let a bad seed germinate in your heart. You're chagrined, as am I. It's not her fault; one doesn't love as one wishes. Don't let that bad seed sprout; the poisoned plant would enlace you entirely.

OEDH

In the gulf of my dolor I'm like a fleck of foam; the void of the abyss attracts me. I can't.

(*He goes back into the house.*)

DARTHULA, *following him*
And King Nann is going to die! May God have pity on us!

(*Laïs and a group of Gauls enter the stage.*)

Laïs. The Gauls

LAÏS
It's nice here.

A GAUL
You did well the accompany us; you have nothing more to fear; you're now the guest of the king.

(*They hasten toward the house. Gauls scattered around the stage gather, speaking animatedly.*)

LAÏS
What Lysippus foresaw is, it's said, really going to happen. These Gauls are slightly light-headed, but they're otherwise amiable companions.

Laïs. Oedh. Darthula. Gauls and Gaulish women

OEDH, *coming down the steps, to Darthula*
I cannot lie; tell Gyptis that she will not see me again. (*To the Gauls.*) Name another chief; I'm leaving.

A GAUL
And who will defend Gyptis, who is being treated as a servant?

OEDH, *running to him*
You're lying!

THE GAUL
We've seen Euxenes' wife disembark.

OEDH
That's impossible.

DARTHULA
And Gyptis?

THE GAUL
She has taken her into her house.

DARTHULA
You can see that it's impossible. You haven't understood what was being said around you.

OEDH
We're going to find out. Everyone, follow me!

(*The Gauls run under the gallery to fetch their weapons.*)

LAÏS, *aside*
Gyptis must be angry, and an angry woman doesn't need a friend beside her. (*Going to Oedh.*) Since this morning, my friends, you've made a lot of fuss about very little.

OEDH
Who is this woman?

LAÏS
A Greek come to... admire your country, which she finds superb. So, you're making a lot of fuss about very little. Leda has arrived in Massalia, that's true...

OEDH
And that's Euxenes' wife?

LAÏS
What does that prove, Gaul? You no longer have last
year's cloak.

DARTHULA
But he loves her, since he's summoned her.

(*The Gauls gather around Oedh.*)

LAÏS
Leda is no longer loved, since he quit her; she has not
been summoned, since she was not expected.

DARTHULA
Why has she come, then?

LAÏS
Because…because Philo brought her.

OEDH
Philo!

DARTHULA, *aside*
Poor Gyptis!

OEDH, *aside*
Philo, a traitor! The best of these Greeks is worthless.

DARTHULA
She's right; it's a lot of fuss for very little. Euxenes has
already chased away this woman and killed Philo.

LAÏS, *aside*
That's what I would have done, in his place.

DARTHULA

They believed themselves obliged to bring big news every time they came back from Massalia. (*To Oedh.*) I'll go to
Gyptis' house and I'll tell you this evening...

OEDH

Shut up.

(*Darthula bows her head.*)

LAÏS

If you want to be seen well by women, my friends, it's
necessary to lose these rather abrupt manners.

OEDH

Take her away; it's not a time to talk without saying anything.

LAÏS, *approaching him*

You think so? (*In a low voice.*) I wanted to talk to you
about Gyptis. (*Oedh takes her a few paces away, while she
laughs.*) I thought so. You love her very much, then?

OEDH

Who permits you...?

LAÏS, *putting her hand on his arm*

Ta ta ta...! I'm a woman who, in matters of amour, can
say anything. I'll begin by affirming to you that between you
and Euxenes, I wouldn't have hesitated for an instant, but she
has chosen Euxenes. What do you expect? We sometimes
make mistakes, just like you. Only, everything wears
away...and everything that is worn away can be replaced.
We're for those who know how to wait. If Gyptis—Gyptis,
you hear!—were to have Euxenes killed today out of jealousy,
she'd mourn him for her entire life, whereas if she took the

thing as she ought to take it, cheerfully... Everything wears away. Do you understand, Gaul?

OEDH
No.

LAÏS
Yes. Don't kill Euxenes; you'd make him a hero. Do you understand, Gaul?

OEDH
No.

LAÏS
Yes.

OEDH
I never give advice. (*He turns and walks away, arms folded. Aside.*) She's telling me: "Don't touch me, liar!" Where does that word strike me? (*Touching his heart, and then his forehead.*) There, or there? That word has never been said to me; I don't know it. I'll see her die pronouncing it, and that will be the end of it, I'll no longer see her; I can no longer send her where faithful spouses go.

LAÏS, *to a Gaul, while pointing at Oedh.*
Is he a chief?

THE GAUL
He's the king.

LAÏS
A king! (*After a moment's consideration.*) That Gyptis is a fool, for having preferred Euxenes to him. (*To Oedh.*) Perhaps I haven't spoken to you as one speaks to a king, but what happens to men happens to kings, and where I come from, Wisdom is represented with a smile on her lips and a flower in

her hand. Love Gyptis as your sister; amity is worth more than amour. (*Aside.*) If those I left behind could hear me they wouldn't believe their ears; I can't believe mine.

OEDH
You're only a cheerful warbler, but a warbler is pleasant to hear. (*To the Gauls.*) I'll go to Massalia alone. (*Aside.*) Devoted brothers, go where faithful wives go. (*The Gauls disperse; her sits down on the first step of the portico, his head in his hands.*) I'll do as she tells me to do.

Oedh. Laïs

LAÏS
This handsome soldier is too sad... I know the trouble well... O Venus the consoler, make ready, in order to heal your servant, the darts that you prepared in order to wound her!

(*She approaches Oedh slowly and kneels before him, her elbows on her knees and her chin in her hands.*)

OEDH, *stupefied*
Get up.

LAÏS
It's like this that one speaks to kings.

OEDH *looks at her and smiles.*
Not in Gaul.

LAÏS
In Greece, it's only women who have kings and they always speak to them like this. I have a favor to ask of you.

OEDH, *lifting her up*
Of me?

LAÏS

Of you. Take me back to Massalia on the rump of your horse; the road is longer than I thought and I'm a trifle weary. (*Oedh shakes his head.*) Oh, I'm well able to hold on to the rump of a horse. (*Showing him her hand charged with rings.*) I'll only touch you with my fingertips; you're a king…you'd be one even in Greece.

OEDH, *softly*

The one who ought to sit on the rump of my horse will never sit there. Spend the night with our women.

LAÏS

But I have to go back this evening; I haven't come to join a husband in Massalia. I followed Philo in order to see new lands; I'm only, as you said, a cheerful warbler, whom winter chases away and spring brings back. I'll go wherever Philo goes.

OEDH

He's leaving again this evening?

LAÏS

He's been poorly received. What do you expect Euxenes to do with Leda?

OEDH

You swear to me the Euxenes didn't summon that woman?

LAÏS

I swear to you that it's Philo who brought her. (*Aside.*) I no longer know, but that Philo is such a liar that he's capable of anything.

OEDH, *aside*

The bad seed has commenced growing in my heart. Nann wants to see Gyptis, Darthula will go to fetch her. It's not to-day that I ought to enter Euxenes' house for the first time. (*He detaches his bracelet and gives it to Laïs.*) You've shown me my route when I went astray; take that to remind you of Gyptis.

(*He goes back inside.*)

Laïs. Then Cathmor

LAÏS

This bracelet is heavy. He's as generous as he is hand-some. Ah! Am I in the process of falling in love, by chance? Where would be the harm? In working for myself I'm restor-ing peace to a household…it would be the first time. O Juno, proud patroness of wives, don't treat me as an enemy! (*Shak-ing her head.*) No, no…that would be too stupid…! It wouldn't be so stupid, though. If Euxenes and Gyptis quarrel, which has probably already happened, I wouldn't pay dear for the houses of Massalia. Let's go and have a chat with Euxenes; I can speak frankly with him. This evening, Leda can take my place in Philo's galley, and tomorrow we'll see whether there are eternal chagrins.

(*Cathmor, staff in hand, enters from the left.*)

CATHMOR, *perceiving Laïs*

They've sent for their wives! So they think this land is theirs. (*To Laïs*) It's only a ball that the wind pushes; the good grain remains in the field, on the threshold of the house.

LAÏS, *as she draws away, aside*

There's a sinister old man, who won't be prowling around here any longer when I'm queen.

(Maidservants emerge from the forest with bundles of wood on their heads.)

Cathmor. Maidservants

CATHMOR
Ah, there you are, girls! You haven't followed her, you've let her leave like a beggar.

When her mother came into Nann's house, great pines were ablaze in order to illuminate the road; around me, a hundred bards were singing; in front of me, a hundred carts were buckling under sacks of wheat and woolen fleeces. She didn't go forth upon the roads like a beggar; behind me, the chief with the blue eyes held her on his gray mare and her maidservants followed her, swinging holm-oak branches.

A MAIDSERVANT
The husband was a Gaul.

CATHMOR, *extending a hand in the direction of Massalia*
Can't you hear sobs in the wind coming from out there?

THE MAIDSERVANT
Let's go look for her.

CATHMOR
Is it her who's weeping? Is it certain that anyone is weeping? I can hear weeping. It's the wing of death brushing my forehead; you'll weep this evening, girls.

(The maidservants pass behind the house. Cathmor heads for the door.)

Cathmor, Oedh. Darthula, Gauls

CATHMOR, *stopping on the first step and striking it with his staff*

A wind has passed through the forest where I was wandering; in that wind the oaks trembled, the kite screeched, and I recognized the wing-beat of the Master's reaper, so I've come to sing the funeral song. (*Oedh enters.*) Who is going to die today? Who? Who?

OEDH, *in a dull voice*
Perhaps me.

CATHMOR

In the grotto where I was hiding like a toothless wolf pursued by foxes, I saw drops of water falling one by one, piecing the hard granite. The mountain was weeping, and its heart was crumbling.

Would you want your heart, when your tears fall, to be harder than a rock? Who is going to die today? Who? Who?

DARTHULA, *entering, aside*
What if it were Gyptis? (*Aloud.*) Don't say those words, bard, which bring misfortune.

CATHMOR

From the summit where I went, like a wounded chamois, to wash my bleeding feet in the blue-tinted snow, I saw the stars breaking into sparks. Do you think that kings weigh more than the stars in the hand of the Almighty?

I have thrown the mountain and the heath over my heart to stifle my chagrin, and I am no longer today the bard with the powerful voice who comes to sing the great deeds of those for whom death is waiting. Who is going to die today? Who? Who?

DARTHULA

Cathmor, King Nann is waiting for you up there, under the oak from which Massalia can be seen.

CATHMOR

The hawk does not let go of the dove; she is not on the road, King Nann.

Since she has been taken from us, I march straight ahead, like a wild boar pursued by dogs. Like a pack, my regrets howl behind me: "She has been taken from you!"

King, why are you looking at the road? Go search for her, if you wish. King Nann, you are like your old bard; age has chilled your veins. You are no longer a kite with bloody wings; like the friend of your youth, you are no longer anything but a crow whose stiffened wings are trailing. You are only any longer able to cry: "They have caught me! They have caught me!" (*The men and women assemble.*)

Madman! I marched straight ahead in the woods and on the heaths, and the leaves murmured: "They have let her be taken!" and the broom said: "They have taken her from you."

(*He takes the path that the king followed, and he crosses the path of the maidservants, who are coming back with bundles of herbs on their heads.*)

OEDH

Shut up, bard. I regret her as much as you do, but there are words that it is necessary, on certain days, not to pronounce before us.

CATHMOR

I marched straight ahead in the woods and on the heaths, and the leaves murmured: "They have let her be taken!" and the broom said: "The men of the clan of Nann are giving their women to those who are passing!"

A GAUL

These strangers confronted us. They drew swords against us.

VOICES
To the sea! To the sea!

CATHMOR
Sing of the blue blade, which loves flesh! Sing of the blue blade!

(*The men gather around Cathmor.*)

OEDH
Who commands here?

CATHMOR
We do!

(*Oedh puts his hand to his sword. Gyptis, followed by Philo, appear on the road to Massalia.*)

A GAUL
Gyptis!

(*Oedh and Darthula run toward her and disappear around a bend in the road.*)

CATHMOR, *indicating her*
The dove has flown away; there are only crows in Massalia now. Come! This evening, on seeing the beach leveled, she will believe that she has been dreaming, and tomorrow she will love a Gaul. Let her not see us leave, in order that she can believe that she has been dreaming.

(*He plunges into the forest; the Gauls follow him.*)

OEDH
You're coming back alone, like a beggar?

GYPTIS
Why should I have myself accompanied? In the land of King Nann, would any man dare to say what I ought not to hear?

OEDH
Women can forgive; men don't.

GYPTIS
I have nothing to forgive; I have come to tell my master that guess are waiting at his hearth.

OEDH
It's true, then!

GYPTIS
Go fetch Euxenes for me.

OEDH
But...

GYPTIS
I beg you to do it, Brother.

OEDH
Your brother...I'll go fetch him; where is he?

GYPTIS
But he's here, with my father.

OEDH
Nann has gone up to the oaks alone.

GYPTIS
It's all true; he lied.

OEDH, *to Gyptis.*
What do you want me to do?

GYPTIS
And me, am I where I ought to be? Have I said what I ought to say? Have I the right to judge my master? (*To Oedh.*) I believed that he was here; I came to tell him that those he was expecting have arrived. (*Smiling sadly.*) He'll be anxious if he doesn't find me when he returns. (*Offering her hand to Oedh,*) Adieu, Brother. (*Embracing Darthula.*) Adieu, Darthula.

DARTHULA
Darling! My darling! (*To Oedh, making him a sign to go away.*) You know what you have to do.

OEDH, *in a vibrant voice*
I know. (*He heads for the road. Aside.*) in the land that I must defend, I want the flowers to open joyfully; if a storm threatens them, my shield extends over them; if a bramble wounds them, my sword cuts it. It isn't Oedh who will avenge himself, it's the chief who will punish.

Gyptis. Darthula

GYPTIS
I have a heavy heart, Darthula.

DARTHULA
You have a heavy hart, my poor thing? Men need, from time to time, to hurt those they love. But they repent very quickly. Tomorrow you will be happy, as you were yesterday. (*Indicating the bench to her.*) Sit down there; it's better when

one has left one's house with a heavy heart, not to go into
one's father's right away. She's very pale, the dear. (*She forc-
es her to sit down.*) Sit down there and think. Think hard, darling. Weep, weep at your ease; no one will know. Tears that
one prevents from emerging choke.

GYPTIS, *getting up*
My place is down there. (*Letting herself fall back on to
the bench.*) Let me rest for a moment, only for a moment; I'll
walk more rapidly.

(*She hides her head in her hands.*)

DARTHULA, *kissing her hair, aside*
Let's prevent Nann from knowing; it's unnecessary for
the men to get mixed up in it.

(*She heads for the oaks.*)

Gyptis. Then Oedh and Philo

GYPTIS
Am I awake? I've come back. I've been in a beautiful
land, far, far away. Now I've come back. I've come back
alone, all alone, from the beautiful country. (*Placing her hand
on her heart.*) I thought that you had stayed there. Shut up.
Until the hour of your death, you must shut up. You're weary?
Sleep, dream if you can, but shut up. sleep, sleep. Shut up,
you're preventing me from hearing; it's no longer amour, it's
duty that speaks in a low voice to spouses. What will the old
king say? His cheek will burn under the insult, and his anger
will be treble. Tomorrow, Massalia will be no more than a
heap of ashes, and it's me who will have lit the torch. And
him? I love him! It's a bad dream. Beloved, I'm stifling, wake
me up!
No, I'm not dreaming. This really is the bench at the
door; happiness has really departed. (*Shaking her head.*) Hap-

piness has departed, but duty remains. I have said: "I shall be the swallow on your roof-beam, until death." As long as he has not expelled me, my place is down there. I am his companion, but I am also his servant. Yesterday, I was only his companion, today I am only his servant. (*She lets herself fall back on the bench and hides her head in her hands.*) Amour runs like a flame in a field of broom; I raised my eyes and I loved him. (*Getting up.*) Above the hearth there is a shining ax! It would be my right; a thrush defends its nest! (*Falling to her knees and sobbing.*) I no longer have a nest! (*She perceives Oedh and Philo, who are fighting.*) Already! Already! (*Philo falls, she runs to him, arms extended, and arrives next to him.*) A day of betrothal requires a drop of blood n the bride's veil; it brings god luck. (*Leaning over.*) But the wound is too deep.

PHILO
No one will ever love you as you deserve.

GYPTIS
Yes; I dreamed that I was the daughter of King Nann; my wedding should be as happy as hers. (*Shaking her bloodstained tunic.*) There was only one drop of blood on her veil; mine is red.

OEDH
Sister, you are avenged.

GYPTIS, *increasingly distressed*
Like the daughter of King Nann, I had a brother, like the daughter of King Nann, I no longer have one. (*She flees, running in the direction of Massalia.*) I'm listening to the voice of my heart; that voice is singing. Sing!

(*Oedh tries to follow her. Philo puts out a hand and stops him.*)

Philo. Oedh

PHILO
Chagrin has put a veil over her eyes, but a kiss will tear the veil. She won't go astray; her amour will guide her. Don't spoil what you have commenced well.

OEDH, *recoiling*
I have fought with you because I had once clasped your hand, but I should have had you killed like a thief.

PHILO
And you would have been right to do so...have I not stolen Gyptis' happiness? So I defended myself poorly, you'll agree. Remorse laid its cold hand on my arm. Euxenes and Gyptis will curse me without witnesses. I would have liked to see Euxenes again, in order to beg his pardon... Life is a strange thing, Gaul... If we meet again up above, I'll tell you things that will astonish you! You've done what I would have done in your place... (*Pointing at Nann and Euxenes, who are coming down.*) Tell Euxenes that I brought Leda because I loved Gyptis... Will you promise? Say so...

(*He dies.*)

Nann. Euxenes. Oedh. Darthula

NANN, *to Darthula*
You have always said things in too many words, my daughter, which ensures that no one understands you very well; but I understood that Gyptis was here, and that's the essential thing. Leaved us (*To Euxenes.*) The newcomers will have talked, and jealousy will have bitten her in the heart. It will be necessary to tell her everything, very frankly. She was wrong to come to complain, she is no longer her own, she is yours. Your fault doesn't excuse hers, but we'll talk to her about it gently; she's still only a child. (*Euxenes perceives the*

cadaver of Philo and utters a cry.) What's the matter with you?

EUXENES, running to the cadaver
Philo!

OEDH, *stopping him with his hand*
It's me who killed him. Before dying, he said: "Tell Euxenes that I brought Leda because I loved Gyptis.)

EUXENES
Ah!

(*He remains immobile. Oedh considers him for a moment, and then kneels down next to Philo and raises his head.*)

NANN
Where is my daughter?

OEDH
On the roads; her house is too small for three.

NANN
On the roads! You hear, Nann? But the blood no longer rises to your cheek, because your heart has no more blood. You hear, Nann? You have come back from where you had gone; you no longer knew but one child, a very small child that a grain of sand would cause to stumble. Do you hear, Nann? Do you understand? Do you understand?

(*He bows his head.*)

OEDH, *kissing Philo on the forehead.*
See you soon.

(*He gets up again.*)

NANN, *raising his arms*

Land of Gaul, I have given you enough blood, render a little sap to the cracked trunk! Breath of our woods, reanimate the lamp that is about to go out! I was the torch, in order that one could search in the darkness; I as the king with the heavy sword, Nann with the open hand. From my aerie the eaglets have fallen one by one; there is only a sparrow now, which sings over an empty nest; a stranger has taken her from me, and today I have thrown her, with crumpled wings, on to the road. (*Marching up to Euxenes.*) Greek, I am the king with the heavy hand; your head is going to roll on the steps of my door.

(*He puts his hand to his sword.*)

EUXENES
Strike; I've merited it.

OEDH
And Gyptis, King Nann?

EUXENES
Strike, before listening to him.

OEDH
Perhaps there are things we do not know. Let's go to Massalia, and if there's a guilty party, let him be punished before all. Will you?

NANN
Yes.

OEDH, *striking a shield suspended between columns.*
Hola, men of Nann!

DARTHULA, *running*
They're with Cathmor in Massalia. May God have pity on us!

IV. IN MASSALIA, IN THE HOUSE OF EUXENES

A chamber paneled in pine. In the middle, a fireplace supported by four pillars. In the foreground to the left, a door leading to Gyptis' bedroom. Ay the back, to the right, the exterior door. Above the fireplace, a Gaulish ax.

Leda, surrounded by her women, is lying on a pile of cushion in front of the fireplace. In a corner, Gaulish maidservants are huddled. The sun is about to set.

Leda. Glycere,. Leda's women. Gaulish maidservants

LEDA
It's cold. Do you think one can live in this, Glycere?

GLYCERE
You couldn't live here.

LEDA
Did he lie, that Philo? Where are the halls sanded with gold? The beds encrusted with carbuncles?

GLYCERE
He didn't say that, Mistress

LEDA
He had no need to say it; one divined it, since, according to him. Euxenes had married the daughter of a king.

GLYCERE
It wasn't him who told you the story of the cup, mistress. When you had him summoned, he even said, smiling, as I remember: "Was the cup gold? It's permissible to doubt it."

LEDA
Is that Gyptis really the daughter of a king?

GLYCERE
I didn't believe it, but now I'm sure of it.

LEDA
Not me. First of all, this morning, she didn't behave like
the daughter of a king. A daughter of a king doesn't run away
without saying anything after having opened a door to you.
You've heard the daughters of kings speaking, in the theater.
A disdained daughter of a king...for she is disdained...why are
you smiling?

GLYCERE
Euxenes wasn't at the port to receive us.

LEDA
Could he know that we were arriving today?

GLYCERE
The sun is setting and he hasn't come yet.

LEDA
He's hunting.

GLYCERE
You think so? He was seen talking to Philo.

LEDA
Why are you telling me this?

GLYCERE
In order to respond to you, Mistress. If, instead of being
a flute-player, I were a great lady. I wouldn't be expecting
anyone.

LEDA

I hate him, that Philo. I should have remembered that he was not one of my friends.

GLYCERE

And that Xantippe, to aid you to await the hour of rendezvous, had given you Glycere (*bowing*), your servant.

LEDA, *striking her with her ivory polisher*
You're mocking me, I believe

GLYCERE

You're forgetting where we are. Glycere salutes you, Leda; she'll go to see whether she will be disdained as you are disdained. You were wrong to quit Xantippe.

(*She leaves.*)

LEDA, *standing up and smoothing her garments*
She'll be buried alive... And Euxenes is leaving me alone! He's with his Gaulish woman. I'll complain. I shall plead. I'm his wife; all women will have to reckon with me. Evidently, he believed that I wouldn't come, that I'd depart again. I'll stay; this house is mine. His Gyptis is only a servant. (*There is a knock on the door.*) Don't open it.

(*A Gaulish maidservant opens it. Arachne enters, followed by Chrysias.*)

Leda. Arachne. Chrysias. Gaulish maidservants

LEDA
What do you want?

ARACHNE
We've been sent by the people. Speak, Chrysias.

CHRYSIAS
The women have told us what to say...

ARACHNE
Shut up. This is the situation. First of all, I'm no longer departing. At first sight, my house didn't seduce me, and I came back to the port in order to embark with Philo and leave tonight.

LEDA
Philo's leaving?

ARACHNE
Don't you know anything? Do you know, at least, where Euxenes is?

LEDA
He's hunting.

ARACHNE
Hunting! He's been abducted by the Gauls. That's why the women, having conferred, have sent me to you. Speak, Chrysias.

CHRYSIAS
The women have said: "The houses are only made of earth, but the coffers are full..."

ARACHNE
Shut up. After having looked carefully, all the women gathered on the beach as they had gathered in Phocea, and they declared that Philo had not lied. This country is a land blessed by the gods; it would be the best place in the world if it weren't for the Gauls...big fellows who can carry a man under their arm. They took Euxenes away like that this morning. Well, these terrible Gauls obey the slightest gesture from Gyptis; to please her they'd bring everything here, their gold

and their precious stones, and Gyptis liked the Greeks. You arrive, she's gone...it's necessary that she comes back. Do you understand?

LEDA
I'll have you whipped tomorrow.

ARACHNE
You'll have me whipped tomorrow! Speak, Chrysias.

LEDA
Someone throw that drunkard out.

ARACHNE
Tomorrow, we're all going to look for Gyptis, and it'll be you who'll be whipped, if you haven't left. Come, Chrysias, Come; let's go render an account of our mission. (*On the threshold of the door, which she slams violently.*) You hear? Whipped!

Leda, Followers, Gaulish maidservants

LEDA
They want me to leave! I'm not leaving; I'll plead. And when I've won my case, I'll go if it pleases me. He'll repay me for everything; I know how it's necessary to talk to him. We'll see, tomorrow, who commands here. Where is my bedroom?

A FOLLOWER, *lifting the curtain of Gyptis' bedroom*
There's only this one.

LEDA, *advancing her head*
It reeks of lavender...pooh! These barbarian women ought to walk barefoot. (*To the follower.*) Extend my veils before the bed.

THE FOLLOWER

There isn't a bed, but the skins of swans in a corner, on a heap of lavender.

LEDA

Bring these cushions, and throw the swan skins and the lavender out of the window. (*Aside.*) Ah, they want me to leave! But Euxenes is a prisoner of the Gauls, that's why he hasn't come. She's said to be ferocious, this Gyptis! (*Aloud.*) Decidedly, II won't spend the night here; this room smells terrible. (*To one of her women.*) Go tell the pilot that we're leaving again, and to inform me as soon as he's ready. (*The follower leaves.*) Oh, burn a few perfumes. (*Aside.*) By leaving today, that Gyptis will know that it's me who didn't want to stay, and consequently, that it was Euxenes who told me to come. She's ferocious, she'll treat Euxenes as he deserves.

(*Laïs enters.*)

Leda. Laïs

LAÏS

Salut, Leda. Where's Euxenes?

LEDA

His royal spouse has asked her royal father to lock him in a dungeon.

LAÏS

That's stupid!

LEDA

You're forgetting who you're talking to.

LAÏS

It's really the lover of Xantippe that I'm talking to? (*Leda makes a movement.*) Oh, I don't hold it against you; he's generous, but tedious. He must be weeping; go console him, Leda; when he wipes away his tears, he'll give without counting. That speech was to define clearly our reciprocal situations. Now, we can talk as two equals, like two friends, can't we? It's as a friend that I've come to talk to you.

LEDA
Oh!

LAÏS
Wait before exclaiming. We're no longer at an age where one loves for the pleasure of loving. What can you hope to gain here? Nothing.

LEDA
Massalia belongs to Euxenes

LAÏS
And it would please you sufficiently to be treated like a queen. Poor Leda! (*Leda makes a movement.*) Euxenes won't throw you in the water. He might be constrained to return to Phocea, and your family is powerful there; he'll support you, then, for as long he hasn't found an honest and discreet way of getting rid of you.

LEDA
He loved me.

LAÏS
When you had a dowry. Don't imagine that Gyptis is going to braid your hair. No, don't imagine that! She's with her father; I left her there. Euxenes isn't in a dungeon; he isn't in the house of his father-in-law, where he's been poorly received. He's observing without being seen, and he said to me: "Laïs, you're a good girl, without prejudice; go find Leda and make her understand that if she spends the night in Massalia, the city will be blockaded by the Gauls tomorrow, and the day

115

after, we'll be constrained to devour one another, for I'm expecting a siege. If she wants to board her galley again quietly, I have a coffer full of powdered gold, I'll give it to her. Is that powdered gold in a coffer or an amphora? We'll go look; let's hurry.

LEDA
I was about to depart, Laïs; I'd sent an order to the pilot—but since he wants me to leave so urgently, I'll stay. This time, definitely. My galley is in the port…since he's so afraid, we'll leave together.

LAÏS
Leave or don't leave; after all, I don't care. I'm not Gyptis' rival, and if I've come to Gaul, it's because the Greeks bored me.

(*She leaves.*)

LEDA
And it's him who earned me those insults; I hate him! I want his Gaulish woman to avenge herself. I want her to kill him—too bad if she kills me afterwards.

(*She goes into the bedroom.*)

Gaulish maidservants. Followers.

FIRST MAIDSERVANT
My legs are trembling.

SECOND MAIDSERVANT, *indicating the bedroom*
She dares to go in there?

THIRD MAIDSERVANT
Fine cushions! Beautiful ladies!

116

SECOND MAIDSERVANT
Let's not make any noise.

(*She opens the door quietly. Gyptis enters abruptly.*)

THE MAIDSERVANTS
Oh!

ONE OF LEDA'S FOLLOWERS, *parting the curtain of the bedroom slightly and seeing Gyptis, in a low voice*
It's her!

(*Leda laughs.*)

Gyptis. Leda. Gaulish maidservants

GYPTIS
It's necessary never to laugh, my girls, at the misfortune of others. Instead of commenting on what doesn't concern us, let's thank the Almighty, who might have punished us, as he has punished the king's daughter.

(*Leda opens the curtain slightly.*)

A MAIDSERVANT
What king are you talking about, Mistress?

(*Leda lets the curtain fall.*)

GYPTIS
King Nann was an old king, who only had one daughter; at sixteen, he married her off. Why, Nann, did you marry your daughter so soon? (*She hears laughter and heads for the bedroom.*) Why laugh? One doesn't know what the king's daughter will do. (*Kneeling down*) She is weeping at her hearth, for the place taken. Weep, Gyptis, but avenge yourself. (*Leda parts the curtains, but a maidservant closes them abruptly.*)

117

THE MAIDSERVANT
Come, Mistress, come.

GYPTIS
The table isn't laid yet? (*She advances toward the hearth and, standing on tiptoe, passes her hand over the ax.*) This is a mirror that my father gave me to celebrate my sixteenth birthday. The table isn't laid yet! That's my fault, I'm late. I've come back from a beautiful land where all the flowers love one another; it's them who sang the song of King Nann... "When his daughter was married, King Nann wept..." Approaching the hearth. He isn't coming! Lord, don't strike me as you have struck the daughter of King Nann.

(*Leda enters. A maidservant runs to place herself in front of Gyptis, another launches herself at Leda.*)

THE MAIDSERVANT
The Mistress is here now.

LEDA
The mistress!

(*A clamor is heard outside, Leda, frightened, returns to the bedroom.*)

GYPTIS, *listening to the clamor, which increases*
That's King Nann, weeping for his daughter.

VOICES, *outside*
To Death! To Death!

A MAIDSERVANT
We're going to laugh.

GYPTIS, *also laughing*

You think so? Lay the table, quickly. He's bringing friends to supper. It's a secret, a great secret. He wants to avenge the king's daughter.

VOICES, *outside*

To arms! To arms! Kill! Kill!

GYPTIS

How the king's daughter would weep; she doesn't want to be avenged! (*The clamors increase, the maidservants clap their hands.*) Instead of laughing, weep; she doesn't want to be avenged.

THE MAIDSERVANT, *sitting next to Gyptis and taking her head in her hands.*

Sleep, beloved mistress, sleep; you're fatigued and your head is getting lost Sleep, beloved mistress.

GYPTIS

I'm not the king's daughter; I'm a woman who is loved. My house is small, but it's entirely mine!

(*The clamors draw nearer. Women's screams mingle with them. Leda launches herself into the room.*)

LEDA

I'm afraid! I'm afraid!

GYPTIS, *without getting up*

Woman, have no fear. Sit down at my hearth. She's expelled you, then, the daughter of King Nann! Getting up abruptly and marching toward her. It's necessary, you see, not to touch our amour.

(*Leda flees to the other end of the room.*)

GYPTIS, *marching solely toward Leda, leaning on a wall*
It's necessary, you see, not to touch our amour.

LEDA, *falling to her knees*
Euxenes! Euxenes!

GYPTIS
Why are you imploring Euxenes? Do you believe that he'll throw you out, when I've picked you up? I'm not in my house, I'm not in his, I'm in ours. (*Turning toward the maid-servants.*) Fear has rendered her mad; she's imploring Euxenes. Doesn't Euxenes always want what I want? Don't the two of us only make a single individual? Isn't Euxenes...can you tell me my name? I've forgotten it.

A MAIDSERVANT
Gyptis.

GYPTIS, *passing her hand over her forehead*
Gyptis! Are you sure? Then I'm the disdained daughter... Why have you told me that I'm Gyptis, the one who is inconsolable? My heart was singing so gaily, and now it will weep, forever, forever! It's necessary for us to go, my girls, our place is no longer here. (*She bumps into Leda.*) What are you doing here? (*Taking the ax.*) I'm avenging myself; it's my right.

(*The followers run away.*)

LEDA, *dragging herself on her knees*
I'll go wherever you wish. I'll be your slave.

GYPTIS, *turning the ax in her hands*
Don't lie. Do you love him?

LEDA
No.

GYPTIS
Then you're nothing but a viper, crawling in his path.
(*Lifting the ax,*) If you'd loved him, I would have had pity.

LEDA, *embracing her knees*
Mercy!

GYPTIS, *dropping the ax*
She isn't even a viper... He should never have loved
you... Get out.

(*She shoves her away with her foot; a maidservant opens
the door.*)

THE MAIDSERVANT
Oh! Look, Mistress!

GYPTIS
And that's because of me!

(*She goes out running; the maidservants follow her. Leda
gets up.*)

LEDA
I'm, afraid! Why didn't I believe Philo? Why did I
come? Perhaps what Laïs said to me just now was true. He
wanted me to go; I haven't gone; if he comes back, he'll kill
me. Anger doesn't rise to his lips, like that Gaulish woman,
but when his hand is raised, it always strikes. I'm afraid of
death! I'm afraid! I'm afraid! (*She runs toward the door, then
stops.*) If they see me, they'll kill me; might as well die here.
Death is the end of everything, the eternal slumber, the dreamless sleep; I have nothing to regret, I've never loved; I've
nothing more to hope for, my mirror has shown me the wrin-
kles. Might as well die today as tomorrow... Dying—that
scares me... That's why I dragged myself at the feet of that

woman; I was afraid! She's going to offer me a place as a maidservant, and her swineherd for a husband. And I'm a Greek, the daughter of a free man! In seeing me fall, it's necessary that that barbarian sees that we're more beautiful than her.

(*She sits down on the floor and veils her face with a flap of her tunic. After a moment, Euxenes enters.*)

Euxenes. Leda

EUXENES, *entering without seeing Leda*
Gyptis! She isn't here. Even if they kill me, I want to see her this evening. Gyptis!

LEDA, *getting up, aside*
He'll kill me. (*Aloud.*) Is it me you're looking for?

EUXENES
You've dared to enter here... (*Taking her by the arm.*) Get out!

LEDA
No.

EUXENES
Why have you come?

LEDA
To laugh at you and your bare-footed queen.

EUXENES
Believe me, Leda, go away.

LEDA
No.

EUXENES, *looking for his sword*
I'm no longer anything but a prisoner fleeing his judge.

LEDA
I did well to come. (*Euxenes picks up the ax that Gyptis dropped.*) Strike my forehead; at least she won't be jealous of a dead woman! Strike! I trembled before her but I won't tremble before you. (*Euxenes drops the ax. Leda holds out a dagger to him which she takes from her bosom.*) It's too heavy? Here!

EUXENES
You've seen her? You know where she is? Tell me, and I'll forgive you.

LEDA
For being Xantippe' mistress? You've known that for a long time, but I only found out today that Gyptis is your mistress.

EUXENES
Listen, Leda; you embarrass me and I hate you. If I killed you, everything would revert to what it was before, but if you tell me where she is, I have jewels and gold, take everything.

LEDA
Keep that with my dowry.

EUXENES, *coldly, heading for the door*
I don't want to see you again, do you understand?

(*Cathmor, staff in hand, appears on the threshold.*)

Cathmor. Euxenes, Leda

CATHMOR
Today is my day! Your city is burning, Greek!

EUXENES
Where is Gyptis?

CATHMOR
Gyptis! I no longer want her to love you.

LEDA
I'll stay with you.

CATHMOR, *to Leda*
Do you love him?

LEDA
I've never loved him.

CATHMOR
Too bad! (*Euxenes tries to move him out of the way, and he shows him armed Gauls on the threshold.*) If I let them enter, they'll kill you. Listen; in front of these men you're going to kiss that woman; then you'll climb back into her galley with her, and you'll never come back.

EUXENES
No.

CATHMOR
Then you'll die.

EUXENES
I'm waiting

CATHMOR
You're brave, Greek.

LEDA, *aside*
I didn't know that.

EUXENES

Hurry up. I'm in haste for Gyptis to know that I love her. You've spoken too loudly, Cathmor. These men have heard. (*To the Gauls.*) Tell her that I was glad to sense her near me, that I loved her as a strong and loving companion, but that today I love her as you Gauls are able to love. Kill me, bard; I believe now what you believe, that tomorrow she'll rejoin me where I shall wait for her.

LEDA, *aside*
And me? I don't want that.

CATHMOR, *to Euxenes*
You're brave.

LEDA

And you, old man, are mad. (*To Euxenes.*) Don't search for your Gyptis any longer; she's killed herself out of shame for having loved you.

EUXENES
Ah!

(*He seizes the ax and marches slowly toward Leda, who recoils all the way to Gyptis' bedroom. Cathmor laughs.*)

LEDA

You're mad, old man. (*She launches herself at Euxenes and strikes him with her dagger. He turns on his axis and falls into Gyptis' bedroom.*) Death is the eternal slumber. She wouldn't have loved him any longer if he'd killed me, and I want her to weep. Is that what you wanted, old man?

CATHMOR
I no longer know what I want.

(*He leaves, followed by the Gauls.*)

LEDA

Death is the dreamless sleep. I didn't have him, but no one will have him. I didn't know that he was brave, I didn't know that he was capable of love. (*Leaning over the cadaver and kissing it.*) You're mine, no one's but mine, and I love you.

(*The curtain of the bedroom falls and hides both of them. After a moment, Laïs enters.*)

Laïs. Then Arachne

LAÏS, *looking round*

He isn't here. When I saw him running so fast I thought he was coming to look for Gyptis. He's as mad as the others. Instead of running so much, he should have departed sooner. King Nann too, Everyone striking, everyone shouting: "For King Nann! For Euxenes!" And King Nann wasn't there, and Euxenes wasn't there! A singular country! And Leda? Euxenes must have delivered her as a hostage. He's a practical man, he came to look for her, that's why he was running so much just now. (*Sitting down in front of the fire, which she reanimates.*) I count for nothing in all this racket. I did what I could to prevent it, and I have no desire to pay for the guilty. There's only one head in all this society, Gyptis. I'll take refuge in her hearth. A singular country! People fight, and then embrace; having embraced, they fight again.

ARACHNE, *entering with a pike in hand.*
Where's Philo?

LAÏS
The Gauls killed him this morning.

ARACHNE

Too bad! I would have liked to kill him myself. To think that he's caused so much bloodshed! For blood is flowing like a river. (*Letting herself fall on a bench,*) What events, great gods, what events! Ad that Gyptis! There's one that I like. Everyone striking, everyone shouting: "Kill! Kill! To the sea! To the sea!" The women weeping. I took this pike from Chrysias; he's asleep, the drunkard; I lashed out in front of me. A woman stands up in the midst of the swords (*She gets up and makes gestures.*) and she extends her little hands. "What are you doing friends?" She parts the pikes as one parts the ears in a wheat-field. Then she spoke. Her voice was soft, mild. We kissed her tunic. Then I see a troop of women running. I recognize Leda's women. An old man, white-haired, tries to speak loudly; Gyptis puts her hand over his mouth; he goes away. I make a sign to the women around me, we set off at a run and we join Leda's band. It was dark, they ran to the water's edge crying like seagulls. We push them, they go. Philo's sailors might have fished them out. The cowards hadn't come ashore. Are you sure that Philo was killed? (*Letting herself fall back on to the bench.*) What events, great gods, what events!

LAÏS
And Euxenes?

ARACHNE
They're searching for him

LAÏS
And Gyptis?

ARACHNE

Disappeared. Suddenly, trumpets were heard and the old king arrived at a gallop on a white horse, sword in hand. To fray a passage he struck Greeks and Gauls alike. All that had happened without his knowledge, by Philo's fault. Then I said to myself; "I'll go get him, that Philo." (*Gyptis enters. Arachne extends her arms toward her.*) Here's the one who saved us!

Gyptis. Arachne. Laïs

LAÏS, *running toward Gyptis*
How pale she is! How cold she is!

ARACHNE
Are you wounded?

GYPTIS
No.

LAÏS
She's gone.

GYPTIS
She's gone!

ARACHNE
And I promise you that she won't ever come back.

LAÏS
It's Philo who did everything.

GYPTIS
Poor Philo!

LAÏS
Now it's necessary to smile, (*She makes her sit down and arranges her hair.*) and to be very pretty, when he returns.

ARACHNE
She loves him as much as that, then? How unfortunate women are! And he wasn't in the places you passed?

ARACHNE
But you're even paler…what's the matter?

GYPTIS
I think I'm going to die.

ARACHNE
Die! Because of a man; you can't think so! No, we don't want you to die.

GYPTIS
I've done what I could.

ARACHNE
She'll let herself die, as she says. (*To Laïs.*) Get out of here. (*Sitting down next to Gyptis and taking her hand in hers.*) Have no more chagrin. I was at Euxenes' wedding; he married her because she was rich and he had debts. He couldn't stand her; in Phocea, everyone knew that. It's Philo who brought her.

GYPTIS
Poor Philo!

ARACHNE, *leaning over her ear*
And don't be jealous any longer; she's dead.

GYPTIS, *disengaging her hand*
Who did that?

ARACHNE
Me.

GYPTIS
You did badly.

ARACHNE, *leaping to her feet*
How unfortunate women are! (*Perceiving Leda standing, her tunic bloody, at the door of Gyptis' bedroom.*) You re-embarked on the water! Wait!

(*She tries to launch herself forward; Gyptis retains her. Nann appears, followed by Oedh, Cathmor and Gauls.*)

Nann. Oedh. Cathmor. Gyptis. Leda. Arachne. Laïs. Gauls

GYPTIS, *aside*
He isn't with them!

(*She goes to kneel, without saying anything, at Nann's feet.*)

NANN
I'm too close to death to judge. Get up, my daughter. I want to die in a ray of sunlight, in the midst of my three chil-dren, with my head on my bard's knees. (*Pointing at Leda.*) Get that woman out of here. Go search for Euxenes, my daughter.

LEDA, *taking a step and indicating the bedroom.*
He's in there!

GYPTIS
There?

LEDA
But he no longer belongs to anyone.

GYPTIS, *leaping forward.*
He's mine.

LEDA, *stopping her with her hand*
I've killed him.

GYPTIS
He loves me!

CATHMOR
When I said him: "Flee with that woman or die," he replied to me: "Strike!"

GYPTIS
He loves me! (*To Nann.*) I believe that our black day is
ended, and that we can go to sleep, my father. Take me on
your knees, as of old, and Cathmor will sing, in order for your
eyes to close more rapidly. (*She puts her arms around Nann's
neck.*) He loves me! We'll give you a beautiful child who will
love you; Oedh will make a soldier of him, Cathmor will make
a bard of him; let's all depart together, to rejoin those who are
waiting for us.

(*She dies.*)

MORGANE

I

The old man has a daughter; he calls her Morgane.[10]

The water has not wet the forehead of the old man; Morgane knows what the virgins of the past knew, and the leaves lean over in order to listen to her.

Her tresses are golden threads, her eyes two woodland cherries, her heart a clear spring.

When she passes over the heath, an eglantine in her hand, the hunter says: "The red deer will come back; the fays have returned." When she runs over the strand, her feet in the foam, the fisherman says: "The azure fish will come back; the fays have returned."

The fays have not returned; they are hiding in the green isle of the western Ocean, the isle that floats on the blue waves.

They fled when strangers traced an unknown sign on the menhirs; the red deer and the azure fish have followed them.

---

[10] This character is L'Estoille's version of a figure from French Medieval romance known in English literature, thanks to Thomas Malory, as Morgan le Fay. She was one of the key archetypes adopted the the salon writers at Louis XIV's court who invented the genre of *contes de fées*. In adapting her to his own idiosyncratic pseudohistory of France, L'Estoille redefines her relationship with Arthur and Merlin, and defines a new relationship with the rider of the white stallion—the Ar-Braz of *La Chanson de l'alouette*—although this prose poem is not entirely consistent with the latter work, in which Morgane does not appear under that name.

Since that day, the strand is mute and the woods are mute.

II

Morgane's heart is a clear spring, but Morgane is a woman; why does she not love one of those men whose hand only caresses the neck of a horse, whose breast is only kissed by the lips of swords?

Water has not wet the forehead of the old man; Morgane loves the past. When the west wind disturbs her hair she cries to the gulls: "Gulls, if you see in his chariot of clouds the warrior dead without a bride, tell him that Morgane loves him."

Since the fays have departed, the dead warriors no longer return on the clouds of the sunset to watch their sons fight.

The woods are mute, the sky is desert.

III

One evening, Morgane was on a cliff at the foot of which the ebb tide leaves a crescent of sand.

She was dreaming, but was she asleep when she saw a great army on the sand and before that army, a chief on a white stallion?

Was she asleep when she saw the white stallion galloping over the waves as if over a meadow?

If she was asleep, when she awoke she said: "That chief is the warrior dead without a bride."

Since the warriors no longer come in their chariots of clouds, the strings of my harp have twisted round my fingers like cold serpents; today they vibrate like cicadas; I have seen Morgane passing, an eglantine in her hand.

IV

The sun is hot; Morgane is walking alongside a stream in the green forest. Her hair is floating loose, her lips smiling at the butterflies, her fingers caressing the ferns.

Then a goldfinch sings in her ears: "I have a palace in the forest bluer than a spring evening, more luminous than a summer evening, more gilded than an autumn evening, more nacreous than a winter evening."

The virgin responds to the goldfinch: "Little woodland bird, you're lying."

The strings of my harp are as vibrant as reeds and sing like cicadas; my heart burns as it burned when I was the bard of the chief with the golden shield.

V

The sun is hot; Morgane is lying at the foot of an oak; the goldfinch perches on a branch and chirps: "Close your eyes, Morgane."

The virgin goes to sleep under the oak; she wakes up in a crystal grotto and the goldfinch sings over her lips: "Our son will be the king of the Bretons, Arthur of the hairy hand."

She responds: "Little woodland bird, you are the soul of the warrior dead without a bride."

You tremble as you open your eyes, Morgane, because you see, between the oaks, a man with a broad brow smile and disappear. Why are you trembling? Can you not see on the grass a sword so heavy that no living warrior would be able to lift it?

VI

Morgane, having recognized the sword that the chief was brandishing as he galloped over the green waves, kissed its hand-guard and rejoined the old man, who was talking to Merlin.

"Father," she said to him, "My son will be Arthur of the hairy hand."

The old man went pale, but the savant Merlin said: "Where is the sword with the golden hand-guard?"

"Under the oak," Morgane replied.

And Merlin smiled, and the old man kissed Morgane's hair.

I have lived many times, I have used up many bodies, I have been the bard of the chief with the heavy sword; his breath has passed between Morgane's lips, the son of whom he dreamed is about to be born. That is why my harp is singing like a cicada; that is why my heart is beating as at twenty years.

VII

Merlin cradles the little child in his arms; a horse whinnies at the door.

"Open the door, Father; my husband is there on his white horse."

"Sleep, my rosebud; your son is as beautiful as the day."

"Open the door quickly, Father; my husband is waiting for me."

"Sleep, my floret; he is already stronger than a mountain bear; he can already lift the sword."

Then she who is a virgin and a mother gets up. She takes the infant with the hairy hands; the door opens; she holds out the child to the man who she alone can see, and then she returns him to Merlin.

When one entered the hall with the blue dome of them man whose bard I was, one saw his throne shining like the sun in the middle of twelve seats as brilliant as stars.

In those days, the earth belonged to the Bretons.

VIII

The horse whinnies at the door

Morgane sits on the luminous mane; an invisible hand holds the reins. The horse gallops in the clouds as in a meadow, carrying Morgane toward the setting sun.

The old man weeps at the foot of the empty bed, but the newborn escapes from Merlin's arm; he brandishes the heavy sword and he says in a loud voice: "I shall be the butcher of my race."

And Merlin says to the old man: "Why are you weeping?"

When I was the bard of the king with the scintillating throne, and I sometimes said: "You do not love, chief; do you not want sons?" he replied to me: "The woman I shall love is not yet born."

He was already thinking of Morgane.

IX

On the western Ocean, an isle as green as an emerald floats on the blue waves; it is the isle where the sylphs and the fays are hiding.

The hero dead without amour has carried Morgane there, and Morgane is now the queen of the sylphs and the fays.

Bards, if you sing of the heroes of the past, you will see Morgane on her opal chariot.

Soldiers, if you fall with a smile on your lips, you will see Morgane on her opal chariot.

BALKIS[11]

For the one whose eyes are my stars, whose lips are the spring from which I drink, whose hand is my support, whose heart is my sap, a poet, while shredding a rose near a spring of clear water in the month of ripe grapes, I have written this,

Listen!

I

In the shade of a sycamore, near an onyx basin from which a perfumed water spurts, between white jasmines and vermilion roses, in the midst of his queens, King Solomon said:

"I am like a slave attached to a mill; I turn in the same circle; where I set my foot today, I shall set my foot tomorrow. I would like to stray to unknown summits and pathless plains.

And near the onyx basin, the brown daughters of the Liban, the blonde daughters of the Caucasus, the serious daughter of Egypt and the foolish daughters of Assur search for what it is necessary to do to dispel the sadness of Solomon.

Is it necessary to dance?" says the Libyan, piercing her tresses with a branch of white jasmine. "Is it necessary to sing

---

[11] Balkis is the name traditionally attributed to the character briefly mentioned in the Old Testament, usually known in English as the Queen of Sheba [Saba in French]. The present prose poem is greatly elaborated from a brief passage in *Fusains*, also echoed in other references to the mythical land of Saba in L'Estoille's work.

of the god of roses?" says the warbler brought from the isle of the evergreen laurels.

"It would be necessary, my blonde bees, to dissipate the ennui that binds me," sighs the disenchanted, "to tell me what I have not heard before; it would be necessary to show me brown swallows, which I have not yet seen.

"I am like the palm tree of the pool that hides between the dunes of the desert; on the motionless waters I only see my shadow on the moving waves; I would finally like to see the white seagull swimming."

Then Lyda the great beauty with shoulders the color of honey, bought the day before, untied her enameled belt, and like a white seagull, slid into the transparent water of the sunlit basin.

And the jealous queens threw their garlands of roses into the basin. Then Lyda the great beauty... "Can you hear it, under the palm trees?"

"It is the wood-pigeons waking up.

All that could be heard was the cicadas moaning under the olive trees and the water falling into the bowl where the petals of the shredded roses were floating.

"It's a stainless ivory, but it's only a woman," said Solomon, stroking his beard.

Then a clear voice spoke on the sycamore: "I have taken pity on your trouble. You want to hear, Solomon, that which you have not heard? Ask your queens the names of those they love." Surprised, Solomon raises his head.

On the sycamore, a hoopoe was polishing its striped wings. "Beautiful bird," the king replied, "Have you arrived from Saba? Say to the one who sent you: "Solomon's necklace lacks a pearl, but Solomon wants the most beautiful."

"You have made a very pretty necklace from these pearls, slightly tarnished by the hands of merchants," said the Hoopoe, "But you are not yet a fine enough jeweler to enclose a drop of dew in a necklace."

Solomon rotated his ring, and the black djinni bowed before him. "I need," he said, "the queen of Saba. Go take her from her palace and leave her in the hall of cedars before sunset."

Then the one who twisted the columns of the temple said: Crows guard her; we cannot take her."
"Tell her that I am asking for her," Solomon interjected.
The hoopoe flew away and the queens reflected...

The eyes of my beloved are the stars that guided me to the embalmed oasis where I am now dreaming.

II

"Who,. then, is this queen whose messengers compare her to a drop of dew? Is she a blossomed rose? Is she a periwinkle, barely opening her modest corolla?"
"She is a blank vellum in a sealed reed, a grain of incense in a golden coffer."

Her father was a sage; when he saw the morning of his last day dawn, he said to the peri who pours the dew into the leaning flowers: "By the sun of amour my heart has been desiccated; to refresh my final hour, put a drop of dew therein."

The old man smiled, the peri leaned over. Then a drop fell from the golden urn. When it touched the still-warm heart the iridescent drop broke, and a blonde child emerged from it, who was the queen of Saba...

The lips of my beloved are the spring where I drank on the evening of the battle. The spring is so fresh that my wound has closed, so clear that I saw coral and pearls gleaming therein.

III

In Saba, the ardent city, which the fires of sunset set ablaze; in Saba, the eternal city where men no longer go, in the depths of a sunlit gulf, where the crimson sea fumes, a bronze palace is flamboyant. It is the palace of the queen.

An unknown architect, in one night, forged the dentellate domes of the palace of that queen, with a brow as high as a poem and eyes as clear as a pool.

In one night he enameled an azure hall in which a hundred palm trees vibrate, as in the desert. Four windows look out at the four corners of the horizon, and a throne of lapis rotates under the azure dome between the hundred trembling palms. It is the queen's bedroom.

She is not a queen like other queens, Balkis with the bronze hair; her gaze is as gentle as a dream, her laughter is as fresh as a kiss.

She is not a queen like other queens, the queen of Saba; she is an iridescent pearl, an inflamed ruby, an opal with vague reflections. She thinks like a poet, she speaks like a prophet and she sings like a bird.

But she is also a woman, since her lips quiver, since her heart beats faster, when wood-pigeons coo on the agate ledges.

When a gardener knows that a blonde cluster of grapes will turn amber on his trellis, he guards it against hornets. That is why, in a bronze palace with dentellate domes and walls devoid of doors, Balkis was enclosed by the unknown architect.

But when the cluster is ripe, the gardener plucks it, and sends it to his master under a white cloth. That is why a door will open before amour in the bronze walls.

But the hoopoe, knowing that falcons lie in wait at the doors of open cages, has said, while polishing its wings: "Balkis is a blank vellum, Balkis is a grain of incense; only a poet is worthy to posses her, only a king is rich enough to pay for her."

That is why the hoopoe flew, without stopping, all the way to the sycamore where it spoke. Is not Solomon the richest of kings and the greatest of poets?

The hand of my beloved retains me when the abyss attracts me. The fingers of that hand are the ivory spindles that will weave my shroud.

IV

Under the shade of the sycamore, the poet king as writing, and the bitter phrases burned his lips and writhed under his stylet like fiery serpents.

His brow furrowed, he wrote: "I wanted to brave the torrent, I wanted to bite the grape, but my mouth is filled with disgust and my teeth have grated."

Then the hoopoe, lying between the queen's breasts, said: "I have returned, Balkis, from the land of Idumea,[12] and in its garden full of flowers I found the poet king."

And Balkis said: Faithful messenger, in this garden full of flowers, what was Solomon doing?" The hoopoe replied: Dreaming of unknown summits and pathless beaches."

"My heart," thought Balkis, "is emptier than the plain; no imprint has ever been marked there; I am the one whom the king of Judea is dreaming amid his queens."

The heart of my beloved is a perfect poem, in which the verses are rounded out like the grapes in a cluster, ripening in the sun under their light vines.

V

Solomon is no longer writing. Without looking at the flowers that are leaning toward his hand in his garden; he is dreaming of inflamed rubies that a jeweler cannot set in a necklace. "Weapons are gleaming in the plan!" cries the sentry on watch on the summit of the palace.

The courtyard was so large in Solomon's palace that an army could camp there at ease, with it camels and its tents, its horses and its elephants, under vaults where armor shines between blue swords.

The soldiers were so alert in Solomon's armies that before he had buckled on his word, brass towers were set up on

---

[12] Idumea was the name given in classical Greek to a region south of Judea, adjacent to or perhaps identical with the kingdom of Edom, most of which lay in the territory of the modern state of Jordan.

the backs of elephants; before he had picked up his helmet, archers had departed on their mares without bridles.

But the women were so curious in Solomon's palace that they massed on the threshold while the archers departed, and they filled the portico while the king threw his tiger-striped cloak over his broad shoulders.

On a chariot encrusted with tortoiseshell, which Pharaoh had given him, in his azure armor, beneath his scintillating helmet, the prophet king is so handsome, that the jewels in his coffer forget that he is their master and the pearls in his necklace forget that they have been bought.

As in the regretted nights of distant lands, a ray of light inflames them, a tear darkens then. Brown pearls and blond rubies accumulate around the proud jeweler. "Take us with you," they say, "Are we not your necklace and the crest of your helmet?"

Solomon was a soldier, before whom the bravest trembled, but he was also a poet; on the sunlit plain he emptied his sparkling jewel-case, and in front of the Judean army he put on his diadem of flowers.

In the sunlit plain, it was the queen of Saba who came to meet Solomon. "King, said the hoopoe, perched on the gilded tusk of the white elephant, one has begun to pity the one who divines everything, and Balkis has come to pose you a problem, in order to relieve tour ennui.."

Solomon bowed, and the daughters of the Caucasus said to the daughters of Liban: "She is red-haired, but she is beautiful. Is she another grape of the dense cluster the Eternal had ripened for the gluttonous lips of the king of Judea?"

"Her voice is vibrant, her teeth brilliant," said the daughters of Egypt to the foolish daughters of Assur. "When she speaks, one might think one were hearing crystal ring on a marble pavement. She will be the merry cymbal of Solomon's orchestra."

And, lips smiling, arms enlaced, while circling the traveler, they sing: "With the amorous sheaf, sunflower of the sands, come and mingle. With the flight of the turtle-doves, lovers of the sun, partridge with yellow wings, come and mingle!"

"I was fifteen years old," responds the queen, when I went to sleep one evening beside my open window; the wall was smooth and high; I thought myself safe, but as I went to sleep, my great beauties, my heart was stolen."

Having spoken thus, one might have thought that a malign smile hollowed out dimples in the amber cheeks of Balkis, but he elephant knelt down, and the bare feet of the queen shone above the head of the wonderstruck Solomon.

In the coral pavilion, under eyelashes the color of bronze, the gaze of Balkis is so soft that the king says to the queen: "A ray of sunlight changes a drop of dew into an inflamed ruby; if you wish, Balkis, I can guide you to the land where the sun shines."

"Solomon, if I followed you to the unknown land, what would you make of the ruby?"

"The seal of my ring, the torch of my late nights, the pommel of my sword, the tip of my stylet, the key to my treasure, the handle of my scepter."

"A thief has taken my heart, on the perforated balcony of my palace of bronze."

"It is necessary to search for the thief."

"I know him Solomon; that thief is a poet; my heart is a prisoner in his cadenced verses, as in a net."

"Since your heart is a prisoner in such a tight net," responds the prophet king, "it is necessary to put there with it your tawny tresses, your fresh lips, and your eyes, in which I see the light shining for which I search on serene nights."

Balkis remained silent, and Solomon said to himself: "I am a good enough jeweler to set a drop of dew in a necklace." He extended his arm.

"Solomon," said the queen, escaping, laughing, "Sit down next to me; it is only my heart that loves you."

I am not a poet. A poet is similar to a red tulip, which hides a heart of soot in a crimson calyx. I am only a fortunate lover, and my poems are the kisses that my beloved gives me.

VI

In the garden of the lively waters, the djinn have built a marvelous palace for the queen, of crystal and nacre.

For a year, every morning, Solomon has taken intoxicating flowers there, saddling jewel-cases, and inflamed poems; but every evening he emerges as soon as the first star peeps under the cool arcades of the nacre palace.

Solomon has never sung the fruits he has savored; the queen knows that, and Balkis of the long circled eyes only loves the poet.

The blonde daughters of the Caucasus, the brunette daughters of the Liban, the pensive daughters of Egypt and he foolish daughters of Assur hid in the bushes, weep on the edges of the basins; for a year, the master, lamenting like a poet, speaks alone, like a shepherd.

One evening, he said to the queen: "My heart remains attached to those tawny tresses; let my lips alight where my heart is a prisoner.

"If I listened to you this evening, you would fall silent tomorrow," responds Balkis, smiling. I only know how to say what you have already heard; tomorrow, under the sycamore, near the onyx basin where icy water flows, in the midst of his queens, King Solomon would be bored."

"The hoopoe has spoken," he thought, very quietly. Then he said to Balkis. "Perhaps you're right; I'm having a beautiful dream, why wake up?"

The next day Solomon brought the queen, as he had the previous day, a bouquet, a jewel-case and a poem. The flowers had opened in the peris' garden, djinn had founded the gold of the bracelets, and the verses would have rendered the nightingale jealous; but he did not mention amour.

He talked about the temple, his fleets, and his soldiers; and the queen with the long circled eyes found that day less short than the others.

The next day, the sun was about to set when the king, his brow furrowed, entered the nacre hall where the queen had been waiting impatiently since morning.

"What's the matter with you?" Balkis said to him.

"I don't know," the king replied; my brow is burning, my head is heavy."

"If that were true, Solomon, you would put your brow in my hands; their coolness would calm your fever."

"No—until tomorrow, my queen."

Maidservants were playing on the steps of the throne; eunuchs were leaning on the twisted columns; what was the queen risking?" "Come, Solomon," she said. "You're suffering, and I love you; put your head in my hands and close your eyes, my poet."

In the queen's two hands, on her slightly tremulous knees, Solomon hid his head. The hoopoe smoothed its wing-feathers.

Leaning on the twisted columns, the black eunuchs smiled, and on the steps of the throne, the maidservants peeped between their slender fingers. "Are you asleep, Solomon?" said the queen.

Solomon did not reply. "Oh, if dared!" said Balkis, tilting her head slightly.

She was an inflamed ruby, an opal with vague reflections, a drop of dew; but she was also a woman, the queen with the bronze hair.

"Before those eyes that gaze at me, I would never dare..." She lifted her fan. Then the eunuchs became crows and the maidservants swallows. The hoopoe, swollen, its head under its wing, seemed to be allowing itself go be lulled by the sweetest of dreams.

"Are you asleep, Solomon?" said the queen. Solomon did not respond, and Balkis kissed his head.

Solomon was not asleep...

Green vines, enlace the wan trunk of the lemon tree; disheveled clematis, sway your embalmed arms like almahs at the tops of the palm trees; at the spring of the palm trees in the shadow of the lemon trees, I am awaiting my beloved.

HÉLÈNE[13]

I

West of the bay of Algiers, near Pescade Point, in a Moorish house, a delightful child lived—the year is irrelevant—who was on the threshold of becoming a woman.

I will not paint you a portrait of that child, for if she were brunette and, by chance, you preferred blondes, or vice versa, you would no longer listen to me. I will simply tell you that Hélène was lying on a divan when Madame Dorothée introduced Captain Jacques.

Captain Jacques was the only friend of our heroine, who, for the convenience of the story, I shall call Hélène, because that was not her name.

As for Madame Dorothée, Hélène called her "Aunt," not knowing any other name to give her. She was a lady about sixty years old, with a venerable face. It was said that she had served as a mother to the girl, and every three months she went to see Maître Leblond, the notary, in order to receive three thousand francs.

Where did that money, for which they never had to wait, come from? Dorothée never said and Hélène had no suspicion. When she searched her memory hard she remembered a large city, where there was a big square, and a large illuminated house where she was taken in the evenings. There, a woman who gave her a lot of bonbons rocked her on her knees.

---

[13] An earlier version of this story was incorporated into *Fusains*, where it was interrupted and incomplete, being confused with the autobiographical passages of that text, the narrative voice staying explicitly that he is Captain Jacques and that Hélène does not exist.

Then she remembered Naples, which she had left when she was seven years old, in order to enter the best convent in Seville. When her education was finished, the superior, a woman as venerable as Madame Dorothée, had urged her strongly to take the veil. Not sensing the slightest vocation, Hélène had refused, and Madame Dorothée had bought the house on Pescade Point for her.

Let us return to our story.

"I thought you were dead, Captain," said Hélène, holding out her hand.[14]

"Mademoiselle, I have returned to life in order to tell you a story."

"A story of the other world?"

"Yes."

"If the story is pretty, I'll forgive you."

"For coming back to life? Thank you."

"I'm listening."

"Do you know Auxonne, the fat green frog that watches the Saône flow by in a melancholy fashion?"

"No."

"Well. I know Auxonne and I could describe it for you if I didn't have to talk to you about Jean Philibert, who spent his days there fishing and his evenings in the company of a yellow parrot. That parrot came from India, where it had been a Brahmin in the time of Solomon, in a pink pagoda on the bank of the Ganges."

"My dear Monsieur, of what malady did you die?"

"A malady of the heart."

"Ah...! Continue."

---

[14] This remark made sense in the version of the story contained in *Fusains*, in which the captain has been away for some time, but does not in the context of the revised story, which develops very differently in order to contrive an ending that the earlier version did not have, and could not possibly have reached.

"That Brahmin had been condemned to a thousand years of existence for having said to a young woman, on the edge of a rice-field, that her eyes were larger than those of Sita, the goddess with the golden eyes. That is why he was able to spend his evenings in the company of Jean Philibert, who was then in love with a moonbeam."

"And was Jean Philibert's love reciprocated."

"Inevitably."

"Inevitably?"

"Yes, inevitably; one is always paid in return by a moonbeam. Look, you're very charming; love a moonbeam. Humans are stupid; they throw themselves, like cockchafers, into the spider-web of amour. They give a tap of the paw here, a tap of the head there, and they change that big gray cannonball, that fine tissue as velvety as flame and as bright as an evening in July, which it's necessary only to touch with one's heart, and only to look at with closed eyes. Whereas, moonbeams... Let's return to the town of Auxonne."

"I'm there."

"Good! One night, Jean Philibert, his hand on his doorhandle, was gazing at the bell-tower where the bells were ringing, and he said to himself: "it's the twenty-fourth of December; is the town celebrating?"

"He opened the door and the parrot cried, in its hoarse voice: 'Noël, Master Jean, Noël!' Let's celebrate, like the mayor and the officers of the garrison."

"'We can have a good time, just the two of us,' replied Jean Philibert.

" Will we not have the lotus flower who came in with you? Be welcome, lotus flower, the Brahmin salutes you.'

"The parrot was addressing a woman whom Jean Philibert had not seen come in. That woman was the moonbeam, about whom he dreamed while the cork of his fishing-line bobbed between the nenuphars of the Saône. He was desolate, because his beard was not perfect.

"The woman sat down by the fire, and in order to warm her little feet better, she lifted her gold-starred muslin skirt a little above the ankle.

"Those little feet were charming; they resembled yours. I'll wager that if you put on a gold-starred muslin skirt, the yellow parrot would say to you, on seeing you: 'Salut, lotus flower!'"

"You think so?"

"I'm certain of it. Jean Philibert, who had only contemplated that dainty ankle in a moonbeam, fell into an armchair, suffocating, and the yellow parrot hastened to say: 'Star of the Orient, your ankle is finer than that of Sita, the goddess with the amber feet. If my master had shaved, he would have told you so already.'

"Trying to understand, but not understanding, how a moonbeam could sit down by a fire, Jean Philibert fell asleep.

"Poor Jean Philibert. He woke up with a start, standing on one foot, in the body of the yellow parrot..."

"Permit me to ask, Captain, how many glasses of absinthe you have drunk?"

"Two, and the second had gum."

"You should also have put gum in the first; you are, I'm afraid, slightly..."

"No, Mademoiselle, I'm not drunk, but...."

"You're yellow, with blue wing-tips?"

"Perhaps... It's stifling. If you'd like to come to Pescade Point, I'll tell you the story of the lotus and the parrot. You'll understand then why Jean Philibert and the said parrot only made a single whole, being, in spoliation, two halves, and why the moonbeam and the lotus flower were only one woman."

"And why do you want to tell me all that?"

"In order to tell you that I love you."

"There's no need; I've known that for a long time."

"But do you know why I love you?"

"Because my ankles resemble those of Sita, the goddess with the amber feet," replied Hélène, with a sigh." There's no need for us to go to Pescade Point. Adieu."

"*Au revoir.*"

"Perhaps."

Hélène stood up and went into her bedroom without holding out her hand.

"She's a little fool, Captain," said the venerable aunt.

"Fortunately, she's only a lotus flower, Madame Dorothée," replied the captain, going out with a beaming smile.

II

They had met one morning on the sea shore, and they had chatted because Castor, the captain's barbet, had licked Hélène's little feet.

That morning, the bare feet of the child—she was only sixteen years old and had just come from the convent in Seville—were shining on the sand like two nacreous seashells.

That morning he captain had gone out thinking: *I must learn Arabic. It's only possible to learn a language well by speaking it, so let's find a daughter of the Prophet who speaks like the Koran.*

As soon as Castor had liked the little feet, their mistress having spoken to the dog in Spanish, Jacques thought: *One doesn't learn anything by trying to learn everything at once; it's necessary to perfect myself in the language of the Cid before spelling out that of Mahomet.*

Captain Jacques was a studious man; he requested a Spanish lesson from the beautiful young woman with the bare feet immediately.

She wasn't a Spaniard; she didn't understand what the captain was asking her in pure Castilian, and she replied in good French: "You have a very nice dog, Monsieur."

The captain understood then that he would have done better to speak French, and while the barbet, who had definitely taken a liking to the bather, played with her on the sand, he said to a venerable lady sitting in the shadow of a rock, whom he had not previously perceived: "You have a charming daughter, Madame."

"She's not my daughter, Monsieur, she's my niece," the lady replied. "She has few distractions, and you're very kind to let your dog play with her."

The venerable lady spoke in French, however, and it as the captain's turn not to understand.

Desirous of studying the problem he sat down beside the lady and ended up accepting a cup of milk for Castor in the Moorish house.

Hélène was a delightful child on the threshold of becoming a woman. She had admirable eyes, those beautiful eyes that say nothing indifferent, those beautiful hard eyes whose eyelids need to be blue-tinted.

Although she had been in the convent in Seville she was as ignorant as a swallow. All day long she played on her sofa with her slipper or watched the butterflies fluttering over the lentisks.

"She's only a child," said Madame Dorothée, while the barbet licked his moustache; she needs a well-brought-up young woman to teach her good manners."

As soon as the captain heard that phrase he fled.

He ran rather than walked all the way to his little room, at the very top of the street of the Kasbah, and he let himself fall on to his stool, saying: "Jean Philibert, you're about to do something stupid."

But after a moment, what he called his yellow parrot, the voice that spoke to him in moments of doubt, said to him: "Reflect, then, Master Jean, and when you know what you want, do what is necessary to accomplish it."

The captain reflected for a week, and then he took from his bookshelf two volumes of the great poets who know how to talk about amour.

As soon as he had them under his arm, the yellow parrot said to him: "You're right, Master Jean; while the sun is shining, a moth doesn't go to burn its wings on candles."

Hélène understood the poets better than he understood them himself.

For a year he went back every Thursday to the Moorish house, and each of his visits lasted six hours, so Hélène said to him one evening: "Since you only have six hours a week to give me, why don't you come every day to spend one hour with me?"

"You're forgetting Sunday, Mademoiselle," the captain replied, gravely. "What would I do on Sunday if I acquired the habit of coming to see you on all the other days?"

Hélène had been quite content with that response. Now she no longer resembles the child who ran barefoot on the sand she resembles one of those delicate and energetic figurines carved in agate by the artists of Syracuse. Her forehead is broader, her eyes open, the corners of her mouth turned up and her hair full of sap, curling over the back of her neck.

She is now a woman, a true woman. She is not a woman like those created by arrangers of words, half-cloud and half-glow, but a true woman with red lips and breasts,

While they read the poets Dorothée gladly goes to sleep, and when the captain stands up and closes the book, she invariably sighs: "What does that prove, then?"

"It proves, Madame Dorothée," the captain invariably replies, "that a girl must be well-guarded..."

Then the venerable lady bows, and Hélène escorts the captain as far as the garden gate. That is the moment when they play for a while with Castor, a worthy dog who does not care about poets and who seems to be quite astonished that Hélène does not embrace his master as she embraces him.

The captain is neither young nor old, nor short not tall, nor handsome nor ugly. He is a little crazy but his madness is not contagious; he believes that the soul is immortal.

III

Hélène has not said *au revoir*, she has said *adieu*, and the captain is walking cheerfully. As he closed the garden gate he looked at his watch and exclaimed: "The office will still be open!"

Only Castor is sad; no one has embraced him; are they annoyed with him, then? He has been very good, though; he needs to be embraced. He pulls the captain by his tunic and then he runs to scratch at the gate.

Dogs often have more intelligence than their masters, but this time, the dog is in the wrong.

The captain hastened his steps; he wanted to arrive before the closure of his office at the home of Maître Leblond, the punctilious notary who gave three thousand francs to Madame Dorothée every trimester. He had made his acquaintance since discovering that detail, so he entered into the matter abruptly.

"What do you know about Mademoiselle Hélène?" he asked.

"Far less than you," replied the notary, cleverly.

"Don't be too witty, Maître Leblond; I'm addressing the notary."

"The notary doesn't know anything."

"How will you draw up her contract, then?"

"Her contract?"

"Yes, if I marry her."

"But this isn't serious?"

"I love Mademoiselle Hélène and I want to marry her, if possible."

"Anything is possible."

"You're presumptuous, Maître Leblond. I'm more modest, and I only want to obtain Mademoiselle Hélène from her
father."

"She doesn't have one."

"Very well. I only want to obtain Mademoiselle Hélène
from her mother."

"She hardly has one."

"That would be perfect, if she had none at all."

"I can only tell you that Mademoiselle Hélène is only
called Mademoiselle Hélène."

"You're extracting a thorn that is inconveniencing me
somewhat."

"Until the day of her marriage she has a pension of
twelve thousand francs, payable quarterly."

"And afterwards?"

"Afterwards, she no longer has anything."

"I would embrace you, if that would give you pleasure."

"Would you care to forget, for a moment, that I'm a notary?"

"Yes."

"You're mad."

"Completely, my dear friend, and mad with joy into the
bargain."

"When is the wedding?"

"When she loves me."

"But..."

"Become a notary again, Maître Leblond..."

As he went back downstairs, the yellow parrot flapped its
wings and said: "She loves you today as you want to be loved;
act in such a way that she loves you forever."

At home, the captain found the venerable Dorothée, who
was wiping her eyes.

"What's the matter, Madame Dorothée?"

"We're leaving tomorrow."

"For where?"

"I don't know. Hélène wants to go a long way, very far."

"When one wants to go that far, Madame Dorothée, one arrives right away."

"I said to her: 'You can't marry; you know that very well, and he loves you. Where do you want to go?'"

"You've explained all that clearly to her?"

"Yes, Monsieur."

"Then there's nothing to be done, poor Madame; go pack the bags."

Dorothée darted a crushing glance at the captain and went out, with her head held high.

"Jump for mistress, Castor," the captain said to the barbet.

"Wasn't Maître Leblond right? When you said that the captain was only a little bit mad, you were looking at him with the eyes of a friend. What, he waited to talk about her contract until the day when he was thrown out?"

"Well, yes, he waited for that day; he had been waiting for a year, and if he hadn't been told to go away, he might perhaps have departed and never come back.

"Captain Jacques had always loved flowers, but he never wore one in his buttonhole. Being here one day and elsewhere another, he could only have flowers that were sold, and those flowers, he said, might be shiny but they reeked of the earth in which they were grown."

"And then, he wanted to know whether the shiny flower of Pescade Point...?"

"Exactly. Those poor flowers that are sold, it isn't their fault, but after all..."

"He only wanted to make Hélène his wife, and that worried Madame Dorothée?"

"Oh, that venerable lady isn't a monster, she's a practical woman. She knows that if Hélène married, the pension wouldn't be paid any longer; it's therefore in her interest that Hélène doesn't marry. Furthermore, she has been closely linked with Hélène's mother. All these explanations would perhaps take us a long way, but what I can affirm to you is that the fresh flower of Pescade Point didn't reek of the earth in which she'd been born."

"I'm increasingly of the opinion of Maître Leblond."

"Become the amiable reader again, who throws away the book after having read it."[15]

V

Madame Dorothée is packing the bags; Hélène is walking in the garden, and every time a branch brushes the gate, she runs.

Castor has the habit of preceding his master and scratching at the gate.

He'll come to bid me adieu, she thinks. She almost pardons Dorothée's stupidity; if Dorothée hadn't said anything, he wouldn't have been able to come.

But if Dorothée hadn't said anything, would she be leaving? She is greatly chagrined; the governess, in her exasperation, has told her many things, which she had divined, but which she did not know.

He'll come, she thinks. *He didn't want to tell me what I thought I understood. If he'd wanted to tell me that, he'd have done it a long time ago.*

She is walking in the garden path, but Castor doesn't scratch at the gate; she is greatly chagrined. "The good sister was right," she sobs. "Under the veil, all are equal. I'll go to Seville; God isn't as demanding as men! I would have liked to see him again, I would have liked to tell him that I wasn't annoyed, but that I was leaving because I loved him."

She is a true woman.

---

[15] Insertions of this kind, which encourage the suspicion that Captain Jacques is not alone in having an internal voice with which he occasionally enters into dialogue, occur frequently in *La Chanson de l'alouette*, and crop up occasionally in other works by L'Estoille.

There are people who claim that poets deprave youth; would you say the same now?

When she returned to her bedroom she wept hot tears, like the little girl she was. On the threshold, she put her hands over her heart; on the sill of the open window there was a large bouquet of bean-flowers.

That window overlooked an olive grove.

"He came back," she sighed, "but he's gone again, because I bid him adieu."

Flowers have souls and they speak; each of them only knows one phrase, but in that phrase there is one of the creator's ideas. Bean-flowers say, with their perfume: "Open your hearts to amour."

The bouquet had a strangely sweet perfume; she respired it for a long time, and then she went to lean on the window-sill. Her eyes searching the clear shade of the olive-trees, and while she gazed, her heart wept quietly: "I love him! I love him, and I'll never see him again."

Then she heard a muffled barking, and she started to smile in the midst of her tars like the child that she was. *They're there*, she thought. *They love me too much for me to be able to quit them.*

She withdrew abruptly, closed the window, blew a kiss to the olive grove and shouted: "Dorothée, we aren't leaving until the day after tomorrow." Then she went to bed, without lighting her candle.

The bouquet had a strangely sweet perfume; she went to sleep and she dreamed.

She dreamed that she went on a moonbeam into the room in Auxonne where the captain was chatting with the yellow parrot, and she said to him: "My ankle is as delicate as that of Sita, the goddess with the amber feet..."

When she woke up in the morning she ran to open her window.

Astonished, she listened.

She no longer recognized the sound of the sea. The waves, as they reached the shore, vibrated like the strings of a lyre; the great sea was singing her a sublime symphony.

Then she said: "He loves me; he will love me forever."

VI

The captain, forgetting all tact, pushed the garden gate before eight o'clock; he had spent the night on the edge of the bean-field.

"The bags are packed but we're no longer departing, *Monsieur le Capitaine*," Dorothée shouted to him.

"I told you that when one goes that far, so very far, one has arrived right away. I'm glad to have encountered you alone, Madame Dorothée, I have a favor to ask of you."

"I'm entirely at your disposal."

"I have a little house in France, with a western exposure, in the midst of vineyards, very clean and well-furnished, where I never go because of Castor."

"Because of Castor?"

"I can't separate myself from him, and he detests cats. Now, that house was given to me by one of my great aunts, on condition that I have a white she-cat cared for there. You have cared so well for Hélène, Madame Dorothée, that you would certainly care as well for the white cat."

"Monsieur!"

"We're going to be married."

"You don't know, then...."

"I know everything, my dear Madame; that's why I dare to ask you to aid the white cat to consume an annual income of six thousand francs—for she has a pension of six thousand francs—and if, perchance, she were dead, you'd procure another; it's only necessary that she be white. You understand?"

"Perfectly... but I'd like to embrace Hélène."

160

"Oh, Madame Dorothée, what would people say if you weren't seen at my wedding? Are you not Hélène's aunt?"

Madame Dorothée blushed.

"You've cared for her as best you could, and you've loved her in your fashion, when no one loved her."

She was not a monster, that Madame Dorothée; she started to weep, and the captain, who was not as wicked as he wanted to appear, whispered in her ear: "We're going to see the white cat."

He whispered in her ear because he had just perceived Hélène, who arrived with a branch of bean-flowers in her hand.

"I expected you yesterday," she said,

"You'd bid me adieu."

"In order to make you return more rapidly. Let's go to Pescade Point to finish the story of the lotus and the yellow parrot."

"I've forgotten it, if I ever knew it."

"I can remember it."

"Then you can tell it to me. Call Madame Dorothée, and let's depart quickly."

Hélène called Madame Dorothée.

"Embrace me," she said to her. "Embrace me as you embraced me when I was little."

Castor was a little jealous; when he saw Hélène embrace Dorothée, he tugged the young woman's dress gently.

"Take my arm," he captain said to her.

"No, I've mistreated Castor; I scarcely caressed him yesterday. We're going to play together on the way. Would you like that, Castor?"

The barbet started describing great circles around Hélène, and they both departed at a run.

"Master Jean," said the yellow parrot to the captain, "march straight or you'll fall."

VII

The captain found the young woman installed on the parapet overlooking the sea.

"Why here?" he said. "We'd be better in the shade."

"No, here. You were saying, then, that the parrot..."

"I was saying stupid things. I simply wanted to say that every man has caressed a dream, and that you're more beautiful than my dream."

"I'm not your dream, then?"

"Bad girl."

"I'll tell you that dream then, since you've forgotten it. I'll begin: In the time of Solomon there was, in a pink pagoda on the bank of the Ganges, a Brahmin proud of his science...is that right?"

"Hélène!"

"One morning, he encountered a poor girl, whom he thought beautiful...is that right?"

"That's exactly right; I remember now. Listen, Hélène; for a week he dared not return to where he'd seen the girl with bare feet, but during that week he composed a poem for her, a poem with a dozen verses, in which he compares her to a wild antelope, to a magnolia the color of milk, to a drop of dew iridescent in the sunlight. When the red cows lay down in the shade he recited his poem to them, and the lines were so sweet that the little cows, their eyes half-closed, followed the rhythm with their heads. Isn't that so, Castor?"

The young woman interrupted the captain.

"On the seventh day," she said, "the Brahmin hid behind the trunk of a tamarind, and the young woman, instead of fleeing, came to sit down beside him...as I am here.

"Then the Brahmin said, as you said yesterday: 'Your eyes are more beautiful than the eyes of Sita, the goddess with the golden eyes.'

"There was a rice-field nearby, but the young woman, pointing at the dazzling Ganges, said: 'That will be our marriage bed...'"

Hélène has stood up; she is on the edge of the parapet.

"I believe you're mistaken, Hélène," said the captain. "The Brahmin said to the woman he loved with all his heart: 'Let's go up the steps of the temple so that God can bless our union.'"

"That's not right. The young woman was of the accursed caste; she couldn't go into the temple; she pointed to the dazzling Ganges..." Pointing at the dazzling sea, Hélène said: "I love you; do you want...?"

The captain put his hand over Hélène's lips. She applied her lips to that hand and repeated, pointing at the sea: "I love you; do you want...?"

"Since you want it," replied the captain, putting his arm around her waist..."

"I'm not the woman of your dream," said the young woman, throwing her arms around him, "but I love you. Make of me what you will."

"In that case, let's go without delay to ask Maître Leblond to draw up the contract..."

VIII

They have been married since yesterday. Castor is very jealous.

MARTHE

A drawing-room on the ground floor in a park, behind the trees of which a factory chimney can be seen. At the back, opening to the park, a glazed door between two windows. To the right, a divan. To the left, a fireplace and a door closed by a curtain. A cradle in front of the window to the right. Marthe is reading a newspaper on the divan, It is the autumn of 1870.

Marthe. Workmen in the park

MARTHE, *getting up*

And that tells me why? (*Throwing away the newspaper.*) I curse this war! I curse those who have declared it. (*Clutching her head in her hands.*) Is it true? Is it a dream? (*A cannon shot resounds in the distance.*) Alas, I'm not dreaming.

A year ago, I entered here on his arm, through that door, proud and happy, and perhaps I'm a widow today. Perhaps a widow! Perhaps! Not knowing whether I ought to hope or die. Not daring to smile at one's son, because, while one is smiling, the father might be writhing under the hooves of horses or under the wheels of a cannon.

Only three months ago he was here, and he said to me: "In three months we'll go to Denmark, to Holstein, near K   , to spend a few days in the house where I was born; then we'll visit the marshes and the strands whose sons don't want to be Prussian." While speaking, he caressed the child and he said: "If Denmark has need of you, France will lend you to Denmark."[16]

---

[16] Denmark had been forced to relinquish Schleswig and Holstein to Prussia in the Second Schleswig War of 1864, a significant annexation that greatly encouraged Prussian ambitions to capture Alsace.

That was three months ago, and today, he's fighting with the Prussians that he hates, against the Frenchmen whose brother he wanted to be. And it's my fault! They all said to me: "This war is only a game of chess between the Emperor and the King of Prussia!" And I believed them, and I said to Karl: "Rejoin your regiment, or they'll believe that you're afraid."

And I was culpable, culpable as a wife and culpable as a Frenchwoman.

(*Jeanne enters.*)

Marthe, Jeanne, Louis. Workmen

MARTHE
You've come from Génoncourt?

JEANNE
Yes. Your father has talked to them. They wanted wine and money. The thieves!

MARTHE, *in a low voice*
The thieves! (*Aside.*) And it's me who sent him with them!

(*She hears voices in the park, and leans out of the window.*)

JEANNE, *aside*
What did that one say? If they stuck to their work, instead of mingling with what doesn't concern them...!

MARTHE
Did you hear what they whispered, in passing?

JEANNE
No, Madame. (*Aside.*) The imbecile who talked will have my news.

MARTHE
Perhaps they didn't say anything. (*Aside.*) It might be the voice inside and I thought it was them saying: "Prussian! There's the Prussian." (*Aloud.*) It's not true, Jeanne, it's not true; I'm not a Prussian and my husband... (*Putting her arms round Jeanne's neck.*) How chagrined I am!

JEANNE
There's reason to be, poor lady, but on the other hand, it's necessary not to exaggerate things; who could have foreseen what has happened? Who would have thought that Monsieur Karl would be recalled to his regiment, and that he'd make war on us?

MARTHE
And it's me who is the cause of everything. He isn't Prussian, he's Danish; you know that, don't you?

JEANNE
I believe you, since you tell me so.

MARTHE, *recoiling*
She's like the others...My God, how unfortunate I am! She doesn't believe me, she doesn't understand.

JEANNE
But yes, but yes. (*Taking her hand.*) My good lady, my good little lady.

MARTHE, *disengaging her hand.*
Leave me.

166

JEANNE

We all love you, we all feel sorry for you; it isn't an old worker at the factory, it's one who arrived yesterday, who said that.

MARTHE

You heard it too, then? (*Wringing her hands.*) And to think that it's my fault!

JEANNE

Think of the little one. Our lady, the little cherub, who'll be ill if chagrin turns your milk.

MARTHE

My head is going astray. Jeanne, it's necessary to take the baby; I can no longer think about him, my head is going astray. I can no longer think about anything but the man I caused to go away.

JEANNE
Monsieur Karl will come back.

MARTHE

No, they called me Prussian; he won't come back. Listen, Jeanne, listen carefully, in order to be able to repeat it. There's a country called Denmark; of that country, the Prussians stole a part a few years ago. Monsieur is from that country. Do you understand?

JEANNE
Yes.

MARTHE

It's because he didn't want to remain Prussian that, two years ago, when my father went to Holstein, he accepted to be an engineer in our factory. Do you understand?

JEANNE
Yes.

MARTHE
Today, he detests the Prussians even more than he detested them then, and when he was recalled he was about to be naturalized as French. Do you understand?

JEANNE
No.

MARTHE
She doesn't understand, My God, what don't you understand?

JEANNE
I don't understand why he went to fight against the French, since he wanted to be French; but that doesn't prove anything; I don't understand much, our lady.

MARTHE
But he was a soldier. In that country, they're all soldiers, I've told you that. Haven't I told you that?

JEANNE
If he hadn't gone, the gendarmes would have come to take him?

MARTHE
Ah, that's it! That's where the fault lies! It's me who made him go. When he said to me: "It isn't my country that's fighting against yours; I'll stay with you," I whispered in his ear: "They'll think you're afraid, my Karl." They're right, I'm a Prussian!

(*Louis stops on the threshold.*)

JEANNE
Who hasn't made a mistake in this world?

LOUIS
It isn't you who made him leave, Marthe; our father and I told him to rejoin his regiment. He couldn't join our army, and when peace was made, fingers would have been pointed at him.

MARTHE
It's me who made him leave... I know it. But I believed you. "This war is only a game of chess, which the Emperor is amusing himself by playing with the King of Prussia, you said to me. They're putting on a big show, it's like a duel... When the shot is fired, they'll embrace..." I believed you. Why did you say that? One only says these things when one is sure of them. Those pleasantries cause too many tears.

JEANNE, *aside*
How many things there are that the rest of us don't understand.

LOUIS
Forgive me, sister; I believed what I said.

MARTHE
It isn't sufficient to believe, it's necessary to be sure of what one says. It's necessary not to say to a poor woman: "All men are brothers," and then go and fight.

It's necessary not to say, when one isn't sure of tomorrow; "All peoples are much the same; you want to be French; there's no urgency. We like you as much as a Dane as a Frenchman. In our next voyage, when we go to Paris, I'll take the necessary steps." One doesn't say that, you hear? In order not to stop work for a week, one doesn't risk causing ones sister to be called Prussian, you hear?

LOUIS
Forgive me.

MARTHE
No.

JEANNE, *aside*
What's the point of it, the war?

(*A group forms outside the door.*)

LOUIS, *aside*
Poor sister!

A WORKMAN, *coming in*
Those from this morning have gone, but others are arriving. The village is full of them. What must we do, Monsieur Louis?

LOUIS, *heading toward them*
I'll tell you.

MARTHE, *launching herself out of the door to the left*
It's necessary that I don't hear it; I'm a Prussian.

A WORKMAN, *in a low voice*
That's true.

JEANNE
Is the good God sometimes not just?

(*Louis draws away with the workmen.*)

JEANNE
Their bourgeois affairs; we can't understand them at all. (*Leaning over the cradle.*) No more than you, darling; but we suffer from it, and you too. (*Looking out of the window.*) What

are they up to, then? They're gathering around Monsieur Louis, who's extending his arms, sometimes in the direction of the town, sometimes n the direction of the Saint-Gilles woods. Wouldn't they do better to go back to work?

If I knew which of them it as who called our lady Prussian, he'd have my news. Is it because of her that this is happening? I'm French, did anyone ask my permission to make war on the Prussians? It's our blood that is shed for these stupidities, though, of which we understand nothing.

Where do they want to go, then? They're tucking their blouses into their trousers, as if they were going to the factory. They're all shaking hands with Monsieur Louis. It's one of them, though, who called his sister a Prussian!

I don't understand why Monsieur Karl has been sent to fight, since it doesn't please him and they couldn't come to get him. These bourgeois have ideas that the rest of us don't have,

They're leaving in twos and threes; where can they be going? (*A tocsin is heard ringing.*) They're ringing at Saint-Gilles, probably to announce the Prussians. What's the point? We'll see them soon enough.

It must be an effect of hearing those bells…one might think that they'd forced women to fill their glasses, in order to drink to the battles in which our conscripts have been killed. They do well to ring at Saint-Gilles; people will have time to stave in the barrels and break the glasses. Ring, ring, churchwarden.!

One might think that they're showing their bayonets, red with the blood of our soldiers, laughing. But our men have rifles too, and they'll show them to us tomorrow with red bayonets. Ring, ring, churchwarden! (*Calling to a group that seems to be hesitating.*) Are you deaf, then, you lot? They're breaking down your doors, drinking your wine, kissing your wives. Ring louder, churchwarden; they're deaf.

You're standing there with your hands in your pockets! Pitchforks and rifles, lads! Is there one who's jibbing. Put my bonnet on him and give me his rifle. When the bell calls, it's necessary for everyone to march.

(She runs forward in order to go out, but she is stopped by Dubreuil, who comes in with Louis.)

Dubreuil. Louis. Jeanne. Joseph. Workmen

LOUIS
We'll set an ambush in the rushes of the river at the base of the Montée des Vorles.

JEANNE
That's it.

DUBREUIL
Are you mad?

JEANNE
Since the tocsin is ringing, it's necessary that everyone marches.

DUBREUIL, *to Louis*
You hear! They aren't as dormant as people say. (*To Jeanne.*) Give me the pleasure of remaining tranquil. (*To Louis.*) It's still the old Gaulish blood, except that it's necessary to talk to them, to lead them.

Ah, they say: "They're roquets who shut up as soon as one throws them a bone!" A beater has sounded, hear the pack howl.

Stay with the child, Jeanne, and while rocking him, make slings and bandages; to each his lot. (*Jeanne sits down next to the cradle.*) May God protect you, children. It's necessary to fight like savages, since they want it. It's necessary to track them like wolves, since that's all they are.

A WORKMAN, *coming in*
They've hanged Jacques.

172

LOUIS
They've hanged Jacques?

THE WORKMAN
From the oak at Génoncourt.

JEANNE
The swine!

LOUIS
We'll hang those who fall into our hands tonight. Afterwards, what will happen will happen.

JEANNE, *getting up*
There are plenty of slings and bandages in the cupboard upstairs. I'll go with the others, our Master.

DUBREUIL
Stay tranquil.
They have a fashion of behaving that's a little too primitive; it's necessary to make them lose the taste for it. Jacques hadn't poisoned wells, he hadn't killed men in their sleep, he hadn't finished off wounded men. He fought in broad daylight, rifle in hand, and they've hanged him! If they'd cleaved his head with a saber thrust they'd have been within their rights, but they've hanged him; they're not soldiers, they're bandits.

JEANNE
It's not on the government, then, it's on us that those fellows are making war. It's necessary to defend ourselves, our Master. It's necessary to sound the tocsin everywhere, as at Saint-Gilles; it's necessary for the people to take up rifles everywhere; it's necessary that the boss marches at the head of his workers, the farmer at the head of his laborers, and that the women march like the men!

(*She tips back her chair and exits running.*)

173

DUBREUIL
We've unleashed the pack.

LOUIS
May it bite.

JEANNE, *on the threshold, extending her hand toward Saint-Gilles*
To the bell, lads, to the bell!

LOUIS
Let's go; it's time.

DUBREUIL
I'm only good for guarding the house. I'll do them more harm by waiting for them than by going with you. (*Seeing a workman chatting with Jeanne.*) Anything new, Joseph?

JOSEPH
They've gone. Let's let them go; if others come, we'll see.

LOUIS
Are you mad?

DUBREUIL
It's you who's saying that, an old soldier in Africa? After all, you're free to do as you please.

JOSEPH
Later, Boss, perhaps you'll regret what you've just said. Let's go, the rest of you. Too bad for those who aren't where they ought to be.

(*Jeanne sits down again next to the cradle.*)

DUBREUIL

I already regret what I said; you're a brave workman, Joseph, but we're in a time when everyone has so much difficulty recognizing the right road that I believed you had mistaken the route.

JOSEPH

The right road is the one that goes straight. Let's be off; the bullets go where the devil pushes them.

LOUIS
Adieu, Father.

JOSEPH
Perhaps they'll come here; stay, Monsieur Louis.

DUBREUIL, *embracing his son*
If we don't see one another again here, we will on high.

(*Louis goes out.*)

JEANNE, *aside*
Joseph is mistaken; that would be too much misfortune

DUBREUIL, *on the threshold*
Good luck, lads. Louis, anger gives poor advice, and I spoke badly just now. Fight like soldiers, like Frenchmen, children. Don't do as they do.

A VOICE
A tooth for a tooth.

Dubreuil. Jeanne

DUBREUIL, *after having watched them draw away*
A tooth for a tooth! We've reverted to a fine code! Whose fault is it? Someone's been hanged, so they'll hang

175

someone, and they won't hang those who merit it. Perhaps it will be the father of a family, whose hungry children are waiting for him, or a man who would have worn away his eyes writing that peoples have no more right to kill than individuals.

JEANNE
Oh, the swine! The swine!

DUBREUIL, *turning round*
You've come back, Jeanne; you're a brave girl. It's necessary, you see, that the women don't get mixed up in it; if they get mixed up in it, we'll become savages.

JEANNE, *aside*
They'll get mixed up in it. If I were sure that Joseph is mistaken. I wouldn't be here.

DUBREUIL, *leaning on the door-post*
Perhaps they'll kill me. How do I know that Karl isn't dead already? Might the house not be empty tomorrow? And I repeated, like so many others: "The Empire is peace!" The very day when we learned about the declaration of war, in the very placed where I am. Louis said: "People counted on us, for so many cannons, so many rifles and so many trouser-buttons; as we wanted to check, and the number isn't there, we're going to have war. A victory will purify the accounts." I said: "You're making a systematic opposition."

JEANNE, *aside*
They ought to be able to see them already, at the bend in the road.

DUBREUIL
It's my fault, and that of all the imbeciles who voted like me. If they put me in front of a firing squad. I'll only be getting what I deserve. They've warned me, like the other *maires*,

176

that they'll shoot me if anyone fires on them while they haven't quit the territory of the commune. I'll be the first one shot, but I won't be the last.

JEANNE, *getting up*
They'll put you before a firing squad?

DUBREUIL
Who told you that?

JEANNE
You, Master; you were speaking aloud.

DUBREUIL
The more men like me they put in front of firing squads, the better; that will be remembered later.

JEANNE, *in a low voice*
As long as Joseph is mistaken!

DUBREUIL
What did you say?

JEANNE
Nothing. Oh, nothing! Save yourself, Master, leave with Madame Marthe, right away. Don't worry—I'll defend the house.

DUBREUIL
I like to understand, Jeanne. What did Joseph say?

JEANNE
Nothing...stupidities...

DUBREUIL
Speak clearly, eh!

JEANNE

It's necessary not to let yourself be shot; Joseph thought he recognized Monsieur Karl.

DUBREUIL

That's not probable, but it's possible; a soldier goes where he's sent. And they're saying that if he hadn't come here in order to serve as a spy subsequently, he wouldn't have gone to rejoin his regiment. They would almost be right to say it, but as it's me who made him go, when they know that, and when I've been shot, they won't say it any longer. You'll explain that to them, my daughter. (*Listening.*) Did you hear that?

JEANNE

Yes; it was a rifle shot, on the road.

DUBREUIL

Well then, everything will sort itself out. I trembled that they might be afraid at the last moment; they're so distressed. But since they've fired, everything will sort itself out.

JEANNE

You think so?

DUBREUIL

Yes, my daughter. They'll come back, indubitably. I'll be shot, and no one will say thereafter that I sent my son-in-law to serve them as a spy. For it's me who made him go. You understand that, at present, but for me, he'd be with Louis and the others.

JEANNE

Well, Master, let me speak frankly. You're wrong. You're going to take Madame Marthe and the little one in the carriage, and you're going to leave right away. It isn't for us, it's for yourself that you want to die, and we need to conserve men like you, to defend us.

DUBREUIL, *mildly*

You're mistaken, Jeanne; if it doesn't serve you right away, it will serve you later. Go find your mistress; it's necessary that everyone is in his placed: the son leading them, the father at the Mairie, the daughter next to the cradle.

(*He picks up his rifle and goes out.*)

JEANNE

He's a man, that one; it's necessary that he isn't shot. There are three hundred of them—a fine affair. All Génoncourt couldn't put a stop to those three hundred reds! I'll go tell them about it, and since these Germans like to drink so much, we'll stuff them in the well. The wells are deep, they'll take the count.

It's necessary not to leave the lady here. (*Leaning over the cradle.*) Wake up, darling, we're going to roll you up in my cape, so you won't feel the cold.

(*Karl, wrapped in his cloak, his head bare, races toward the cradle and kisses his son. Jeanne utters a cry of fright.*)

Jeanne. Karl

KARL
Don't say anything.

(*He goes out rapidly.*)

Jeanne. Marthe

JEANNE

Monsieur Karl! He ran away without kissing his wife! He knows that they're going to shoot his father-in-law, and he's taken off his uniform in order to go and join Monsieur Louis! What ideas these bourgeois have!

MARTHE, *lifting the door-curtain*
Who were you talking to? (*A rifle shot resounds in the garden. Marthe puts her hand to her heart.*) Oh!

JEANNE
You felt the shot?

MARTHE
Here!

JEANNE, *aside*
He's killed him. (*Dubreuil appears on the threshold, rifle in hand.*) Woe, woe!

(*She runs into the garden hiding her head in her hands.*)

Dubreuil. Marthe

DUBREUIL
Woe indeed—but whose fault is it?

MARTHE, *in a dull voice*
Karl has been killed!

DUBREUIL
What's happening is ugly enough, let's not let our imagination make it worse.

MARTHE
That rifle shot...?

DUBREUIL
I was defending my house.

MARTHE
It's you who fired. You haven't killed him?

DUBREUIL
Didn't he slip into this park like a thief?

MARTHE
I felt the shot in my heart.

DUBREUIL
Take the child and carry him to my sister's house by the path through the wood.

MARTHE
No, Father.

DUBREUIL
I haven't often given you an order, Marthe.

MARTHE
Come with us.

DUBREUIL
They'll certainly need me at the Mairie. I'm going there. Take the child and go, quickly.

MARTHE
I'm the Prussian! You're expelling me.

DUBREUIL, *drawing her to him*
You're my daughter, chérie. It's necessary, for one second, to forget everything and kiss me, as you kissed me before. People think they're parting for an hour, and they never see one another again. It's the first time we haven't spent the night in the same house. Kiss me, as you kissed me when you were a child, and forgive me.

MARTHE
Oh, father!

DUBREUIL
Say to me: "I know that you thought you were acting for the best in making Karl leave, and I don't hold it against you."

MARTHE, *putting her arms around him*
You've never caused me any chagrin.

(*Karl, tottering, stops on the threshold.*)

Karl. Dubreuil. Marthe

KARL
Marthe! Marthe!

(*Marthe runs to him, with a scream, her arms extended; before she reaches him, he collapses.*)

MARTHE
Who has killed you?

DUBREUIL, *in an extinct voice*

Me!

ALSA

I

The Rhine is growling in the fog; the poplars are buckling under the frost; hail is rattling on the windows of the ground-floor room.

In the ground-floor room, vaguely illuminated by the fire, are a tall old man with a bald head, a withered woman, a pale young woman and a bed with serge curtains.

Behind the curtains, a wounded man is moaning; amour has made the virgin pale; the mother has seen her sons die; the old man is a hundred years old.

The old man is thinking; the mother is weeping; the virgin is dreaming; the wounded man is sleeping; the Rhine is growling dully; the poplars are buckling under the frost; hail is rattling on the windows.

II

The old man says:

"Their chariots came like a whirlwind. Their horses passed by, lighter than eagles. Their quivers were like an open sepulcher, and their swords devoured us like a lion, penetrating all the way to our soul."

The mother sobs:

"Accursed be the day when I was born; accused be the night when I was conceived."

The virgin sighs:

"As an apple tree is between the trees of a forest, so was my beloved between the young men. I sat down in his shade, and his fruits were sweet to my lips."

The wounded man murmurs:
Eternal, have pity on me, for I am devoid of strength. Eternal, sustain me, for my bones are all a-tremble."

In the squall, which bends the poplars, the great voice of enchained Alsace weeps.

III

The old man says:
"He had built on mud, and his walls have collapsed; he had leaned on reeds, and he has fallen to his knees; he had sown on the edge of a marsh, and snakes have crushed the ears of his wheat.

"We have suffered, by the fault of one alone; but let us not cry: 'Lord, Lord, why hast thou smitten us?' We are the ones who raised up the one who has lowered us."

The old man says:
"They had searched for gold in the mire of the stream, and fever has softened their marrow; they wanted to climb the stairway of the others, but the steps were worn away and in order to climb they were obliged to heap up the cadavers of our sons.

"We have suffered, by the fault of the thirsty; but let us not cry: 'Lord, Lord, why hast thou smitten us?'

"We are the ones who sculpted the cup in which our blood is fuming."

The old man says:
"We had laughed at those who sang the praises of the flag; then they thought that it was nothing but a scrap of cloth, and everyone has chosen his own. We had laughed at those

who said: 'Death has a tomorrow,' and then they trembled when it was necessary to die. We had laughed at those who prayed; then, when the darkness came, no one lit the beacon to show us the route.

"Lord, Lord, thy hand has weighed upon us, and it has crushed us; thou art the Good, even more than thou at the Just. Thou hast not treated us as the wild antelope, but like the indocile ox; it is not thy dart, it is only thy spur that has touched us."

IV

The mother sobs:
"When all four of my sons were around me I was like a city flanked by towers. Who could have gone all the way to my heart, to steal my treasure?
"Three are dead, and the last is going to die.

"When all four of my sons were around me. I was like a vine charged with ripe grapes. The valiant said: "The wine of these grapes will be red." The sage said: "The wine of these grapes will be good.
"Three are dead, and the last is going to die.

"When all four of my sons were around me, I was like a jeweler in the midst of golden necklaces; with eyes shining with desire, the young women extended their hands toward me...
"Three are dead, and he last is going to die.

"I am the dismantled ruin, the tree cut down for fire-wood. The thieves have entered and the spider in spinning its web over the cases of the golden necklaces."

V

The virgin falls to her knees, and three times her forehead strikes the floor. Her black hair sweeps the ashes of the hearth, her folded arms writhe and a lament rises from her entrails to her lips.

She says:

"Lord, I wanted to hold the dolor at bay, but my heart has softened within me.

"Yesterday, I was asleep, but my heart was alert, and I heard my beloved knocking, who said: 'Open the door my sister, my friend, my dove, my perfect; the dew is wetting my brow, the pearls of the night are sliding from my hair.'

I awoke, but I said to my heart: 'Go to sleep.' And I did not open the door, of which I would have liked to have been the threshold, beneath the feet of my beloved.

"Today, I am the spring from which the doves have never drunk...O my beloved!

"Today, I am the solitary palm-tree...O my beloved!

"Today I am the masterless tent...O my beloved!"

Her hair sweeps the ashes of the hearth, and in the squall that bends the poplars, the great voice weeps of Alsace enchained.

VI

On hearing the fiancée of the dead man, the wounded man woke up. He had not yet had time to have a fiancée himself, and he felt himself dying.

Like the water-lily that plunges into the water, he plunges into his dolor.

He says:

"In order to defend his house, to protect his vine, a man has blood in his veins and marrow in his bones; but this house did not belong to me, this vine was not mine.

"Why have I been struck? I was not the ivy of this house, the cep of this vine; a son of Israel, I was only a reed, languishing in a foreign land; only an olive tree transplanted in the vineyard of a master."

The Rhine is growling dully; hail is rattling on the windows.

VII

The Rhine is growling, and in the squall, Alsace is weeping. Listen:

"To the table where hunger does not sit down I have come after the others; but out there, the platter is never empty. Oh, the fine feast! The white tablecloth! The pleasant welcome! Do not forget me!

"A broad place was made for me, and, as I did not understand the songs that rose from the cups very well, my neighbors smiled at me and wove their coral necklaces in my blonde tresses. Oh, the fine feast! The white tablecloth! The pleasant welcome! Do not forget me!

"I only had one sheaf, I have given it to you; do not forget me! A sheaf of cornflowers and golden ears; do not forget me!

"They said: 'It is ours.' That is not true; have I not sown my cornflowers in your feasts, and my golden ears in your battles? Do not forget me!

"Do not let the cornflowers fade, do not let the foreigner mingle the white flour with his black bread.

"I shall never forget; do not forget me!"

187

VIII

The Rhine is growling in the fog; the poplars are buck-ling under the frost; the hail is rattling on the windows; in the squall, Alsace is weeping; the old man raises his bald head.

The women have talked in low voices in order not to be heard; he speaks in a loud voice, in order that others will listen.

He says:

"O my son, retain my words within yourself, do not forget my lessons; wrap them around your neck, keep them on the table of your heart.

"It is not the lion but the jackal that howls when it is sated. It is not the proud charger but the wild ass that flees when it has eaten the oats.

Has this house not warmed you? Has this vine not allowed its heaviest cluster to hang down as far as your mouth? Why would you have allowed the crows to soil the roof that has sheltered you? Why would you have allowed the fox to devastate the vine that has given you wine to drink?

"The lips of the foreigner distil honeycombs, his palate is milder than oil; but his heart is as bitter as absinthe, and his tongue wounds like a two-edged sword; never forget that, my son!

Never forget the nurse who has rocked you, and if your blood is flowing for her today, do not forget that she smiled while you bit her breast."

Then the wounded man, raising himself up, says:

"It was not me, it was the fever speaking; if I live, I shall not forget anything."

The old man extends his trembling hands toward the flame, and the entire past is flamboyant before him in the flames of the hearth. He too has traveled far, with the others, his sack on his back and his rifle over his shoulder; then he returned. He was a fine connoisseur; he sold cattle!

Someone had said to him what Laban said to Jacob: "If you want Rachel, accumulate new louis!" He had accumulated new louis, and he had had Rachel.

No one had attempted to steal his louis, no one had ever insulted Rachel; Alsace was not for him the land of exile, but the hospitable tent where he found bread and salt.

Alsace is the Rachel of the great vanquished; in giving it the blood of his veins he has only been paying his debt. If he last of his sons does not die today, let him be ready to die tomorrow; one must render without counting what has been given to you without counting.

He extends his trembling hands to the flames; hail is rattling on the windows.

IX

But the Rhine is growling, and its voice dominates the whistling of the squall. Listen.

"Between two worlds, the master has hollowed me out; woe betide whoever crosses me! I am not the Gaulish river, I am not the German river, I am the Master's river.

Those who cross me do not return; they die or they forget. The Romans crossed me, the Franks crossed me, and the German forest stifled the Romans and the Gaulish vine intoxicated the Franks.

"My waves are neither German not Gaulish, and in my fogs roll all the dreams of conquerors who have tried to touch the Master's boundary-marker.

I am what separates the vision from the dream, the why from the how, the flower from the root, the melody from the voice.

I am the river where those must drink who believe too much, and those who do not believe enough, those who forget nothing and those who have forgotten everything; to some I

189

render memory, and to others hope. I am the river of the past, I am the river of the future; but I am not a wager, I am a barrier; woe betide those who cross me!"

In the squall that is bending the poplars, the great voice of enchained Alsace is weeping.

X

The sobs of the captive mingle with the growl of the irritated river; the poplars vibrate under the squall; the hail rattles the windows and in the room vaguely illuminated by the reflections of the fire, the kneeling virgin strikes the floor with her forehead,

Then the old man extends his hand toward her and says: "Daughter of my brother, get up; on the throne of the old willow, the Eternal has set a nest of moss for your bruised heart.

"The wind of the desert has dried up the spring at which the doves would have drunk; you shall be the ever-clear cistern from which the maidservants draw water for the evening feast.

Leave your youth, like a flower, on the grave of the dead man, and put your shoulder under the hand of the one who will avenge him; you shall be the palm tree that shows the route, the tent that will provide shade.

"Daughter of my brother, get up; you are of my blood, it is necessary that you have sons, who will be what I have been. They will love what I have loved, and they will not forget the hand that held out bread and salt to me, the hand that does not strike and does not steal."

In the squall that bends the poplars, the great voice weeps of Alsace enchained.

XI

The squall flees northwards; the poplars straighten up again; the crescent shines in the sky, which turns blue, and a broad silver furrow is traced on the silken Rhine; but a lament mingles with the call of the curlew.

"Do not forget me! Do not forget me!

"O my beautiful river, if I am forgotten in your green arms, carry me away. Take my vines and my meadows; sow sand where my golden wheat germinated.

"Do not forget me! Do not forget me!

"O my beautiful river, if I am forgotten in your green arms, carry me away. Take my bastions and my bell-towers; sow sand where my azure flax flourished.

"Do not forget me! Do not forget me!"

XII

A bright sunbeam entered through the window of the ground-floor room.

Then, the woman who had lost three of her sons said:

"You are the master and I am the servant; I must be silent when you have spoken; but I cannot hold back my tears. My eyes are like the ravine when the snow melts, like the meadow after the storm."

And the old man said:

"Let the man who is afraid of the dark not look toward the place where the sun set. But where it will rise.!"

Then the virgin, having put up her scattered hair again, knelt down beside the wounded man, and, putting his feverish hand on her hair, said: "Our sons will remember."

"Woe betide those who have crossed me," growled the irritated Rhine.

MEYRIN[17]

I

The sun rose, and the virgin with the dark eyes sang under the palm trees:

"Like the swallow, my heart has two wings, two sharp wings; toward the great river it flies... It has flown so far, so very far that it will never return again!"

The sun rose, and the poet with wan cheeks said under the palm trees:

"When I was rich I went around the river and I took it into the arid plain, where the sun burned the merchants.

"The plain became a garden; but when I passed before the merchants sitting in the shade again, a poor man, they cried: 'Look at the madman!'

"Then disdain entered into me, and I became a camel-driver.

"When I saw, in the desert, the road bordered by cadavers, I said to the chief: 'Let us find a new route.'

"He left me alone, and when I returned, after having found one, he cried: 'Look at the madman!'

The virgin, having raised her eyes, perceived the poet.

"For what are you searching?" she said to him.

"Since you have been here I have been searching my memory for a dream that I had.

---

[17] This item is an extensively-rewritten version of "Le Poème du fou," published in 1867 in the *Revue des lettres de de l'art*, in the series indexed therein as "Fusains," which was abridged when adapted into the book version of *Fusains* in 1868.

"It was further away than Gizeh, further away than Memphis, further away than Thebes, going up the Nile; I lay down in a round valley, which resembled a cup of amethyst half full of sand.

"While I slept I dreamed about a woman who resembled you. I dreamed for such a long time that the sun drank my water-skins.

The Nile was nearby, but the crowd drinks from the Nile and I only like new cups; I lay down in the sand and, while the vultures soared above my head, I said to them in beautiful verses:

"When you perch on my still-warm forehead, wings dangling, in order to eat my eyes, you will see in my eyes the image of my beloved; her sweet face is engraved in streaks of fire in my pupils.

"Since I have contemplated that star fallen from the sky I am like a man blinded by the sun, who sees in the darkness the star at which he has gazed."

"He's a madman!"

"You are only saying what others have said; listen to the end of my dream.

"Extended on the plain I gazed at a cloud, which seemed to be descending from the sky.

"When that cloud touched the earth, three almahs emerged from it.

The thinnest was holding a cup, the most beautiful was naked to the waist and the palest was holding a flute.

"The thinnest said to me: 'Drink, and you will never be thirsty.' I replied: 'My amour is a fresh spring, from which I drink long draughts.'

"The most beautiful said to me then: 'Come into the shadow of my arms.' I replied: 'My amour is a garden, in which the tree with golden fruits grows,'

"The vultures stretched out their bald necks,

"Then the palest of the almahs played the flute, and the vultures alighted on my forehead.

"They have eaten my eyes; that is why, young woman, I bump into the stones of the road as I go along. Would you care to lend me your eyes, in order that I may see the azure sky and the limpid spring again?"
"He's nothing but a madman!"

II

The virgin sat down at the foot of a palm tree and sighed:
"Like the ocean, my heart has waves, great green waves and great blue waves; but the wind of solitude weeps there and its kisses make me weep.

"Why does my heart have waves, on which nothing can float?"

The poet lies down, his eyes turned toward the sun, as in the valley the color of amethyst, and he says:
"Life has nothing as good as the dream; that is why the poet is the foremost among men.

"He is the richest, he is the most beloved; what he wants he dreams, and his dream is more beautiful than reality.

"No one has wanted to love me! The daughter of the sultan will love me. The daughter of the sultan is more beautiful than the moon; I shall write for her a poem as profound as the night.

"When my poem is similar to a rose-bush I shall perfume my mouth and I shall sit down before her on an embroidered carpet. I shall light cassolettes to my right and my left, and I shall speak my verses slowly, marking the measure.

"The daughter of the sultan is as blonde as a honey-bee, but my poem will be s fresh as an asphodel; I shall sing it softly, nodding my head, and the blonde bee will descend from the sky.

194

"If she does not give me her hand to kiss when I have sung a thousand verses, if she does not give me her lips to kiss when I have sung ten thousand verses, I shall say: "I am mad…!" and I shall no longer love her."

Then the virgin sad:

"The verses of this madman lull me. They fall one by one, all equal, with the same sound, like drops of water on the tent. They lull me; I believe I can hear the woman who put me to sleep in her perfumed haïck in the happy times when I lived as merrily as a sparrow.

The poet said:

"Light of my eyes, put a cushion under your elbow, light your nargileh, take your little feet out of your green slippers and listen to the poem that I have written for you. Sister of blonde ears of wheat, let my verses caress your soul with their wings as they fly way.

"Close your azure eyes, blonde sister of ears of wheat, and my verses, while flapping their wings, will sway your soul, as the evening wind sways fields of barley.

"Listen to my poem; you are the daughter of the sultan, but it is the song of amour..."

While the poet sings, Meyrin thinks she sees blue birds passing, and white storks.

The blue birds said to her: "If you wished, Meyrin?"

"But you have not wished, Meyrin," replied the white storks.

The poet said:

"I have only sung a hundred verses, and you are giving me your hand to kiss? You have divined, hen, that my heart is a fresh oasis, where the flower of amour blooms brilliantly? You have divined that my heart is a profound sea, in which the boat of our amour will never run aground?

"You are giving me your fingers, more transparent than cloudless amber! You are giving me your fingernails, more brilliant than a drop of blood on a golden stirrup" You are giving me your wrist, slimmer than an ivory flute, and I have not yet declaimed any more than a hundred verses! Oh, my poem, which is no longer running like a hare, which takes ten paces and looks around, run like the white camel, which traverses the desert without stopping.

"Sweet incense of my soul, my verses will be ardent coals, and your heart will change into an embalmed cloud."

The virgin has drawn nearer, in order to hear better; she has slid to her knees, in order to approach soundlessly.

The poet falls silent; her hand on her breast, she sighs:
"My heart has roots like aloes; where it has flowered, it will die."

The poet resumes:
"Alight, nightingale, on that pomegranate bush, the bloody eyes of which are gazing at the sister of my soul. Grip in your little feet a branch with very smooth bark; withdraw your pretty gray head into the feathers of your neck and sing your most beautiful song of amour; you will sing what my beloved has said."

Meyrin believes that she sees blue birds and white storks passing.
"If you had wished, Meyrin!" say the blue birds.
"But you have not wished, Meyrin," reply the white storks.
"It is no longer about me that he is thinking; I am the cup that has been broken because the water therein was troubled; the rose that has been thrown away because its thorns wounded!" says Meyrin, getting to her feet.
Then the poet retains her gently by means of her trailing scarf.

196

"You don't want," he says to her, "to hide like the lover who is waiting; you want, like a proud wife, to stand upright on the threshold? Come with me to see the kadi.

"Come, you shall be the shadow of my body. Come, he will read the two verses and you will attach the pleats of your veil to my name, and your veil will be retained by a solid pin.

"Come with me to see the kadi, blonde sister of the roses."

"Am I as beautiful as a dream?" says Meyrin, with a sob. "It is no longer about me that he is thinking!"

And the poet responds: "Can you hear the kadi murmuring: 'You want me to say the two verses and you have nothing in your hand but a handful of ashes!'

"Can you hear the crowd shouting: 'Look at the madman!'

"Yes, I am mad; I have sown in the furrows of others. Yes, I am mad, I have emptied my head in order that the sun might shine therein, in order that the desert wind might extend its wings therein.

"But what do the cries of the crowd matter to you? Let the crowd speak! Your heart will find, in my empty hand, a garden where the reeds are singing."

He opens his hand...

"That is not sand," he says, "it is my heart, which is falling from my open hand."

III

Then the poet said:

"What are you picking up there, young woman? It is nothing but the heart of a madman."

"It's a frightened nightingale, which an owl has wounded while it was singing. In order to warm it up again I want to put it between my breasts, and if it does, I shall die."

"It's nothing but the heart of a madman."

197

"It's a frightened nightingale; when my lips have smoothed its crumpled wings, I shall place it in a white lilac, and if it flies away, I shall die."

"It's nothing but the heart of a madman!"

"It's the nightingale that sang to me in spring. Since I have heard it, the sky is bluer, the sand is softer and I want to die if it does not sing any longer."

"It's nothing but a bloody tulip with a calyx full of soot!"

"In that calyx I have wept; like diamonds my tears have glittered there. A beautiful flower for my hair!"

"It's only a dry thistle!"

"How soft it is, thistledown! Like a warbler, I shall make my nest of it."

"It's nothing but an empty sepulcher!"

"I shall lie down in it, O my beloved, and my sweet dream will have no awakening."

ROSALIE

The parlor of an Alsatian farm. At the back, windows opening on to an orchard. To the right, a door leading to the kitchen. To the left, a door leading to Rosalie's bedroom. A table in the middle,

FRITZ, *climbing through the window*

I nearly foundered within sight of port.

Those rogues have good legs, but they dared not jump into the river. They fear the water, like the drunkards they are.

It was, however, me, a year ago, who placed the plank that I was so glad to pull behind me just now. It's thanks to Rosalie, who was passing then, that I forgot to nail it; if I hadn't dropped my hammer while gazing at her, instead of being here I'd be in prison.

What I'm doing isn't good; I'm entering Monsieur Hantz's home like a thief...but if I'd come in through the door, like an honest man, the gendarmes would have nabbed me! For the Prussian gendarmes I'm no longer an honest man, and I must have the word *refractory* written on my forehead, since those who had never seen me before started chasing me. It's true that I turned round maladroitly as soon as they marched my direction; I lacked *sang froid*.

Damn! They didn't recognize me, since they didn't know me; they won't come to search here immediately, and in half an hour I'll have gone...gone forever. (*Noises are heard in the kitchen.*) Is someone coming? Since I entered like a thief this house that ought to be mine, let's continue as I've begun.

(*He slips into Rosalie's bedroom, closing the door quietly. Rosalie comes in.*)

HANTZ, *from the kitchen*
So, you're going to be reasonable?

ROSALIE
I'll try. (*She looks around.*) My heart is beating rapidly, as when I found him leaning on that window sill.

HANTZ, *from the kitchen*
You'll receive Guillaume?

ROSALIE
I'll receive him as he merits. (*Quietly.*) I dreamed about him last night; I'll wager that he'll come.

HANTZ *entering*
You'll receive him as the son-in-law I've chosen.

ROSALIE
Then I won't receive him. (*Hantz raises his hand; Rosalie puts her arms around him.*) Because you only have one daughter, me, and I don't want Guillaume for a husband.

HANTZ, *pulling away*
I forbid you to embrace me.

ROSALIE, *recoiling, pouting*
I won't embrace you again.

HANTZ
When I'm angry.

ROSALIE
You're always angry, since you no longer love me.

HANTZ
I no longer love you!

ROSALIE
You only have one idea: to get rid of me.

HANTZ
Come and kiss me.

ROSALIE, *kissing him*
But you're still angry.

HANTZ
You're still thinking about that Fritz?

ROSALIE
Yes.

HANTZ
A vagabond!

ROSALIE
An outlaw.

HANTZ
A coward, who ran away in order not to be a soldier.

ROSALIE
A Prussian soldier.

HANTZ
It's necessary for him to be a Prussian soldier, since we're Prussians today.

ROSALIE
He's doing as I would, who wants to remain French.

HANTZ, *running to the door and looking in the kitchen.*
Fortunately, there's no one here to hear you.

ROSALIE
Too bad.

HANTZ
I too would rather have remained French; I did all I could
for that, but since it wasn't my fault I've resigned myself.
Come on, listen to me

ROSALIE
I am listening to you, Father.

HANTZ
Do you speak German, or French.

ROSALIE
I speak German and French.

HANTZ
Good; like me. So, you're as German as you are French;
it ought not to matter to you whether Alsace is in France or in
Germany.

ROSALIE
It matters a great deal to me.

HANTZ
Because of Fritz?

ROSALIE
Because of Fritz.

HANTZ
An imbecile!

ROSALIE
Guillaume isn't an imbecile, of course?

HANTZ
He's the burgomeister, while Fritz, with his ideas, has had his property sequestered.

ROSALIE
And he's obliged to do a day's work in order to live.

HANTZ
He'll die of hunger.

ROSALIE
That's why I want him for a husband.

HANTZ
They're all mad! He doesn't even think about you any more, since he hasn't dared to come to see you.

ROSALIE
Are you sure about that?

HANTZ, *undoing his cravat*
You know that anger might give me a heart attack

ROSALIE
So, dear father, it's necessary for you not to get angry.

HANTZ
You know that once I'm started, I'm like March beer. What do you know about it? One doesn't talk back like that to one's father (*Approaching her.*) You're lying, You're lying— if he'd come to see you you'd have told me. I know you.

ROSALIE
So you're no longer angry, then? You still love your Rosette, then?

HANTZ
I love her too much.

ROSALIE
And your Rosette renders it to you.

HANTZ
That's not true.

ROSALIE
If I didn't love you, would I be here?

HANTZ
Where else would you be?

ROSALIE
In France.

HANTZ
With Fritz?

ROSALIE
With Fritz.

HANTZ
Name of a pipe!

ROSALIE, *putting her hands on his shoulders*
Since I'm not there...

HANTZ
If he set foot here...

ROSALIE
You'd go to fetch Guillaume, the burgomeister, in order to hand him over.

HANTZ
Oh, no…! But I'd break his back.

ROSALIE, *putting her arms around him.*
How polite you are!

HANTZ, *pushing her away*
Truly, the girl is mad.

ROSALIE
Then it's necessary to forgive me everything.

HANTZ
I have a great deal to lament...

ROSALIE, *returning to him*
Let me console you, dear Father

HANTZ, *retreating all the way to the door.*
You're a charmer…but I'm stopping my ears. (*From the doorstep, having slammed the door.*) You're going to marry Guillaume, because I wish it.

Rosalie. Fritz

ROSALIE
Poor Father, he can't be malevolent, and yet that malevolent beast has bewitched him. It will pass. Before that horrible war he said to me: "You'll marry Fritz because I wish it." (Fritz opens the door quietly.) I said: "Perhaps, perhaps." Perhaps means neither yes nor no, and I know that it's necessary to contradict him a little in order to affirm his resolutions.

205

(*Fritz blows her a kiss as she leans on the table. Fritz takes a step forward and then stops.*)

FRITZ, *aside*
What if my abrupt appearance were to do her harm?

ROSALIE
Why has my father made himself Prussian? Because he didn't want to quit his house... What if I set fire to it? But he also likes his orchard, his meadow and his vineyard.

FRITZ, *aside*
I daren't.

ROSALIE
I'm only a woman; I don't understand very much of all that; but Fritz said: "I can't be Prussian." I can't be Prussian either. (*Getting to her feet.*) That's indisputable. (*Perceiving Fritz.*) Him!

(*She puts her hand on her heart and totters. Fritz leaps forward and catches her in his arms.*)

FRITZ
My beloved Rose

ROSALIE, *uttering a sigh*
It's finished. I love him with all my heart, you see.

FRITZ, *kissing her hair*
And me!

ROSALIE, *disengaging herself from his arms and smiling*
We're speaking from a little too close together.

FRITZ
It's been such a long time!

ROSALIE
It's been too long. (*Fritz draws nearer.*) How did you get in, Monsieur?

FRITZ
Through the window.

ROSALIE
Go back the same way.

FRITZ
Oh!

ROSALIE, *pulling him by the hand*
Let's go, quickly, (*Fritz bestrides the widow; she draws his head toward her and kisses his forehead.*) You'll be a charming husband. (*Fritz holds out his arms; she raps him on the fingers.*) Everyone for himself, Monsieur. How I love you! Why did you come in through the window?

FRITZ
Because...

ROSALIE
Because you didn't dare come through the door. Because you were afraid of my father, timid wretch.

FRITZ
Because the gendarmes were pursuing me.

ROSALIE
The gendarmes! (*Taking him by the hand.*) Come quickly. (*Fritz leaps.*) Where to hide you? In my bedroom. Quickly, quickly!

(*She shoves him into the bedroom and locks the door.*)

FRITZ, *through the door*
The gendarmes aren't here yet, my little Rose.

ROSALIE
It's just that...just that...

FRITZ
Just what?

ROSALIE
I love you, my Fritz; I'd like to tell you that, and I don't say it so well when I see beside me those long arms ever ready to open... Then my heart beats rapidly and my eyes are troubled... You'll regret it later, my Fritz.

FRITZ
And you?

ROSALIE
I won't regret it.

FRITZ
Open the door, Rosette. I love you as you love me.

(*She opens the door.*)

ROSALIE
There's no danger, then. Why did you come, at the risk of being caught?

FRITZ
To say goodbye to you.

ROSALIE

Goodbye... oh, the vile word! If that's all you had to say to me, you've had a wasted journey; that word I won't hear. (*Fritz shakes his head sadly; Rosalie puts her hand around his neck.*) Can you say it to me now, that word?

FRITZ, *pushing her away gently*
I already have so little courage.

ROSALIE, *drawing him toward the table*
I certainly hope so. Sit down there, in the master's place—your place. (*Going round to the other side of the table and sitting down facing him.*) Here's mine. Now listen. You're going to ask my father for me; he'll say no.

FRITZ
Alas!

ROSALIE
Shut up. He'll say no. Chagrin will grip me; that would be wrong...

FRITZ
I shouldn't have come back.

ROSALIE, *thumping the table*
Insupportable! So, as I was telling you, I'll weep for a month, two months, and my father will be furious. I'll become very pale, very thin. (*Fritz passes his hand over his forehead, Rosalie leans forward and takes Fritz's hand over the table, which she lowers.*) I'll have done wrong, and I'll become ugly; that will be my punishment. (*Fritz utters a sigh.*) It won't last, for my father will say to me, one evening: "I've sold the house, I've sold the orchard, I've sold the meadow and I've sold the vineyard; let's get away." Which means: "Go and marry Fritz." Fritz won't be very far away, because I don't want him to go to America like the others.

FRITZ
You don't want that?

ROSALIE
I don't want that. (*The noise of a carriage in the court-yard is heard. Rosalie gets up swiftly.*) The gendarmes! (*Pushing him into the bedroom.*) Don't budge from there, whatever you hear.

FRITZ
But...

ROSALIE
Whatever you hear...

(*She closes the door quietly, and then starts shifting plates on the dresser, while singing.*)

Rosalie, Then Hantz

ROSALIE
Between the tall reeds
When the sun slips through
A lady of the waters,
On the rippling Rhine
Lets herself be gently lulled...
(*In a low voice*) My father is with them...I'm afraid.

(*Approaching her bedroom door:*)

Whatever you hear
Mariners,
Don't turn your heads.

(*Going toward the kitchen door and listening.*)

The beauty with the blonde hair...
(*Quietly.*) It's only Guillaume.
Of an amour is in quest,
And all her lovers.

(*Opening her bedroom door slightly and blowing a kiss to Fritz.*)

Whatever you hear,
Mariners,
Don't turn your heads.

(*Hantz comes in abruptly. Appearing not to have heard him, Rosalie slowly closes the door.*)

And all her lovers,
So joyful,
When the sun slips
Between the tall reeds,
On the rippling Rhine...

(*Turning toward her father and raising her arms to the heavens.*)

In the morning, under the water,
They'll be sleeping eternally!

HANTZ
What are you singing?

ROSALIE
The song of my lovers:
In the morning, under the water,
They'll be sleeping eternally!

HANTZ
Fool! Have you reflected?

ROSALIE
Yes.

HANTZ
You'll do as I wish?

ROSALIE
Yes, Father, as long as you always end up wanting what I want. If you wanted that right away, how nice you'd be!

HANTZ
Never! (*Calling.*) Guillaume! (*Guillaume comes in.*) Plead your case. You're nothing but an imbecile if you don't win it.

Guillaume. Rosalie

ROSALIE
You've arrived at a good moment, Monsieur Guillaume.

GUILLAUME
Mademoiselle...

ROSALIE
I'd like you to take an urgent letter to the post office.

GUILLAUME
Certainly.

ROSALIE
It's for your friend Fritz.

GUILLAUME, *disdainfully*
Fritz!

ROSALIE
He often mentions you to me.

GUILLAUME
Then he writes to you…often?

ROSALIE
Often… He's leaving for America.

GUILLAUME
Bon voyage.

ROSALIE
Thank you.

GUILLAUME
That's not necessary.

ROSALIE
Yes it is, since I'm going with him.

GUILLAUME, *anxiously*
What about your father?

ROSALIE
He's absolutely opposed to it.

GUILLAUME, *reassured*
In that case…?

ROSALIE
I'm counting on you to make him change his opinion.

GUILLAUME
You're very cheerful this morning.

ROSALIE
I've been waiting for this day for such a long time.

GUILLAUME
Me too.

ROSALIE
I wouldn't have believed it.

GUILLAUME
Listen, Mademoiselle Rosalie; you know very well that I love you; that I'm the burgomeister; that your father looks upon me kindly; that my vineyard has a reputation...

ROSALIE
Merited, Monsieur Burgomeister; so, let me give you some advice. Go away.

GUILLAUME
Ahem!

ROSALIE
Immediately.

GUILLAUME
Where?

ROSALIE
Far away.

GUILLAUME
Why?

ROSALIE
Because I'd be the cause of your misfortune, for sure, and perhaps your death.

GUILLAUME
Fritz doesn't frighten me.

(*A noise is heard in Rosalie's bedroom.*)

ROSALIE, *recoiling in a measured fashion as far as her
door.*
*Whatever you hear
Mariners...*

GUILLAUME
Thought I heard…is that a lover?

ROSALIE
Better than that; it's Fritz. (*Standing aside.*) If you have
something to say to him…?

GUILLAUME, *troubled*
If Fritz were there, I'd only have to go away.

ROSALIE
That would be wisest,

GUILLAUME, *laughing*
You're trying to scare me.

ROSALIE
You're the burgomeister. But believe me, go away; if
you were unfortunate enough to marry me—which, fortunately, seems improbable to me—I wouldn't give two sous for
your skin.

GUILLAUME
Get away!

ROSALIE
On emerging from the church on your arm, in the midst of your friends the Prussians. I'd sing the *Marseillaise.*

GUILLAUME
The *Marseillaise?*

ROSALIE
And the *Rhin allemand.*[18]

GUILLAUME
Oh no!

ROSALIE
Oh yes! And as you love me passionately, and you wouldn't want me to go to prison alone on my wedding day, you'd sing the *Marseillaise* with me.

GUILLAUME
You're making fun of me.

ROSALIE
Who knows?

GUILLAUME
Well, you're wrong; I've sworn that you'll be my wife, and you will be.

---

[18] *Le Rhin allemand* is a poem by Alfred de Musset, published in the *Revue de Paris*, a patriotic response to a translation of N. Becker's bellicose *Rhinelied* that had appeared in the publication, to which Alphonse de Lamartine also wrote a response. Musset's poem became famous, being set to music by several composers

ROSALIE

You're showing your teeth? The proverb doesn't lie: Crooked hands, bad teeth.

GUILLAUME

I love you too much; when you mock me, I emerge from my natural state.

ROSALIE, *bowing*

Your servant, Monsieur Burgomeister. May God maintain you in joy, and return us to France. (*On the threshold of the kitchen door, pointing to the bedroom.*) If you want to talk to Fritz, don't be embarrassed.

(*She leaves the door open behind her and draws away, singing.*)

Whatever you hear
Mariners...

GUILLAUME, *heading for the door*

I must know whether there's someone there. (*Stopping.*) What if there is? (*Laughing.*) She knows full well that if he comes, I'll have him pinched. (*Going toward the dresser.*) Ten years in prison, if you get caught. And you'll get caught, if you love Rosalie, which is quite possible, after all.

I thought that there was only one silver platter, but there are two of them. That old Hantz is a hoarder. Oh, you love Fritz, child! Love him, if that amuse you; I don't care a fig. I don't love you, I love your father's meadow and orchard and his silver plate. But as it's necessary to take you into the bargain, I'll marry you, Beauty. Here's some brand new cutlery. Perhaps they're only ruolz?[19] (*Looking attentively.*) They're silver. Oh, the rich old man!

---

[19] Ruolz was an alloy imitative of silver named after Henri de Ruolz (1808-1887), who was a Romantic classical composer

I'll marry his daughter, that's certain, but the silverware, that can be given away; it's necessary to have the lover put in prison. Twelve new sets of cutlery and six little spoons, plus a dozen old ones that I know, make... (*He counts on his fingers.*) And you'd like to marry Fritz! You'll bait the mousetrap in which we'll catch him. If you say yes he'll get away with ten years in the fortress, but if you don't say yes right way, I'll have him shot.

Well, that's a new goblet, a new platter, a dozen new sets of cutlery. A new goblet! It's certainly solid silver. And she wants to marry Fritz...! He'll be shot. The fellow isn't patient; I'll put him down, as burgomaster, in the exercise of my functions; a fistful of bullets will pay him back for two or three pairs of slaps.

(*Hantz enters,*)

Hantz. Guillaume

HANTZ
You please me, Guillaume; your vineyard is adjacent to mine; the waters of my meadow emerge from yours; but my daughter is weeping, and it's necessary to sacrifice ourselves, you understand.

GUILLAUME
Let's not be hasty, Monsieur Hantz. You're a faithful subject of the Emperor?

HANTZ
Certainly. Why wouldn't I be a faithful subject of the Emperor?

---

before being forced by the loss of his family's fortune to make a living as a chemist. Extensively employed in the manufacture of cheap jewelery, it became a significant symbol of fakery, referenced in that way by Victor Hugo and other writers.

GUILLAUME
Because you were a devoted servant of the other one.

HANTZ
Devoted! Devoted....

GUILLAUME
That's remembered in high places. It will be necessary to efface that... As burgomeister, I've been asked questions.

HANTZ, *slapping him on the shoulder*
As long as you're there to reply to them.

GUILLAUME
You'd have nothing to fear; but there are facts.

HANTZ
Facts?

GUILLAUME
Undeniable facts.

HANTZ
I assure you that there have never been any

GUILLAUME
You might be responsible

GUILLAUME
Your daughter.

HANTZ, *aside*
Always that Fritz. (*Aloud.*) I don't understand what connection there might be between my daughter and my fidelity to the Emperor.

GUILLAUME

The person who doesn't prevent a crime—and desertion is a crime—and who doesn't aid in the arrest of a criminal—and a deserter is a criminal—becomes criminal themselves, Monsieur Hantz.

HANTZ, *aside*

I'll explain that to Rosalie. (*Aloud.*) When Rosalie is your wife, it's you who'll be responsible for her.

GUILLAUME

If she were my wife, she'd no longer be occupied with Fritz.

HANTZ
Evidently

GUILLAUME, *uttering a sigh*

But she isn't yet my wife. Certainly, Mademoiselle Rosalie would be a faithful wife, but it's necessary that she be, immediately, a devoted—which is to say, a loving—wife, for I might be in a delicate position.

HANTZ
Because of what?

GUILLAUME

Because of you, Monsieur Hantz. You're not believed, in high places, to be a faithful subject; as Maire, you're too much in view. If I became your son-in-law, it would be necessary for all my acquaintances to be in order, in order not to be suspected myself; in consequence, I'd be forced to absent myself, and with a wife who wouldn't have married me with enthusiasm…you understand.

Decidedly, I'm renouncing the honor of entering into your family.

HANTZ
But no, no; everything can be arranged.

GUILLAUME
If Fritz became your son-in-law, what would people say?

HANTZ
He will never be my son-in-law.

GUILLAUME
I can't see any means of preventing it.

HANTZ
You're forgetting me, Guillaume.

GUILLAUME
One can acquire a son-in-law whether one wants it or
not.

HANTZ
That's stupid, Guillaume.

GUILLAUME
People can marry legally in America without parental
consent. It's so far away!

HANTZ
Your suppositions are devoid of common sense.

GUILLAUME
It wouldn't be your fault, but no one would believe it.
You'd be immediately suspect...from there to arrest...and se-
questration...

HANTZ
Devil take all conquerors!

GUILLAUME

If someone heard you! (*Running to the kitchen door*,) You might have been heard, You're too frank, Monsieur Hantz; that's what makes me tremble. If Fritz were to be imprisoned, as a deserter...

HANTZ

That's up to you; are you not burgomeister?

GUILLAUME

I'll take charge of it. On the day when he comes to see Rosalie, you'll inform me?

(*Fritz opens the door violently.*)

Fritz, Hantz. Guillaume. Then Rosalie

FRITZ

Scoundrel!

GUILLAUME, *aside*

A bad business.

HANTZ

Where have you sprung from? My daughter's bedroom! Name of a pipe! Rosalie! Rosalie!

ROSALIE, *entering, to Fritz*

And our agreement?

HANTZ

Since when has he been there?

ROSALIE

Since yesterday evening.

HANTZ
A thousand million billions!

FRITZ
It's not true.

ROSALIE, *pretending to weep on his shoulder*
You want to abandon me now!

HANTZ
Let him try!

(*Rosalie turns away to smile.*)

GUILLAUME
I believe...

FRITZ
Get out, or else...

GUILLAUME, *recoiling*
I'm the burgomeister, the representative of the Emperor.

FRITZ
I don't care about the Emperor, or his burgomeister.

(*He takes a step forward.*)

GUILLAUME, *still recoiling, aside*
No slaps, without witnesses.

HANTZ
Let's not be hasty.

ROSALIE, *shutting the door in Guillaume's face*
That's it.

Hantz. Fritz. Rosalie

HANTZ, *hiding his face in his hands*
Rosalie! My daughter!

ROSALIE
It's not true.

HANTZ
It's not possible.

ROSALIE
I'm saying that to you, but I won't say it to others. For everyone except you, Fritz spent the night in my bedroom.

HANTZ
You wouldn't say that.

ROSALIE
I've already said it to the burgomeister. It's therefore "official," to speak as he speaks.

FRITZ
Forgive me, Monsieur Hantz, I only wanted to say adieu to Rosalie before departing for America.

ROSALIE
A charming country, Father, where the wheat grows of its own accord.

FRITZ
The gendarmes were pursuing me; I came in by that window,

HANTZ

There's only one way of sorting this out now; you have to marry Rosalie immediately.

ROSALIE
That's the only means. Leave quickly, and I'll catch up with you.

HANTZ
Leave?

ROSALIE
Certainly. Guillaume will do as he said. Arrest...then sequestration...

HANTZ
What will become of our property?

ROSALIE
The Emperor's. That will be more convenient; when the Prussians are thrown out, we'll find all our money in the same pocket.

HANTZ
This is serious!

ROSALIE
There's one another means.

HANTZ
Speak

ROSALIE
Take Fritz by the collar and take him to prison.

FRITZ
Adieu. Until better times!

HANTZ

I've already noticed that all honest men think like Fritz; I'd be a stain amid the others. We'll go to America.

FRITZ

I can hear Guillaume and the gendarmes.

HANTZ, *going out swiftly*

Get away; I'll stall them momentarily. We'll catch up with you. You have my word.

Rosalie, Fritz

ROSALIE, *at the window*

There are two of them on watch.

FRITZ

It will be necessary to wait ten years for me, my Rosette.

ROSALIE

Ten years is a very long time.

FRITZ, *sadly*

So it's necessary not to wait for me.

(*Rosalie runs to unhook the rifle from above the fire-place.*)

ROSALIE

I'd rather die than go without seeing you for ten years; let's defend ourselves; they'll kill us.

FRITZ

I don't want them to kill you. I don't want them to kill me. I value life, since I know that you love me so much. The

226

gendarmes are watching the window but it's Guillaume who's guarding the door, and the frontier isn't far away, See you soon, my Rosette.

(*He extends his arms to her. Hantz opens the door.*)

The same. Hantz

HANTZ, *to Guillaume, who is in the kitchen*
I'll bring you the response. (*To the young couple, after having closed the door.*) And me—aren't you going to embrace me? (*Rosalie throws her arms around Hantz's neck,*) I want you to embrace me too; you're my son-in-law.

Now, this is what Guillaume proposes: Fritz having not been able to spend the night in your bedroom, since the gendarmes were pursuing him less than an hour ago, he'll forget the slightly sharp words that have been exchanged—those are his words—and promise to let him escape if you'll marry him within a week.

ROSALIE
What did you reply, Father?

HANTZ
That I'd propose the bargain to you.

ROSALIE
And you thought...

HANTZ
I know what you're worth. Give me the rifle; that isn't your response, it's him that I'll seek out.

FRITZ
You won't do that, Monsieur Hantz

HANTZ

227

He's only a Prussian.

ROSALIE
Can't the three of us get the better of that imbecile? (*Opening the door.*) Monsieur Guillaume!

The same. Guillaume

FRITZ
Rosalie!

HANTZ
Let her do it.

ROSALIE, *to Guillaume*
Bargain concluded.

FRITZ
Oh!

(*Hantz makes him a sign to shut up.*)

GUILLAUME
Really?

ROSALIE, *looking him in the face*
A man only has his word, Guillaume, and when he breaks it, a woman has the right to slap him in front of everyone. I will do that as I said.

HANTZ, *showing the rifle*
And I, faith of a Hantz...

GUILLAUME
All right, all right; put the rifle back on the nail.

ROSALIE
So you're going to send those two gendarmes wherever you wish; then I'll climb into your carriage, with Fritz, and you'll drive us to the frontier. If we find gendarmes *en route*, I'll slap you, first before them...

GUILLAUME
I believe we won't make a good household, and...

ROSALIE, *raising her hand*
A man only has his word, Guillaume...

FRITZ
Mademoiselle Rosalie...

ROSALIE
Shut up. I don't want tongues to wag, and I don't want anyone to say: "He was arrested in her bedroom."

FRITZ
I won't have been arrested in your bedroom.

(*He tries to leave.*)

ROSALIE
Yes, for you're going to go into it.

FRITZ
No.

ROSALIE
I want it (*In a whisper.*) I beg you.

GUILLAUME
You're making mock of me.

ROSALIE
The wine is drawn, Guillaume; it's necessary to drink it.

GUILLAUME
Laugh heartily...

ROSALIE
Who laughs last. (*Pushing Fritz into her bedroom and locking it with a key.*) You won't get out this time.

Hantz. Rosalie, Guillaume

ROSALIE
You have concluded with me, Guillaume, a bargain that I wouldn't have dared to propose to you; you'll keep it. You'll conduct Fritz to the other side of the frontier, and in a week, I'll be your wife, but...

GUILLAUME
Ah! There's a but.

ROSALIE
But I won't love you.

GUILLAUME
And...?

ROSALIE
You'll see...

GUILLAUME
You're definitely too smart for me; I've made a bad bargain. We'll take him to the other side of the frontier, and you'll render me my word.

(*Someone knocks.*)

The same. Fritz. Gendarmes

ROSALIE
Come in.

A GENDARME
We have him, burgomeister. He jumped out of the window and came with us very meekly

ROSALIE
It will be a long ten years, Fritz, but I would have done what you have done.

HANTZ, *to Guillaume*
Cain!

ARGENTINE

A Norwegian Tale

I. In which a fay is bored

At the entrance to a large grotto opening somberly over a blue gulf, a fay is gazing at the icebergs descending from the pole

It is the time when the men of the North go back up the rivers of the west in their boats.

"How bored I am, how bored I am," she says. "If I were a woman and I had a friend I would go to weep over her heart, but I'm only a fay. I have no tears, and my friends have no hearts..."

She sits down on the spangled sand licked by the azure waves; her hair the color of ears of wheat hangs downs all the way down the ground, her periwinkle-blue eyes shine like sapphires.

Her pink foot is playing with her green slipper; she is dreaming, her hands folded over her knee.

Then a chubby, plump, rubicund being in a blue satin doublet with black stripes appears, out of breath.

"But it's Grésil!" she exclaims, the sniffling monarch of the steppes.

"You said it, Argentine; I'm Grésil, the king who commands the spirits of the earth, as Perce-Neige commands the spirits of the ice,[20] and I've come to ask for you. Your silver thread is under the ice, it's true, but it's in the ground, so you don't belong to Perce-Neige, you're mine, and I want you for a wife."

---

[20] The French common noun *grésil* signifies hail, and *perce-neige* is the flower known in England as a snowdrop

Argentine is about to laugh...but she thinks that her smiths and her elves are far away, in the depths of the grotto, and that Grésil has a merited reputation for being angry and brutal, so she responds to him rapidly; "Since you want to marry me, it's necessary for you to prove your love to me; go and find Perce-Neige for me."

"In her polar palace?"

"Yes; when you return you'll have permission to kiss my fingertips."

"I'm on my way..."

He swells up like a balloon and rises up to the crest of the cliffs.

"When he comes back," said the fay, "He'll have found Perce-Neige, who'll defend me."

Soon, two large heads with bristling moustaches emerged from the sea. Those two rounded heads were the heads of two seals harnessed to a coquille Saint-Jacques. Perce-Neige descended from it.

"Greetings, Queen," said Argentine, bowing. "Good day, Sister," she added, throwing her arms around her.

Perce-Neige is pretty, but she does not resemble Argentine. Small, slender and brunette, her smooth tresses have no reflections; her eyes, with lids slightly raised toward the temples, shine like velvet; her lips are red and her cheeks gilded.

Perce-Neige is a strawberry from the Northern thickets; Argentine is a peach from the gardens of the Orient.

When only Finns lived in Norway under leather tents, in the lands of the Orient, in a city surrounded by walls of copper, there were twelve men equal in strength and in courage, so tall and so handsome that they were said to be gods and named the Aesir. The city was pierced by twelve golden gates, in order that each of the heroes could go in and out as he pleased.

They were the first among men, and their neighbors were jealous of them; when they were drinking together in their marble palace, around a round table, on twelve similar chairs, the jealous men killed their wild boar and their fallow deer with arrows. So, one evening, after a long feast, they said to one another: "Let's go where we can hunt in peace."

The next day they went out through their twelve gates, each having his lineage behind him.

Then they cut the copper walls with swords and each of them took one of the golden gates in order to make it into a shield.

They loaded the fragments of the walls on to carts and they marched northwards on their horses with black legs. They passed like a river of milk.

When they arrived in Norway—it was in spring, they had passed over the sea on the ice—they said: "This land is beautiful; its mountains sparkle, its lakes are as blue as the distant sky, its forests murmur and its waterfalls sing. Let's stop."

Their golden shields shone so flamboyantly that the bewildered Finns fled, crying: "They're the sons of the sun!"

But the Aesir, rude with the strong, were gentle with the small, they loved birds and flowers, sylphs and fays; when they departed, the sylphs, who slept there in the calyxes of roses, and the fays, who hid there in the stars of brambles, said to the rose-bushes and the brambles: "Grow so high and so dense that no one can approach the holy city any longer.

The rose-bushes branched like elms and the brambles interlaced like the mesh of a net.

Then the dreamy sylphs and the laughing fays said to the wood-pigeons; "Take us on your wings and let's go to rejoin them.

On seeing them, the fays of the North fled with the reindeer to the pathless solitudes....

When the leaves reddened in the crowns of the beeches, and the spray of the waterfalls sparkled like little rubies, when the mist silvered the reeds of ponds, when the long glaucous blades glided in the blue fjords, the wood-pigeons said to the elves whose flowers withered and the fays who were cold: "Let's go spend the winter in the lands of the sun."

Only the youngest of the fays, the one who was born out there on the eve of the departure, did not want to go; she had no memories.

Then the brunette daughters of the pole came back from the pathless plains, and Perce-Neige, their queen, met her on the shore.

"Since you only like Norway," she said to her, "be our sister. I'll give you a silver palace where the flowers will never wither."

"I'd like that," said the blondest of the daughters of the Orient.

That is why she is called Argentine, and why, in the midst of her brunette sisters, she resembles a spring of honeysuckle on a carpet of myrtles.

Argentine told Perce-Neige about her troubles.

"In sum, I'm bored," she concluded, "And…I'd like to weep."

"In spite of my advice, then, you've gone into the world of humans?" said the queen, sadly.

"I only went there once, eighteen years ago. From the edge of a forest of firs, all white with snow, I saw a child as beautiful as daylight in a cradle lined with swansdown. He was cold and I carried him quickly into my grotto, and...."

"And now?"

"He's still as beautiful as daylight.

"I understand then. You love him."

"If I were a woman, perhaps he'd love me…and I would certainly love him…but I'm only a fay."

"Friend, as long as we remain in our domain, we're immortal, but if we love in the land of humans, we become women.

"I could cry then when I'm sad!" exclaimed Argentine, clapping her hands. "look; can one see Noël without loving him?"

She showed her a handsome adolescent.

He advanced, smiling; the brunette Queen of the North launched forth in her shell.

II. In which we learn who Noël is...

Eighteen years before that day, Otto the Valiant, whose maple-wood boat flew like a seamew, had left Emma the beautiful in his castle.

As he quit her he had said: "The laborer reaps the field he has sown; the sea is the field of the men of the North; the red boats are our plows, the blue swords are our scythes; it's harvest time, I'm leaving. I'll bring you back golden rings, and pearl necklaces as a toy for the child. I'm departing without dread; my name is written on my door, and no one would dare to touch what belong to Otto."

Emma accompanied her husband to the shore. She had buckled his breastplate of scales, she wanted to untie the cable that moored the boat, because the old songs say: "She who buckles the breastplate will unbuckle it, and she who unties the cable will tie it up again."

Otto's companions were waiting for him; there were a hundred, perhaps two hundred; they were the elite of the northern warriors.

On seeing him so strong among the strong, Emma said to herself: "Who would dare to touch what is his?"

With tears in her eyes but confidence in her heart, she went back to sit down in the hall paneled in fir-wood, next to a cradle lined with swansdown.

The summer has passed, autumn is finished, the geese have fled the frozen ponds, the wolves have come in packs; Emma is weeping.

Where is Otto the Valiant? Has the tempest broken his boat? Has the mud of the river entangled it? Is his cadaver rolling beneath the glaucous waves? Is he sleeping under the reeds?"

Where is Otto the brave?

His boat is dancing on the waves like an iridescent bubble, his boat is gliding over the sea like a duck-feather; it is far away, far away where the sun sets. Upright at the curved prow, leaning on the dragon's head that rears up open-mouthed, Otto is still as handsome as a fir-tree, as white as an eider, and as strong as a salmon. He is so strong that his boat is full of golden rings; he is so white that the foam seems gray on his arms; and he is so handsome that the daughter of the sea is singing before his boat: "Otto, Otto, if you wanted…I have a palace of emeralds decorated with sapphires."

"You don't have Emma's eyes," replies the Northern warrior.

"Otto, Otto, in the depths of a wife's eyes, one reads: *Perhaps*; in the depths of mine one reads: *Always*."

Leaning on the red dragon, he dreams about Emma's eyes, as clear as a spring, and Emma's blonde hair, as delicate as spider-silk; but the undine sings so sweetly that her song lulls him, and the boat follows the undine into the depths of the west.

"Otto, Otto, if you wanted…I have emeralds in my palace, and pink anemones."

"In my castle I have a fine white carnation," replies the Northern warrior.

And he cries to the helmsman: "Steer for Norway!"

The boat rears up like a charger under the bit; like a docile charger it turns. The rigging stiffens, the sail stretches, and the joyful men ship the oars.

Otto can no longer see before him the undine with the ivory shoulders; he is thinking about the white carnation that he has left back there, on a swansdown cushion.

"Harder! Harder, companions!" he shouts, while pulling the oar.

"What is this white carnation, then?" wonders the undine. "If I had it in my palace, perhaps he would come."

Like a seamew, the boat flies. The coast is blue in the distance; it shines in the moonlight. It is Christmas Eve.

Then the undine stands upright on the waves; she must have that white carnation. In the radiance that bathes her she glides over the shore, she climbs all the way to the castle, the black silhouette of which is standing out against the steely sky.

A window is shining at the top of the tower; a woman is leaning over a cradle.

"There, she says, "are Emma the blonde and the white carnation that Otto cannot forget. When I have that beautiful carnation in my palace he will come in search of it.

"Woman with blue eyes," she shouts. "Otto is on the shore."

The blonde Emma shivers and runs to the window, from which the shore and the sea can be seen in the distance. Over the bay, of which the moon makes a mirror, the black boats are gliding.

Without kissing her son, and without taking her cloak, Emma runs to the shore, and the undine takes away the beautiful white carnation.

The undine swims in the moonlight, but the moon is rising toward the fir-woods and the pale radiance makes the shore distant.

Soon, out of breath, she sighs: "I'm a daughter of the waves, I stifle on land. Like the azure-tinted jellyfish that the sea abandons in the hollow of a rock, I shall die if the sunlight touches me, and this radiance is carrying me away."

Toward the firs the radiance rides; between the trunks it glides, on the stiff needles it is shredded.

The undine utters a cry; her shoulders are bleeding and the beautiful white carnation escapes her arms...

The moon rises into the sky; behind the mountain the radiance descends, carrying the undine away to the endless snowy plains.

Under a juniper bush, in his swansdown cradle, the white carnation is still asleep.

In the depths of the wood the hungry wolves are howling. Here they come.

Then the earth opens up beside the juniper bush, and a fay emerges from the narrow crevice.

The child utters a plaint and the fay sees him, as dainty as a carnation.

"What's the point of looking any further?" she says. "At the first step I've found a flower as beautiful as one can imagine."

Into the opened earth she carries the white carnation; the bells are ringing for Christmas.

That is why Argentine's beloved is named Noël.

III. In which Noël chats with his godmother

"What do you want, Noël?" the fay asks the adolescent, who is gazing in surprise at the huge seashell sinking into the gulf.

"I've come to drink from the spring."

"You don't find the water insipid? Men, your brothers, drink hydromel from golden cups."

"Is it good?"

"It appears so.

"I'd rather drink this beautiful running water from your hands. I'm very thirsty, godmother."

"Don't call me godmother any longer."

"What should I call you?"

"I don't know."

"You don't know whether hydromel is good, and you don't know what name it's necessary to give you. Let's stay as we are, godmother, let's call one another what we call one another."

"Men fight against monsters and giants."

Noël smiles; Argentine has made a nacreous cup with her hands.

He's certainly the son of a knight, thinks the fay. *He smiles at the idea of combats; when he has a sword, he'll want to make use of it.*

Noël is still thirsty, but she touches the wall of the grotto with her finger. The granite wall opens up and she draws the glutton into an immense forge, in which bearded dwarves broader than they are tall are extended around anvils, sleeping in their otter-skin capes.

"On your feet, idlers!" cries Argentine, stamping her foot,

Awoken with a start, the dwarves run to the forges, to the hammers and to the bellows, and the foremost smith, picking up a handful of jewels, says to his irritated mistress: "Look, we've been working hard."

"Forge me a sword for Noël," replied Argentine, without looking.

"In gold?" asked the dwarf.

"A sword for killing giants," said Noël, negligently

"You'll also need a very warm tunic, which rain cannot penetrate," the fay interjected. "While they forge, let's go see the spinners."

As they went to see the spinners, in the utmost depths of the grotto, Argentine said: "I'd like to see you on a fine horse when your sword is flamboyant. Would that give you pleasure? Let's go to the abode of the spinners, then, to find a tunic that the rain won't penetrate."

Under Argentine's finger, the depths of the grotto open up, and they enter into a round chamber where a hundred spinners are chatting.

"To your spindles, gossips!" say the fay, frowning.

But the mistress runs forward, fine fabric in hand, and, placing it on the hair the color of wheat she cried: "How pretty you are under that!"

"It's true that you're very pretty under that," Noël approves, taking a step back in order to see better.

Argentine smiles and strokes the cheek of the dainty spinner, as thin as a reed and as brown as a rush. "You're good

240

workers. Now it's a matter of weaving for Noël a very warm tunic, which the rain won't penetrate."

"So he wants to return to the human world?"

"Argentine wishes it," sighs Noël, "but she'll come with me."

Argentine does not want to depart with Noël for the human world, she wants to join him there, because she wants to be loved not as a fay but as a woman.

"You're a man, and you'd be afraid all alone!"

The spinner laughed.

"Oh, you think I'm afraid?" said Noël, piqued. "Well, I'll depart alone; but as soon as I've killed a giant I'll return, because, you see, godmother, I don't find water good when I don't drink it from your hands."

The dwarves have forged a beautiful sword with a steel blade, a gold hand-guard and a silver scabbard. The spinners have woven an asbestos tunic that has no colors and al reflections, a tunic mild to the eyes, rude to the touch, as supple as deerskin and as hard as a shield.

When he had donned the tunic and buckled on the sword. Noël said: "I'll kill a giant, since you desire it, that's decided, but how shall I find one? In that unknown world I'll be like a blind man."

"You'll soon find a guide," replies Argentine, slightly hesitantly.

If she had been a woman, she would have blushed.

"But how shall I recognize that guide? Will it be necessary to say to all those I encounter: *I've come to kill a giant; show me one, if you please?*"

Argentine does not reply. She is thinking.

"Godmother, Godmother, let's stay as we are; the giants haven't done anything to you. I love you so much, you see, that no godmother will ever have a nicer godson."

"Shut up, we're talking seriously When you arrive up there you'll find a squire, very thin, as befits a young man.

Fie! The fearful fellow, who seeks a thousand pretexts to remain."

"I have no need to seek a thousand pretexts; I have a hundred thousand good reasons.—but the sooner I leave, the sooner I can come back. Adieu, Godmother."

The elves who bear a flame on the forehead, those who follow the seams of silver under the ground, had carved a broad stair inside the mountain. Noël went up the stairs two by two.

As soon as he disappeared into the somber path, Argentine clapped her hands.

In the blink of an eye, smiths and spinners, miners and hairdressers surrounded her.

"I need a suit of armor," she said to the smiths, "And hosiery," she said to the spinners.

The mouths of the fat dwarves opened all the way to the ears, and the eyes of the dainty spinners lowered modestly.

"Why laugh, ugly wretches? And why look like that, stupid sluts? I want to be the squire of the man I love."

"She loves Noël!" cries all of that petty society. "Hurrah! Hurrah!"

And the otter-skin bonnets fly into the air. "Hurrah! Hurrah!"

And the hammers of the elves ring on their foil. "Hurrah! Hurrah! She loves Noël! Hurrah! Hurrah! Oh, the beautiful wedding! Hurrah! Hurrah!"

And the dainty spinners, as brown as rushes, draw the pale burnishers with fingers dusted with silver into a mad round dance.

IV. In which Noël sees the human world again

Noël is in a fir-wood. In front of him extends a snowy plain limited by high mountains, which crown a castle with sharp turrets.

The shadow of large clouds running across the sky puts ashen trails over the plain; the mountain, with sheer slopes, resembles a chipped saw, and the towers taper like black tears.

"A nasty country," he says, "I'm turning back," when a young woman falls into his arms, exclaiming:

"I'm dying!"

As an enormous bear was trotting behind the young woman, Noël spread his arms wide and the lovely child slipped on the snow.

He marched upon the wild beast, brandishing his sword.

Argentine's smiths are good smiths; the bear is laid out dead next to the fainted beauty.

It appears that women are fearful, Noël thinks; and he kneels down in order to lift the pale head. *But they're pretty*, he adds, on seeing the rosy color return to the cheeks. *Not as pretty as my godmother, but very pretty all the same.*

"Where am I?" sighs a soft voice.

"In the snow," Noël replies, "between a dying bear and a boy who admires you."

"Thank you, Messire," says the unknown woman, bounding to her feet.

"Are you afraid of me, as you were afraid of the bear?"

The beauty smiles slightly and blushes deeply.

"I don't know," Noël continues, "whether all women resemble you—you're the first one I've seen—but I'd like them to; you're good to look at."

The unknown woman blushed a little less and smiled a little more. "You've come from the land of the fays, then, Messire?"

"Just now."

She was no longer blushing; she laughed.

Two more young women, who arrived running, stopped, trembling, before the cadaver of the bear.

"Women are decidedly fearful," murmurs Noël, "but they're as pretty as fays."

"Oh, no," says the unknown woman. Then, addressing the newcomers: "I was about to be devoured when this knight..."

"I'm not a knight, I'm Noël. I've come to kill a giant; as soon as the giant is slain, I'll return whence I came."

"Be careful, Hildewige," whispers one of the young women, "he's an elf; see, his doublet has all the colors of the rainbow."

"He's a brave man," replies Hildewige, and, turning back to Noël: "Who sent you to kill a giant?"

"My godmother. I do everything she wishes, because I love her. But I also love you; I sense it. What is your name?"

"Hildewige. I'm the daughter of Otto, whose castle you can see over there."

"Are there any giants in your father's castle?"

"No."

"Too bad. I would have been glad to chat with you along the way, but I'm in haste to return to my godmother."

"I understand."

"I'll come back up to the earth in order to see you. I sense positively that I love you. That doesn't annoy you?"

Hildewige recommenced blushing.

"You aren't saying yes or no," Noël continues. "You're too pretty for anyone to cause you pain; say that you're not annoyed."

"No."

"Then it's settled; I love you—not in the same manner, but almost as much, as my godmother. I'll certainly come to see you one of these days."

A sleigh stopped beside them. Hildewige climbed into it with the two women.

"There's a tourney at the castle tomorrow," she says, taking the reins, "and I'll expect you," she adds, launching the shaggy ponies at a gallop.

Noël watched the sleigh fly away in the snow cloud.

"I'm sorry to see her go away," he said. "Almost as sorry as I was when I quit my godmother. I love her...that's astonishing. It's astonishing for me, who doesn't know anything, but it didn't seem astonishing to her. What am I going to do now? I can't always be running from Argentine's grotto to the castle. It's necessary that they live together. If the castle is nicer than the grotto, Argentine can come to the castle; if the grotto is nicer than the castle, Hildewige can come to the grotto. Since they both want me to love them, they have similar tastes; they'll certainly please one another."

The sun slid behind the mountain; the sleigh disappeared in the evening mist.

"Let's go to sleep," sighed Noël. "This snow is as soft as down, the little spinners have woven me a tunic that the north wind doesn't traverse, and that bear will make me a soft pillow."

He lay down, with his head on the bear's belly, and went to sleep.

V. In which it is understandable why Noël loves Hildewige

Eighteen years ago, when Otto went into the high room in the tower with Emma, the swansdown cradle was no longer by the fireside.

"Wife, what have you done?" he said.

Pale, her eyes haggard, the mother ran to the widow, crying: "The elves have stolen him; I've got to get him back!"

Then Otto remembered the daughter of the waves.

"I told her where my treasure was," he murmured. "What has happened is my fault."

He hugged the crazed mother to his breastplate, put a kiss on her eyes and departed, without taking the time to empty the cup that his cup-bearer held out to him.

His companions are celebrating his return; he is alone on the maple-wood boat, the red dragon of which is plunging its scaly breast into the foam. He returns whence he came, into the depths of the sunset.

His back to the mast, which is bending under the north wind, he cries into the darkness: "I am Otto, do you hear? Can you hear me, queen of the waves?"

But his voice is lost in the noise of the waves breaking heavily.

The boat quivers all the way to the keel; like a deer struck by a spear, it lies down on its side; Otto is on an iceberg tossed by the waves,

"They're going westwards," says the warrior. "They're going where I want to go."

And, fearlessly, he shouts into the darkness:

"I am Otto, do you hear? Can you hear me, queen of the waves?"

But his voice is lost in the noise of the wind whistling between the thin needles of the errant iceberg.

At daybreak, Otto sees on the summit of the floating mountain a giant with a white beard holding the tiller of a rudder. As he is never afraid, he shouts to the giant:

"Steer toward the sunset!"

Only Otto the Brave could speak thus, thinks the giant; *for a long time I've desired to measure myself against the strongest of men.* And letting go of the tiller he says. "We'll wrestle one another; the loser will be the slave of the victor."

"Gladly," Otto replies.

They wrestled until sunset, and then all night, and all of the following day. At the end of the second day, however, the giant, being thirsty, wanted to break off a fragment of ice, and his right arm let go of Otto's back briefly; the warrior recovered his breath and squeezed his adversary's sides so forcefully that he made him cry for mercy.

"You'll obey me, as I would have obeyed you if I had been vanquished," said Otto. "Resume your place at the tiller."

"Where is it necessary to go?"

"To the emerald palace of the daughter of the waves."

"You won't find her in her emerald palace any longer; the moon's rays have carried her into the snowy steppes of the endless plain."

"Then take me in that direction; it's necessary that I find her."

After a week, perhaps two, the iceberg ran aground in the depths of a narrow gulf bordered by frozen ponds.

"You can return where you were going," said Otto then. "I'm returning your liberty; I'm proud of having wrestled with someone as strong as you."

"Since you're as generous as you're brave," replied the giant, I'll tell you a secret that humans don't know. On the far side of these lakes, in a forest of birches, under a stone slab supported by three others, there is a woman older than the world; ask her for what you seek; she knows everything."

Otto traverses the frozen lakes and plunges into the forest of birches.

He had been marching for a week when he was attacked by crows with steel claws and bronze beaks. He swatted them away with his hand as one chases away flies in summer.

He marched for another week, and a wolf larger than a two-year-old colt barred his route. He seized it by the ears and rubbed its muzzle in the snow.

"Wolf," he said, "I could strangle you if I wished, but I'll let you go if you take me to the old woman who knows everything."

The trembling wolf replied: "Follow me."

Otto followed him and they arrived at the entrance to a grotto. The old woman, crouching before an iron spinning-wheel, was spinning hair.

"I don't have the hair that you're seeking to spin," she said. "Go away."

"Listen. Old woman," said Otto. "I've felled the giant with the white beard, I've swatted your crows as ne chases

247

away flies, and I've held your wolf by the ears; if you tell me what I'm seeking, I'll give you my golden necklace."

"And if I don't want to?"

"I'll force you to speak."

"Madman! I'm Death!."

"I'm not afraid of death."

"You're going to fight me?"

"Instead of talking so much, let's begin; you have no sword so I won't draw mine."

"You're a brave man! Listen: return to your castle; when a rosebud opens there, amour will bring the white carnation you seek."

He left Death spinning with her iron wheel.

When Otto returned to the high hall, Emma was still weeping.

"Weep no more, white seamew, my sweet teal," he said to her, "weep no more. Give me a rosebud, and when the rose blossoms, we'll see the one for whom you're weeping night and day."

Emma was worthy of a brave man; she was like the white seamew, whose wings are not tarnished by anything, like the multicolored teal which only has one amour in its life; her heart was swollen by tears, but her lips smiled night and day...

When the maidservants brought the waiting warrior the fresh rosebud, Emma closed her large bright eyes. She was a white seamew, who opened her wings; a gentle teal who only had one amour in her life.

Emma soul went to the land without winters; while passing over a marsh whose reeds were rustling in the wind, she heard a voice.

The voice wept: "You who have wings, carry me as far as the waves that are singing out there; I am the daughter of the sea. The desiccated reeds are bruising my breast, the mud

248

of the marsh is hardening my hair; I am the daughter of the sea."

"It is my tears," Emma replies, "that have burned the reeds, it is my sobs that have caused the mud to rise all the way to your hair; the one you stole will bring you back, if he wishes, to the singing waves."

Otto's heart sighed in the tower: "If a sword were not necessary beside roses that bloom, I would follow you, my white seamew. Remake our nest on high, my sweet teal!"

Today, the fresh rosebud has blossomed; Hildewige is a rose.

That is why Noël, who loves his godmother so much, also loves the blonde girl with such blue eyes; that is why the wild rose, which has flourished under a sword, has inclined without dread toward the stranger whose eyes are as blue as her own.

VI. In which Argentine regrets what she wanted

As soon as Noël falls asleep with his head on the bear, Argentine emerges from the shadow of a fir-tree. She is wearing the pretty costume of a page, half-yellow and half-black, a slender sword and an otter-fur cap with an eagle feather. In order to resemble a page more closely, she has cut her hair.

"I no longer want to be a woman," she sighs. "Women are all liars and coquettes. She's brazen, that Hildewige! He must love me, in order not to have followed her to the castle. He was right, this morning; let's stay as we are. I'll take him back very quickly, and tomorrow he'll think that he had a dream."

She is leaning over him when she straightens up abruptly, putting her hands to her cheeks.

"Did the flap of my cloak touch you?" says a little shrill voice. "I regret it, but it's your fault; I had such momentum that I couldn't stop."

It is Grésil.

249

"I carried out your commission, but when I came to collect my salary, I found the house masterless and your servants laughed in my face. Hee hee," he continues, on perceiving Noël, "I'm beginning to understand. There's a fellow that it's necessary not to leave asleep under the stars; I'll drape an alcove for him so comfortable that he'll no longer want to emerge from it."

"You're forgetting who I am." Argentine interjects.

"And you're forgetting that you're no longer in your own domain. On the land where I reign, you have no strength and no power. If you're interested in this fellow, swear to marry me incontinently, or he'll serve as breakfast for the wolves tomorrow."

So saying, he shakes his mantle and the snow begins to swirl.

"Noël!"

If you wake him up, I'll blind him—look!"

And the snow falls more thickly

"You always want to cause me pain; you don't love me, as you claim," sighs Argentine.

"You're no longer at home; you're where I'm the master; I prevail over you."

Argentine is in the cloud that serves Grésil as a palace.

"You can see that my palace is too large for me alone," sniggers the chubby elf. "You can stroll around it at your ease."

"And he'll die in the snow!" sighs the fay.

"Indubitably."

If a fay could weep, tears would stripe her cheeks, she has so much chagrin. She has so much chagrin that her lips say what her heart is saying: "I love you dearly, Noël."

"Blow! Blow hard!" cries the elf.

Genii, swollen like balloons, send whirlwinds of snow over the forest.

"I'll be your wife," cries Argentine, "if..."

"If?"

A white radiance fills the gray palace, and Perce-Neige appears, mounted on a swan.

"If I wish it!" says the Queen of the Pole.

"You're queen in your abode, but I'm king here!" growls Grésil.

"You're a villain and a liar."

"What?"

"Have you, yes or no, asked for me in marriage?"

"I have asked for you."

"And what was my reply?"

"Go take a walk."

"Have you taken a walk?"

"That's all I've done."

"You have, therefore, as a smitten suitor, obeyed my orders. Here's my hand."

"Are you serious?"

"I don't like questions. My court awaits yours. If a single one of your subjects—my subjects, I mean—is lacking, we'll have words. Go and get suitably dressed."

"Perce-Neige, I render you your promise."

"I've said yes; you've said yes. Yes, it's too late."

"It's too late!" sighs Grésil, and he goes out, grumbling.

"Oh, my sister," says Argentine. "you're sacrificing yourself for me?"

"The marriage isn't made yet. An eider had seen you carried away; he warned me, I came immediately. But where were you going in a doublet with a sword at your side?"

"I no longer want to be a fay, since a Grésil can abduct me. When I'm Noël's wife, he'll defend me."

"Every being obeys its destiny," sighs Perce-Neige. And stamping her foot: "Grésil! Grésil!"

"I'm running," says the elf.

"Slowly…I like quick people. Take Argentine back whence you took her."

"But…"

"I don't tolerate observations. Go quickly, and come back the same way."

VII. In which Noël finds a squire

The sun rises—a pale sun—and Noël wakes up.

"Those spinners," he says, have woven a fine tunic; I didn't feel the cold. I'd gladly have breakfast. Where can one have breakfast on earth? Argentine promised me a thin squire to serve me as a guide, but I don't see him. I ought to have accepted Hildewige's hospitality yesterday..."

He was about to head toward the castle, the black towers of which were visible, when he perceived a dainty page.

There's the promised squire, he thought, joyfully. But he ran forward, crying: "Godmother!"

"Greetings, Messire," said the dainty page.

"That costume suits you," Noël replied, circling the page. "Truly, truly! But one thing astonishes me!"

"Do you need a square to hold your horse and furbish your sword?"

"Why have you cut your hair?"

"I was wearing a helmet, Messire."

Noël smiles. "Come on, Argentine..."

"My name is Muguet."[21]

"You're joking?"

"A small person should have a small name."

It's another idea she's had, Noël thinks. *It's a sequel to yesterday's; since it amuses her, let's pretend not to recognize her.* "It's agreed, Muguet," he said, finally, "You're my squire. To seal the bargain, come and kiss me."

While kissing the dainty page, who hoists herself up on tiptoe, he laugh. "Do you know my godmother?" he says.

"I don't know, Messire."

"She's a crazy little fay."

---

[21] The French common noun *muguet* refers to the flower known in English as a lily-of-the-valley.

"That'll be why a fay said to me yesterday: 'Go forth, Muguet, and when you see a handsome knight, be his squire.'"

She's making fun of me, Noël thinks. *My turn, now...* "Muguet, you've arrived just in time; you're going to take a message to the castle that is standing out blackly against the snow; you'll find a beautiful demoiselle there..."

The dainty page shivers.

"What's the matter with you? I'm not charging you with a disagreeable mission. Hildewige is good to behold, and, coming on my part, you'll be well-received."

"Where did you meet that beautiful demoiselle?"

"Curious child! Let it suffice for you to know that I saved her life."

"Already?"

"Already. You're sighing? You would have liked to see that? Have no fear, in my service you'll see many more. I wanted to spend my time slaying giants, but on reflection, I'll spend it saving beautiful demoiselles. We'll amuse ourselves a great deal, friend Muguet. But here she is,"

Hildewige was approaching in a sleigh.

"I was wrong not to believe Perce-Neige." sighs Argentine.

"Greetings, Hildewige," says Noël.

"Good day, Noël," replies Hildewige.

Hildewige! Noël! They greet one another as if they had grown up together, thinks Argentine.

"I wanted to revisit the place where I was so frightened," says the young woman. "I didn't think I'd encounter you here, but I hoped to find you when I returned; my father is expecting you. Did you sleep here, then, in the snow?"

"And I slept there very well, dreaming about you."

"Is this your page," she interjects, indicating Argentine.

"He's nice, isn't he?"

"He looks like a girl."

"You think so?"

"You must give him to me; he seems better made for playing the viol than wielding a sword.

"What do you think, Muguet?" asks Noël, laughing.

"I don't want that!" cries the page.

"My father, to whom I recounted my adventure, would like to thank you," said Hildewige. "When I told him that you had a fay for a godmother..."

"For a godmother!" cries Argentine, sharply.

This page isn't a page, thinks Hildewige.

She returns abruptly to her ponies and departs at the gallop, after having blown a kiss to Muguet.

"She has also seen that you're not a page," says Noël. "Let's sit down in the warm, between the bear's paws, and talk seriously."

He draws her to him gently, on the soft fur.

"What do you want?"

"Nothing," Argentine replies, bowing her head. She has so much chagrin that she does not perceive that she is weeping for the first time.

"You're annoyed with me," Noël continues. "You think that I find Hildewige pretty. Don't deny it! Certainly I find her pretty, and I love her already, but I don't love her in the same way that I love you"

"I'm only a fay!" sobs Argentine.

"If you were a woman, do you believe that I'd love you more? Since yesterday, I no longer understand you, and when I rack my brains trying to understand, it fatigues me. Hold on! She's asleep...isn't she pretty? She's even prettier than Hildewige."

Then an old woman followed by a wolf larger than a two-year-old colt appeared.

"Noël," said the old woman.

"You know my name?"

"I know everything."

"Since you know everything, tell me what Argentine wants."

"She wants to be your wife."

254

"You mean my fay. She can't be my wife, since she's a fay."

"When she wakes up, she'll be a woman."

"I don't know whether it's necessary to say *so much the better* or *too bad*. My head is hurting! What gave her the idea of sending me to travel the world in order to follow me here? We were so comfortable down below!"

"Let her sleep and go to the castle; it's necessary that she doesn't see you when she wakes up."

Noël hesitated, but he thought that if she woke up a fay, she would find him very rapidly, and if she woke up a woman, she would wait for him.

"I'll watch over her," said the old woman. "Take my wolf."

"If anything happens to her, I'll strangle you," said Noël.

The old woman would have smiled if she had been able to do so; she sat down in the snow, and Noël headed toward the castle, holding the wolf by the ear.

VIII. In which many things are explained

In the great hall of the castle, at the foot of a platform on which Otto and Hildewige were sitting, a large carpet had been extended to serve as lists.

On the steps, the castellan's old companions were crowded silently between their wives and daughters; at the back of the hall, the servants of both sexes were heaped up; the bare-chested champions were waiting. But Hildewige did not give the signal; she was hoping to see Noël.

Hildewige is nicknamed the Rose of the North.

She is not one of those pale roses that lean over, shivering; she is a mossy rose with gleaming leaves and nacreous petals. She has the fine hair of Emma the beautiful and the glaucous eyes of Otto the strong; when she puts on her skates, her greyhound can hardly follow her over the ice of the lake, and when she takes the tiller, the dragon with the great wings seems to be playing like a seal between the rocks of the coast.

She has the gentle smile of Emma the beautiful and the proud gaze of Otto the strong. When her white fingers spin wool, her heart sings the beautiful poem in which the blue steel of swords rings, in which the sound of oars striking the long waves of the North Sea can be heard.

Her heart is like a spring in a granite hollow, like a clear spring whose bed can be seen, and sand over which the shadows of clouds and the shadows of the wings of gyrfalcons pass without leaving any trace.

Like the blonde virgins who sing the Eddas she would have liked to follow the brave men who reap the foam of the waves to distant shores, but she has the heart of Emma the beautiful; next to her pensive father she remains the swallow that twitters in summer, the cricket that laughs on the hearth in winter.

But time is passing. In order to say to the men "Do well!" she is rising sadly to her feet when Noël appears, holding the huge wolf by the ear.

Otto shudders; it seems to him that he recognizes the wolf of the old woman with the iron spinning-wheel.

Before such a brilliant assembly, Noël ought to be shy, but nothing of the sort; he cuts through the servants and the warriors with his head held high, marching straight toward the platform.

He bows to Otto, smiles at Hildewige, and says to the wolf, indicating an empty place near to the cushion the color of dawn on which the virgin's feet are placed: "Lie down there."

If he's the person that I believe, thinks the old man, *He's entering my castle like a ray of sunligh*t. And addressing Noël: "You're going to wrestle; I'm wagering on you."

"Me too," says Hildewige.

In the midst of the warriors, Noël is like an ash-twig among knotty elms.

"We'll take the bet!" cry the men of the North.

"Your swords against a kiss," says Hildewige.

Remarking that the wrestlers have bare torsos, Noël takes off his tunic, and as he does not know where to put his sword, he hands it to Hildewige.

The men smiled, but the old man, seeing that golden hilt-guard and that silver scabbard, on which birds and flowers are enlaced, murmurs: "He's the person I'm waiting for; only an elf could have forged such a sword..."

"Let's go; do well, Noël!"

Noël does not know how to wrestle; when the first man leaps forward, his arms extended, he takes the two arms by the wrists and parts them as he would have parted two sprig of gorse barring his path.

The warrior tries to seize him but he lifts him up gently and holing him in the air, he says to Hildewige: "What is it necessary to do with him?"

"Give him to me," replies the virgin gaily.

"Here he is!"

And he sets the warrior down between the paws of the wolf, whose muzzle creases.

When he turns round, the lists are empty.

Otto cried: "It's him!"

Noël did not understand why everyone was astonished by such a simple thing.

He had put his tunic on again and buckled his sword.

"You're my son," said the old man.

"You're my brother," said Hildewige.

"You'll be our chief," said her suitors, glad no longer to have him as a rival.

"Excuse me!" Noël exclaims. "I'm very touched, but I don't understand anything of what you're saying."

"Has a fay," the old man interjected, "kept you under the waves in an emerald grotto?"

"A fay found me under a juniper bush and I grew up next to her in a seam of silver. It's necessary, in order for you to inform yourselves, to go and find the old woman who knows everything; at this moment she's guarding the sleeping Argentine."

"I have no need, my son, to seek any longer. You are Hildewige's brother. Kiss her."

"Gladly. This castle is a fine castle; brave men fill it; I'll go fetch Argentine."

"I'll go with you, Brother," says Hildewige.

The rose now has a solid support, thinks the hero of the North. *I can go to rejoin the beloved of my youth, and rediscover on high the happiness of old.*

To the servants, he says: "Children, set the table..."

To his guests he says: "Friends, sit down around me; I have fought bravely; I have the right to repose."

IX. In which everything recommences

Hand in hand, they marched over the white snow.

"I shall love your fay," said Hildewige. "She's a pretty sparrow, and I shall make her a lovely nest."

"Her dwarves," said Noël, "will forge you a golden ring, and among the brave men who love you, you shall choose."

"I don't want a golden ring, I want a maple-wood boat, which will hold all three of us."

"To go where, my sister?"

"To go forward."

Hand in hand, they marched over the white snow.

"You were not mine yesterday, today you are mine," said the old woman, breaking one of Argentine's hairs; "I shall spin on my spinning-wheel the days that remain to you. Will they be long? I don't know—what does it matter to me? I shall spin the days that remain to you."

She fled, rustling like a dry leaf.

Argentine woke up, and called to Noël.

The she saw before her a white reindeer, which said to her. "Since you're only a woman now, I'll take you where Noël is coming to search for you.

"Let's go," Argentine replied.

While they were chatting, hand in hand, the great wolf had run away.

When they arrived in the forest they no longer found the old woman, and nothing remained between the bear's paws but the bonnet with the eagle feather.

"Oh, my brother!" said Hildewige.

"Don't torment yourself," Noël responds. "She's a little jealous. She's sulking somewhere nearby... Argentine! Argentine!"

"Perhaps the wolves have come?"

"Wolves don't eat fays. She's sulking, I tell you. Argentine! Argentine! She doesn't know who you are; she's sulking. But she's jealous; she'll be at the castle this evening. Perhaps she's already there...? She's certainly there...let's go back quickly."

The young woman took away the cap.

On the back of the white reindeer, Argentine dreams, and the more she dreams, the more the past seems to have been a dream that is gradually fading away.

Was I a fay? She could almost doubt it. But she knows that she loves, and she is going to where Noël will come.

Having arrived on the edge of the sea, the reindeer stopped.

"I can't take you any further," it said, "but if you're not afraid, I can see a salmon that can take you over the sea."

"Since I'm going to where he will come, let the salmon carry me."

As it quit her, the reindeer said: "In your husband's house, it's necessary to have the footfalls of a mouse and the hearing of a hare."

The salmon swam toward Denmark.

When Hildewige and Noël went into the great hall, the table was laid.

"Console yourself, my daughter," said the hero the North; "the woman who knows everything said to me: 'When the rosebud blooms, amour will bring you the handsome white carnation. The woman has brought you to me in order to love me, you will find her again.'"

Then he sat Noël down to his tight and Hildewige to his left.

"Friends," he said then to his guests, "Noël will be what I was, because the grafted apple tree cannot yield a wrinkled apple." Then, addressing Noël: "You must not forget that it is necessary never to ask for what cannot be done; if you want to be the pilot, it is necessary to know the reefs; if you want to be the sword of your men, it is also necessary to be their shield. Remember, my son, that the strongest hydromel is made with the sweetest honey; if you want to be obeyed, command mildly..."

The hero of the North spoke thus for a long time, while his guess assuaged their hunger. When no one was any longer touching the dishes, he stood up, and after having hugged Hildewige and Noël, he went out without saying where he was going.

On the back of the salmon, which is speeding like an arrow, Argentine dreams, and the more she dreams the more the past seems to have been a dream that is gradually fading away.

She is going to where Noël will come, she no longer knows anything else.

Over the green sea the salmon glides like an arrow; having arrived at the sand of the shore, it stops.

"I can't go any further," it said, "but I can see a mare that can take you where Noël will come to look for you."

While the young woman, who is twenty years old, and only one day old, mounts the dappled mare, the salmon says to her: "In your husband's house, it's necessary to be like amber, which burns without leaving any ash, and like salt, which preserves the summer catch for the winter."

While the mare traverses the endless plains it is as if Argentine is emerging from a dream, not knowing whether she is awake or still asleep.

After having crossed forests and rivers the mare stops beside the dense thicket of rose-bushes and brambles that encircles the city of the Aesir.

"I'm returning whence I came," it says. "In your husband's house, be like the plain that gives us wheat, like the hill that gives us honey."

Then a fox yaps;

"Follow me; I've hollowed out a path through the brambles, a winding path between the thorny stems of the white rose-bushes. Follow me, young woman, into your husband's house; you shall be as lively as the grouse and as brave as the quail."

The sated guests had taken their leave. Noël was alone with Hildewige under the ash-wood beam of the high hall, by the fireside where the beautiful Emma, the beautiful dead woman, had rocked the cradle lined with swansdown with her foot.

"What will you do now?" said Hildewige.

"Search for her until I have found her."

"I would go with you," replied the daughter of the dead woman, "If I were not for the old man the staff that moves aside the stones of the road, the mirror in which he sees the days of old."

"Brother, bring us your bride; she will be received in our house like the warm breeze of May; she will be fêted like the first catkin of the willow."

X. In which what has been seen before is seen again

Argentine has followed the fox into the narrow path under the brambles, the somber path beneath the flowering rosebushes; she is in the city of the Aesir.

The past is no more, for her than a fading dream; she is twenty years old and only one day old. She has forgotten Noël's name but she remembers that someone is coming to search for her, and that memory is in her heart, like a drop of dew in the calyx of a anemone.

"That's not a fay," said the sylphs. "That's a woman."

"It isn't a woman," replied the wood-pigeons, "it's the Norwegian blonde who has come to search for a ray of sunlight in her cradle."

"She's still our sister," said the laughing fays. "She's still Argentine, the dreamer with blue eyes; she is welcome in the city of the Aesir."

The fays had brought her to the palace without a roof, where the wood-pigeons build their nests in the marble friezes, where the twelve heroes sit down every year on the twelve seats around the round table.

The Aesir were gathered there, talking about the past before full cups. Behind them, standing against the wall, their great golden shields were flamboyant, like twelve suns, illuminating the room.

On seeing her enter, Thor with the heavy hand said to Odin the one-eyed, who is presiding at the table: "You who divine everything, can you tell me what I am seeing?"

Then Balder, the hero who sings like a swan, said: "It's the flower of spring, grown down there on our tombs."

But Argentine replied: "A fox guided me, a mare brought me, a salmon carried me, a reindeer abducted me, and someone I'm waiting ought to come to look for me here. Greetings, heroes!"

Then Odin, having reflected, said: "Let's squeeze together, so that there's room for her."

As there were only twelve seats around the table. Odin put his bronze helmet with great silver wings on the floor beside him. It was higher than the seats,

Balder made a cushion of his brilliant scarf, put it between the two wings and sad to Argentine: "Sit down, white ermine of the land of snows. Sit down among us, the most beautiful of our daughters, the freshest flower of the land that we gave to our sons."

Then Thor, the smith, saw that the helmet was too high. And he put his hammer under Argentine's feet, like a footstool.

It was a fine feast.

Odin, who divines everything, having reflected, said: "It's Noël, the son of Otto the Brave, who will come to search for you."

Then Balder, whose cup was empty, took the tortoise-shell harp hanging from his belt between his blue sword and his jade dagger, and he sang the great deeds of Otto, the hero of the North. Then he sang the amorous laments of the daughter of the waves and the chagrin of Emma the Beautiful when she no longer found the swansdown cradle by the fireside. When he said how the white carnation had been found under a juniper bush in the snowy forest while the bells were ringing for Christmas, Argentine cried:

"I remember now. Before being a woman I was a fay; but I love him today even more that I loved him yesterday."

And Odin the wise said: "In your husband's house, you shall be the lamp that drives away the thief, the ember hidden beneath the ashes, which reignites the fire."

The stars fell behind the mountain, and the Aesir got up in order to go to join them.

Argentine remained alone with the wood-pigeons, the sylphs and the fays in the marble palace.

XI. In which Noël sets forth

Argentine, Noël thought, *is certainly in the grotto. She's sulking, but she isn't annoyed; she will have left the door to the crystal staircase open.*

In the depths of his heart he was a little sad, but he could not help saying: "It's a good day; I've rediscovered a father who is a famous hero, a sister whom all the brave men are disputing; I've discovered that the strongest are not as strong as me. If that little fool hadn't turned her brain upside down, my father would have blessed us, Hildewige would have kissed us, and, the dinner having been served, we'd be married...."

"And by now, instead of retracing this path through the snow for the fourth time, I'd be helping Hildewige arrange my sparrow's nest coquettishly."

A pack of wolves was devouring the cadaver of the bear; they did not disturb themselves.

Where the crystal staircase had opened the day before, he saw nothing but a white carpet, without a crease or a wrinkle.

She's definitely annoyed with me, Noël thought. *She's left me to freeze in the snow.*

A terrible anger took hold of him. Seeing a wolf by the tail, he swung it around like a sling and struck the others with it, which were looking at him, bristling. They fled, howling.

And he cried: "I no longer love her; she's a fool, and wicked. I'll choose a wife among the beautiful demoiselles that lowered their eyes at the table...and if ever she takes it into her head to be jealous, I'll..." He threw the cadaver of the wolf a hundred paces away. "If she ever decides to behave like Argentine..." He wept hot tears. "But she won't be jealous and I'll love her dearly, as I would have loved you if you'd wanted, Argentine..."

He would perhaps have wept more if a cloud of Grésil hadn't whipped his cheeks.

"Argentine! Godmother!" he murmured. "Be kind; I'm no longer angry with you. Open the grotto for me; the weather on earth is frightful. I'm the son of a hero, I'll be a hero my-self, since a grafted apple-tree can't bear wrinkled fruit; I'm the brother of a sister whom the brave dispute, and I love you more than all of that. Come on, Godmother..."

It was not Argentine who appeared but Grésil, in gala costume.

"Have you seen Argentine?" Noël asked him

Ah! He's still here. that youth, the cause of my marriage, thought Grésil. *I was looking for Argentine but I find him; I prefer that. Wait, wait...!*

"You're asking for Argentine?" he finally said.

"Yes. I've rediscovered my sister, but Argentine didn't know that Hildewige was my sister, and she was jealous...you understand? She was chagrined, and..."

"She's consoled herself; I'm returning from her wed-ding."

"That's not true."

"Do you believe that I'd be traveling the world in a satin doublet if I weren't returning from a wedding?"

"That's true," sighed Noël...and he fainted.

"I'm going to be able to avenge myself! Without Argen-tine, I wouldn't be the unfortunate husband of a true devil. What shall I do with this youth? Since she loves him, I'll mar-ry him off..."

Grésil spread out his white mantle and wrapped Noël in it.

When Noël came round he was in a large plain, on the edge of a lake with desiccated reeds, the warm water of which was fuming; teal were swimming there.

"Thank you, Grésil," sighed Noël. "You've understood that I could no longer live, and you've brought me to the only place where I could drown myself in such cold weather."

And without thinking, without thinking about the old man, or Hildewige, he threw himself into the clear water.

The lake was deep, he arrived breathless in a green grotto where an undine was weeping.

265

The undine recognized the white carnation and uttered a scream.

"We'll weep together," said Noël. "The woman I loved has forgotten me."

"If one died of amour, I'd be dead," sighed the undine.

She took him in her arms and rose up to the surface again.

Thanks to the doublet woven by the dainty spinners, Noël had only wet his hair; its curls, burnished by the water, were dangling over his shoulders.

It really is the white carnation, thought the undine; *I thought I was seeing the man I loved when, in the spry of the waves, at the prow of his red dragon, he went bare-headed where the wind pushed him.*

Noël, still slightly stunned, admired her; with her aquamarine eyes flecked with gold, her ivory shoulders and her hair brilliant with reflections like a new sword, she was as beautiful as moonlight.

"You're the living portrait of Otto the Brave," she told him. "You're not one of those one forgets."

"Alas!"

While they were speaking, the lake froze,

"Was it the flame of your eyes that warmed it up?" Noël asked.

"It was my tears. For twenty years I've been weeping night and day for my emerald palace. If you wanted to carry me to the nearest shore. I'd guide your boat and show you the paths that lead to the land of gold."

"My beloved's hair was so shiny that I find gold dull; if I had heaps of it I'd trade it for one of her hairs."

"You're not one of those one forgets; return whence you came and let me weep, since you don't want to take me away."

"Argentine told me, when she loved me: 'Noël, never make anyone cry; tears burn the hearts of those who cause them to flow.' I don't want you to weep..."

He carried the daughter of the waves away in his arms.

For weeks, and then for more weeks, as a falcon carries a dove, over the snowy plains, through forests, he carried her. The nacreous arms of the undine were wrapped around his neck, her fine hair brushed his cheeks, her heart beat against his heart; but he only thought of Argentine.

And was the daughter of the waves thinking again about the man who had disdained her in the mist of the sunset?

The heart of a woman is like a gulf; no one can fathom its depth. On Noël's breast, the undine allowed herself to be cradled as if on the waves, for weeks, and then more weeks, like a seamew asleep on the green wave.

But without wearying, night and day, she sang to him what the waves sing to the keel of ships, and the cutting edges of oars, and when Noël reached the shore, he knew what the reapers of the sea know.

On the edge of the sea bewailed for such a long time, before unknotting her arms, the undine hesitated. If he had not been thinking about his beloved, Noël might perhaps have felt the arms tightening around his neck; but he was only thinking about Argentine, night and day; he put her down gently where the waves died in a pink fleece of foam.

As she plunged into the sea, the undine said to him: "The woman you love will be like a pearl, which dies when its master no longer wishes to wear it."

"Where shall I go now?" said Noël.

He raised his head and saw, on the mountain, the pointed turrets of Otto's castle.

If what the undine said is true, he thought, *Argentine will have returned there...*

For weeks, and yet more weeks, he had been listening to the songs that render the heroes of the North strong; he was no longer a child, he was a man.

"A woman belongs," he said, "to the man who can take her; amour is the harvest of glory; I want the woman I love; neither the waves nor the earth can hide her."

He climbs with a firm step toward the castle perched on the high cliff, like a fishing eagle.

XII. In which Noël finds Hildewige and Otto again

Hildewige is under the vault of the first courtyard; she is coming back from the hut made of bark chips where the witch reads the future on a reindeer-hide drum.

In a dream she had seen Argentine and Noël in a marble palace filled with wood-pigeons under a flamboyant sky, where roses bloom in winter and summer.

She told the wise woman what she had seen in the dream and the wise woman threw a white pebble, a black pebble and three grains of wheat on to the drum covered with signs. The white pebble responded "Soon," the black pebble responded "Never," and the grains of wheat responded "Perhaps."

She is returning home pensive.

"The signs of the future," she says, "are not written on drumskins, the words of the future do not fall from the ringing of little bells; the future is what the brave make it, the future is a blank skin that one etches with one's sweat, a bell without a clapper that sounds under the sword. I shall say to the old man, who is leaning like a mossy fir-tree: *O my father, my cherished father, I would like to sleep on your knees like the she-cat that guards the hearth, but it's necessary to find Noël. When I've found him, I'll come back very quickly, and you will be in your house like an apple-tree laden with apples that everyone envies.*"

She arrives in the middle of the courtyard as Noël emerges from the vault.

"Have you seen her?" he asks, before greeting her, before sending her a kiss with his hand.

"No, Brother, but Father has seen the old woman who knows everything; he will tell you where she is."

268

"Since we know where she is, we'll bring her back here."

Noël is no longer a child; for weeks he has heard the songs that render strength; those songs are speaking in his heart, and their refrains are flowing in his veins.

The old man is sitting by the fire, but his spirit is far, far away, in the land of clouds, whether the gentle teal has built its nest.

Why is his spirit alone near to her? Why, since he is thirsty for death, does he not drink from the ivory cup?

Because the old woman with the iron spinning-wheel has said to him: "The rosebud needs a sword for support, and Noël is only a rush in a rapid river; can he contend with the current that bears him away?"

When Noël entered the vast hall, the old man saw that he was no longer a child, but a man.

It only requires a week, he thinks, *to ripen barley; it only requires a week to redden the berries of the service tree.*

"Father," Noël says to him, after having placed the wrinkled hand on his head, "I would like to be the cup in the depth of which you will rediscover your memories, but amour has burned me and I am nothing but ash. When I bring back to your roof the woman I love, you shall have a golden cup, as fresh cup, for your old age."

"The old woman has told me, child," the hero of the North replies, "that it is necessary for you first to make the giant with the white beard cry mercy."

"If the thing can be done, it will be."

"But a pilot is necessary to guide your boat; the giant is sailing on an iceberg in the Sea of Darkness."

Then Noël sang what the waves say to the keels of bots and the cutting edge of oars, and what the wind weeps to stiffened rigging.

"Who taught you those songs?" asked the old man.

"The daughter of the sea that I carried over my heart for weeks, with her arms around my neck."

Then the old man got up, as straight as a pine and as strong as an oak. "Hildewige," he said, "bring me the largest cup, full of hydromel."

He emptied it in a single draught, as straight as a pine and as strong as an oak, "Noël," he said, then, "give me my sword."

As straight as a pine and as strong as an oak, he cleaved the bench with a single stroke.

And he said: "I am not falling apart piece by piece like an old boat in the mud of the port; like the red dragon with wings outspread, I am breaking on a reef..."

He was dead.

XIII. In which the city of the Aesir is seen again

Argentine is living alone with the wood-pigeons, the sylphs and the fays.

The wood-pigeons bring her wheat, one grain at a time, the sylphs give her honeycombs, and the fays, while playing, pick up oranges and peaches for her in the evergreen orchards. Her days are long.

She sits on the marble steps pensively, trying to remember the days of old, but the past is nothing for her but a forgotten dream; she is no longer a fay but a woman.

"Beautiful friends," she says to the wood-pigeons, "if I had your wings, I would fly from sunset to dawn, night and day, until I had found the man for whom I hope."

The wood-pigeons reply: "Wait! He will come."

But she is no longer a fay; she can no longer understand the language of the wood-pigeons.

Why did the reindeer abduct her? Why did the salmon bear her away? Why had the mare brought her?

"Spring is commencing," coo the wood-pigeon. "Sylphs, it's necessary to depart; the larches must be verdant out there; fays, it's necessary to depart."

"If we leave her," the sylphs reply, "who will give her honey?"

Then a chariot drawn by two cats descended from the sky. It brought Freya, the protectress of lovers.

"Argentine," she said, "It's me who bridled the reindeer, it's me who sent the salmon and it's me who saddled the mare; I'm the goddess of love. You must weep, as I have wept, if you want to love forever."

Having spoken thus, the blonde goddess, whose eternal tears fall in golden pearls, ascended again into the sky, and Argentine said to the wood-pigeons: "Fly away, so that I may weep."

The wood-pigeons have gone, bearing the sylphs and the fays away to the lands of the North.

XIV. In which Grésil is seen again

Why has Grésil married? He has none of the pleasures of marriage and all the annoyances; he is only the humble valet of his better half. It is forbidden for him to idle at the foot of cliffs because he crumples the saxifrage there; he must not linger in the forests because he fades the violets there.

He can only wander at his leisure over deserted shores and pathless plateaux.

One morning, he was running between the sunlit sand and the utterly black sea—it was in April—when he perceived a boat dancing on the waves.

"Let's distract ourselves a little," he says.

He blows, and the waves crackle under the hail, the hull groans, the mast bends, but the boat continues its route directly.

A vigorous helmsman is holding the tiller, he thinks. *It's necessary that it capsizes; I'm too bored!*

He blows so strongly that the yard-arm dips into the water, but the boat holds straight to its course. Then, furious, he launches forth.

A woman is holding the tiller, and Noël, leaning on the dragon of the prow, is gazing at the waves insouciantly.

"IT's you!" howls Grésil. "You're standing up to me! Wait!"

He blows so forcefully that the torn sail flies away and the tiller breaks in Hildewige's hands.

The sharp rocks of the coast were very close. Grésil could already see the man he hated broken against the cliffs when the undine appeared in front of the boat. She placed her hand on the timbers and the boat stopped like a horse under the weight of the bit.

"Where are you going?" she said.

"I'm seeking the giant with the white beard," Noël replied.

"I'll take you to where he is."

While the undine, with her hand on the timbers of the ship, which is following her meekly, glides over the water, Grésil returns to his palace of clouds.

He finds Perce-Neige there.

"Where have you been?" the fay says to him. "You're never at home."

"I've been for a stroll. Am I not master of taking a stroll when I want to? You pretend to be my wife, but I don't know. If we're united let's separate. I'll take back my liberty and I'll render yours to you."

She touches him with her crystal scepter, and his misty mantle turns into a block of ice, under which he groans, crushed. His servants and his subjects come running; the scepter touches the vaporous walls of the palace, which congeal, and they are all prisoners around the immobile elf.

"I love you too much to let you wander the world," says the laughing queen.

"Oh, my cherished spouse," gasps the elf, "I'll always obey you. Return my liberty, and I'll be your slave."

The queen touches the mantle and the walls of ice with her finger, and they become clouds again.

"You see what I can do," she says. "Go in search of Argentine."

The elf departs over the snowy land.

The boat cleaved the waves over which ice-floes were floating, and the undine sang to the attentive Hildewige the poems of the sea where palaces are hidden beneath the seaweed and pearls fall in cascades into nacreous basins, in the depths of blue abysms.

They had been traveling for a week, perhaps two, when they perceived the giant with the white beard on an errant iceberg.

"Giant," Noël shouted to him, "I've come to wrestle with you. I'm the son of Otto the Brave."

"I can't refuse what you request," replied the giant. "If I'm vanquished I'll be your slave, but if I'm the stronger, you'll be mine."

And the contest commenced.

Hildewige, standing in the prow of the boat, and the undine, hanging on to the timbers, watched anxiously.

The contest lasted for a long time. Only Otto the Brave was strong enough to defeat a giant; Noël was vanquished.

"You're my slave," said the giant, "but I'll be generous, as your father was. You'll be free if the beautiful young woman who is weeping on the boat brings me two golden apples."

"I'll bring them to you," replied Hildewige. "Be patient, Noël."

Noël wept, not in chagrin but in shame.

"You're a rude companion," the giant said. "When you have your adult strength, we'll wrestle again. The beautiful young woman is certainly worthy of being your sister; she'll bring the two golden apples and we'll try our strength as two friends."

While the undine pushed the boat, Hildewige dreamed of the land where the golden apples ripen, and Noël listened to the giant telling him the secrets of the first day,

273

Grésil was searching for Argentine throughout Norway. Not having found her, he went to search further afield.

XV. In which Hildewige encounters the Viking fleet

"Do you know," said Hildewige, "where the golden apples ripen?"

"I don't know," the undine replied. "I'm the daughter of the Northern seas; but I've seen them shining in the hands of Vikings returning in summer from the lands of the west. You're my sister, Hildewige, my beloved sister, and I want to free Noël; we'll follow the route of the fleets and we'll end up finding the tree of the golden apples."

One morning, at sunrise, Hildewige perceived boats.

"Who are you?" shouted a warrior as handsome as the day from the leading boat. "Who are you, who are traveling against the wind with neither oar nor sail?"

"I'm Hildewige," the virgin replied. "I'm the daughter of Otto the Brave."

"Otto was my father's companion," said the Viking. "They mingled their blood in the cup; they loved one another. You are as beautiful, Hildewige, as Freya the blonde goddess; if you want to climb into my boat, you shall be queen and I shall be king."

"Viking, I won't climb into your boat; the boat is the house of the laborer of the waves, and a virgin should only enter her husband's house. I'm going to the land where the golden apples ripen."

"It's far away, that land, and the sea is an untamed mare; you have neither sail nor rudder; you'll be its plaything."

Then the undine raised herself up, smiling; she had seen Hildewige's cheeks blush when the hero of the North spoke to her.

"Viking," she said, "I am the pilot of Otto's daughter."

And the boat without a sail and without an oar glides like a salmon between the black boats full of valiant warriors.

"Companions," says the Viking, then, "you have sworn to follow me as the reapers follow the man who goes into the field first. Today, I'm no longer a reaper; I'm a hunter pursuing a roe deer; I release you from your oaths."

The fleet continues its route toward Norway, and the Viking follows the boat without oars pushed by the daughter of the waves.

That Viking is the bravest of the heroes of the North; in his house he has heaps of gold and piles of silver, amassed at sword-point.

Then Hildewige' cheeks take on the hue of the eglantine of the woods, and the undine sings while pushing the boat:

"Fortunate the woman loved by a brave man! Fortunate the woman whose house had a sword for a bolt!

"Fortunate the mother loved by a brave man! Fortunate the woman whose children have a shield for a cradle!

"They have no need to release dogs into the enclosure by night; they have no need to put thorns in the gaps in the hedge; a blue sword guards them, and the scintillating flowers of a shield stop thieves better than hedges of plum-trees."

Hildewige thought: "If Noël had a brother, there would be two turtle-doves in the nest of two hawks."

For weeks they had been sailing toward the sunset when a warm current, azure in color, caressed the undine's flanks.

"I can't go any further," she said. "This sea is no longer my domain; unknown routes are opening before me."

"I've followed these routes!" cried the Viking. "Climb into my boat, Hildewige; you will be my sister."

"A man who is afraid of nothing never lies," said the undine. "Sit down without dread in the shadow of the brave man's sword; I shall return to where Noël is captive, and I'll tell him that you'll return, bringing his ransom."

"A woman," thought Hildewige, "is not like a rose, which allows itself to be picked by whoever wants it."

And she climbed into the Viking's boat.

Hildewige is sitting at the foot of the mast, between the warriors with white arms.

Then the Viking, in order to abridge the hours, and in order that no one will hear his heart speak, picks up his maplewood harp The bold reaper with the red scythe has read, during his sleep, the runes engraved on the tongue of the Dragon, the god who makes verses vibrate.

He has picked up his maple-wood harp, and while the warriors ply the heavy oars in cadence. He sings:

"Mistress of the house, open the door to the one who is knocking; his feet will not sully the sanded floor; his feet have never touched the mud of roads.

"Mistress of the house, open the door to the one who is knocking; for weeks he has not slept beneath a roof, and his heart is only a rock polished by the waves.

"Mistress of the house, it is not a beggar who is knocking; he had golden rings and silver necklaces, bracelets of coral and enameled belts.

"Mistress of the house, it is not a thief who is knocking; he has only harvested his field, but his field is limitless, it is as long as his sword.

"Mistress of the house, my furrows are always sown, the crop always ripens there, and the waves of the ocean are the cattle in my cowshed..."

While he sings, the bronze shields ring against the planks, the ash-wood oars dip into the sea devoid of ripples, and Hildewige's heart beats gently.

The sun was flamboyant; a burning wind inflated the sail; the warriors were asleep; Hildewige was holding the tiller.

Then a streaming, emaciated, breathless being appeared, sitting on the yard-arm.

"If you are the elf of these unknown seas, what do you want?" Hildewige said to him.

"Alas, I am Grésil, the elf of Norway. Under this fiery sun I am dissolving into water; let me hide for a moment in the shadow of your sail."

"Where are you going, so far from home?"

"To search for Argentine."

"We're also searching for her."

"It's necessary for me to find her; my wife wants it. Never marry, young woman... In the shade of your sail I can breathe a little... Never marry, believe me; I'm no longer anything but a shadow, no longer anything but skin.... Never marry; now I'm cooked, and if I return to my palace I'll freeze."

"I recognize you," said Hildewige. "Noël has mentioned you to me."

"I can only go away, then—but I was so comfortable!"

"If you want, we can travel together. Inflate the sail when you've got your breath back, and we won't tell Perce-Neige that you tried to drown Noël."

"I'll inflate your sail night and day; since you're going in search of Argentine; when you've found her, I'll have found her too. But don't say anything to my sweet wife... Don't marry, young woman."

While the warriors sleep, the elf inflates the sail and the boat flies so rapidly that in the morning it runs aground in a peaceful cove, where the green trees are shining with golden apples.

"Wake up, Viking," the virgin says, launching the docile boat over the fine sand; "wake up, we've arrived; I can see golden apples shining on green trees."

XVI. In which Hildewige and Noël continue their voyage

While Hildewige is going to the lands of the sun in search of golden apples, Noël is on the iceberg with the giant with the white beard. But the giant has not forgotten Otto the Brave, and he does not treat Noël as a slave but as a companion.

"You'll soon be free," he tells him. "Hildewige will certainly bring your ransom, and then we'll wrestle again, and the victor will remain the friend of the loser."

That giant was of the race those whom Vainamoinen, the god of Finland, had expelled from Lapland a long time before the coming of the Aesir; he sang to Noël of the days of Creation, and Otto's son engraved the songs in his memory, after those that the undine with the blue-green eyes had taught him.

He now knows how the world emerged from an egg laid by an eagle on the knee of Vainamoinen; he knows why Imarigen, the eternal smith, being unable to find a wife to his liking, forged one of silver. He knows why the luminous Aesir have exiled from the heavens the gods of vague form, who are still wandering, deformed and monstrous, in the mists of the North.[22]

Noël is no longer a child, he is a man. He is a man who has not allowed the fresh flower of his youth to fade; he will be as great as those who only have one amour in their life.

The hours are long for him on the iceberg, which is floating in the eddies of the Pole; he is always looking toward the sunset. On the sea, where white icebergs pass by like gulls, he is searching for a black dot.

But the icebergs, like gulls, come and go, and he does not see his sister's boat on the sea.

One morning, while the giant is still asleep, he sees two moustached seals drawing a large seashell. Perce-Neige emerges from it.

"What are you doing here, Noël?" says the astonished queen. "Are you no longer searching for Argentine?"

"I was searching for her, beautiful queen, but today I'm a prisoner. The giant has defeated me, and I must give him two golden apples for my ransom."

---

[22] These details are taken from Elias Lönnrot's synthesized Finish epic *Kalevala*, but the eternal smith is there named Ilmarinen.

"Then you're free," relies the fay. "I've brought Immer golden apples from my garden; you can give them to him."[23]

"Alas, beautiful queen, the apples that he wants ripen in the lands of the sun; they can't ripen in your garden."

"You don't know, child, that my palace is mirrored in a blue sea that never freezes, in a warm sea where the whales come to nurse their infants. Over my palace on high the sun only sets once a year, and while it shines for six months, oranges ripen in my crystal greenhouses."

The giant woke up. "Be welcome, Perce-Neige," he said. "What have you been doing for such a long time?"

"Immer, I'm married. I've married Grésil."

"When we were gods, I as known as 'the Wise'; it's said that one chooses badly when one has been searching for too long."

"It was necessary. I'm taking Noël away; here are two golden apples for his ransom, and here are two more for the good advice that you're going to give us, father of wisdom. We're looking for Argentine—where is it necessary to go?"

"It' necessary to go to where Freya, the blonde goddess, has a temple surrounded by a golden chain; it's necessary for you to ask her to bring you the one whose wings have been broken by amour."

Having said that, the father of wisdom said to Noël: "Your ransom is paid; would you like us to wrestle again now, like two friends."

"I'd like that," Noël replied.

And the contest commenced. But the songs had inflated Noël's heart, their refrains were flowing in his veins, and he was no longer a child. After having wrestled for a week, he said to the giant:

"I believe, Immer," that we're as strong as one another.

"I believe so too," said the fay. "Clasp hands like two friends."

---

[23] The name given to the giant, Immer, is German for "forever."

They held out their hands, and Perce-Neige said: "Now it's necessary to go to Freya's temple without delay."

"What about Hildewige?" Noël replied.

"I'll wait for her, while chatting about the past with Immer, who still knows what other people have forgotten. Mount my seashell; my seals will take you to the round beach where, under the gray ash-trees, a golden chain surrounds the temple of the goddess of love."

Noël climbed into the huge seashell.

While the seals were drawing Noël, the Viking's ship, full of golden apples, was heading for Norway.

It soon reached Immer's iceberg, the undine pushing it again. The days seemed short to the blonde virgin; the Viking's eyes were bright and their gaze slid over Hildewige's cheeks like a kiss.

XVII. In which Noël enters Freya's temple

The bells of the periwinkles were ringing in the spring, the wood-pigeons were arriving, carrying on their wings the dreaming sylphs and the laughing fays.

After having caressed the round heads of the seals that had brought him to the beach. Noël is wondering what path to take when a rustle causes him to raise his head.

"Oh, wood-pigeons, beautiful wood-pigeons," he says, "you who are come from afar, have you seen my beloved? She resembles the chamois of the rocks, the squirrel of the woods, the ermine of the snows. Her cheeks are pink apples, her lips strawberries, her teeth white currants; when she speaks, one thinks that one is hearing a pearl necklace; when she moves her head, one thinks one is seeing a golden shield shining.

"The blonde chamois, that lovely squirrel, that chaste ermine," the wood-pigeons reply, "can only be the one who is waiting in the city of the Aesir."

"That's her," say the sylphs.

"And here's Noël!" exclaim the fays, letting themselves slide like raindrops over the wings of the wood-pigeons.

They surround Noël.

"You're as dainty as mice," the child who has become a man says to them, "on seeing you I thought I was seeing grains of wheat flying from the hands of the sower in a ray of sunlight. If you have seen the one who has caught my heart on the hooks of her eyelashes and the net of her hair, tell me."

"When she wept night and day over her troubles, we said to her: 'Has your Noël wings like a butterfly, then? Does he know a thousand songs, like a nightingale? We understand now why she was weeping night and day; it's a bard that she loves, a butterfly of the flowers of dream, a nightingale of nights of amour. If you want to rejoin her, you who can, like the Master, give a body to your dreams, it's necessary to create a horse with wings, with feet like a swan's in order to swim, a horn on the forehead in order to defend her and a silken mane in order to carry her...'"

"I'm not what you say, I'm only Noël, and very sad; I'm looking for the temple of Freya, the friend of lovers."

"It's over there in that ash-grove; follow us," coo the wood-pigeons. "We're the chicks of the good goddess."

Noël follows the wood-pigeons; under the green ash-trees he sees a golden chain surrounding a great stone circle. In that circle, strewn with silver sand, there is only a sword leaning on the trunk of a rose-bush.

Noël stepped over the golden chain fearlessly; he had no soot in his heart. He marched over the silver sand without leaving footprints; he had no mud on his feet. He parted the branches of the rose-bush without soiling them; his hands were unstained. And he read the runes engraved on the blade.

The runes said:

Amour is the harvest of tears, the grain of the brave, the bread of the strong.

Then I must be loved, thought Noël.

But he did not see Freya,

I shall see her soon, he said to himself. *The father of wisdom told me so, and a worthy man does not lie.*

He went to sleep at the foot of the rose-bush.

Noël has a beautiful dream; he is in a silent city where twelve palaces are aligned around a marble palace. He climbs the steps of the temple, and at round table, on a cushion the color of the rainbow, between the silver wings of a bronze helmet, he sees Argentine sitting, surrounded by twelve heroes.

"Do you know the man who is coming in Argentine?" says the one-eyed hero who is presiding over the feast.

"It's the man for whom I'm waiting," replies the fay who has become a woman.

"Oh! Godmother! Godmother!" cries Noël.

It is a beautiful dream.

Then he is in the silver grotto, in the midst of the spinners as brown as rushes as the squat dwarves with otter-fur caps; the spinners have hands full of brilliant veils made of silken fabrics; the dwarves are weighed down by necklaces and bracelets in beautiful red gold, and elves with flames on their foreheads are carving the final step of a crystal staircase.

Argentine says to him: "Will you never regret the fay when she is your wife?"

It is a beautiful dream, but the most beautiful dreams come to an end; Noël wakes up.

He is in a fir-wood, the branches of which are sparkling in the sunrise, and next to him, on the moss, in her page's doublet, Argentine is asleep; her hair has grown again, it is the color of wheat.

I wasn't dreaming, Noël says to himself. *Freya has returned the woman I love to me.*

Argentine wakes up.

"Have you slept well, Muguet," he asks her, laughing.

"I don't know, Messire," replies the dainty page, throwing her arms around him.

They had been searching for one another for such a long time that they could embrace!

XVIII. In which Noël returns to his house

The pointed turrets of Otto's castle were shining on the mountain.

"Let's go home," said Noël.

"I'd never dare in this page's doublet... If only I had my cap, it would hide me a little."

"Don't look for it; Hildewige took it away on the evening when you were jealous. Let's go, Muguet; you wanted me to be a knight, and every knight must have a page."

They walked, chatting gaily about the future and the past; Argentine was a woman with the soul of a fay. Noël was telling her how he had found the undine when Hildewige appeared at a bend in the path; the Viking was beside her, and all the castle servants were behind her.

"We were coming to meet you," said the Northern virgin, running to Noël. "Be welcome, Master. And you, Muguet, come and embrace me; your mistress is waiting for you, her spinners have brought her marvelous robes and her dwarves have forged so many rings, so many bracelets, so many belts and so many necklaces that the great hall is full of them.

"Brother," the Northern virgin continued, indicating the Viking, "here, if you wish, is your brother. He's a worthy man, Muguet; I've slept alone on his boat for weeks, lying in his shield. If you want to remain a page and travel the world, he'll gladly take you."

Oh, Hildewige, Hildewige!" murmured poor Muguet.

"But while the two brothers chat," Hildewige continued, "You can accompany me; Argentine is waiting for me to fasten her necklace."

"Oh, what a dainty page!" say the companions of Otto the Brave.

"He has a woman's hair," their daughters respond, "and hands so small that they could never hold the hilt of a sword."

"Let's walk quickly," said Argentine. "What if sometime were to guess...?"

"No one will ever guess," said Hildewige, smiling.

They walked so rapidly that Noël found them waiting for him on either side of the door. Argentine had put on a dress inlaid with silver, and bowed, blushing.

"But where has Muguet gone?" he said

"Your page, my brother, is a scatterbrain," Hildewige replied. "He said to me just now: *My master is getting married; he'll no longer travel the world. I love traveling, myself.* And with that, he left."

"That beautiful fay resembles someone we've seen before," said Otto's companions

"Might she be the sister of the slender page?" whispered the women of the castle.

During the meal, Hildewige told the story of her voyage in search of golden apples; she had just related how she had found Perce-Neige on the giant Immer's iceberg when a seamew flew in through an open window. It was holding two identical necklaces in its beak.

"I recognize the white messenger of the daughter of the waves," said the Viking. "Brother, one of those necklaces is for your bride, the other is for my beloved.

"Is she very beautiful, that undine?" Argentine murmured in Hildewige's ear, very softly.

"You'll see her at our wedding; Perce-Neige has invited her." Then, addressing Noël: "This, Brother, is what the queen said to me on Immer's iceberg: 'I'll expect you; Grésil will come to fetch you. His palace is large; you'll be at ease there with all your guests.'"

"We'll leave right away!" Noël exclaimed. "Do you want to, Viking?"

"Let's go and dress, then" Hildewige interjected.

284

While the two brides were putting on their wedding dresses, the two men talk about the future, cups in hand.

"What shall we do?" says Noël.

"If you wish, we can go together to harvest the waves," replies the Viking.

"My beloved is a flower of the lands of the sun," Noël remarks. "I'm afraid that her cheeks might fade in the fog."

"Personally, I have no fear of that for Hildewige. She's Otto's daughter."

The sky darkened.

"Here's Grésil," said the Viking. "Let's go and fetch our brides."

XIX. In which everyone goes to the wedding

Grésil's palace passed over forests and plains. It traveled rapidly; the elf was in haste to arrive, Perce-Neige having said to him: "I believe that we're not well-matched spouses; when we've married these young people who love one another, you can take back your liberty and I'll take back mine."

Grésil does not feel well; he would be amiable if he could.

In the great hall with walls of down and a floor of ice, he hastens to look after his guests; he turns round in order to sneeze, and his sniffling subjects have been forbidden to cough.

While passing over the birch forest, Argentine sees the fays of the Oriental gardens chatting with the sylphs.

"If only we had them at our wedding!" she sighs.

Then Grésil, ever gallant, stops his palace and Argentine says to her former sisters: "Would you like to come to my wedding? I have this cloud for a carriage. Would you like to come with me to Perce-Neige's palace?"

The fays clap their hands—they dream of nothing but dancing. The chilly sylphs, seeing that Argentine has bare arms, take a chance and go with her,

When they were all reunited, the hall of Grésil's palace is almost full, and as it was rather cool, in spite of the down lining the walls, the parquet being slippery, everyone begins to dance.

"When I'm divorced," said Grésil, losing his head in the midst of the twirling roses, "I'll choose a companion among these cheerful fays "And he, the grave Grésil, sketched a minuet; his stupefied servants did not know what to think, and his chubby elves whistled dance tunes.

Finally, they arrive at Perce-Neige's palace: a marvelous palace, all crystal and amethyst.

Between high cliffs crowned with glaciers, a warm sea of a darker blue than the sky, slumbers indolently. It is the polar sea, for which men have been searching for such a long time, the sea into which the great river of the ocean flows.

The queen's palace is on a salt cape as brilliant as a ruby; its domes taper into pointed bell-towers and it broad, scintillating porticos emerge from waves that lick them.

Swans, eiders, mallards, teal, gulls and seamews design living flowers over the azure gulf, flower-bed with sinuous pathways, the rockeries of which are furnished by brown whales.

For six months the sun rotates without setting, like a fiery wheel, crumbling the glaciers, and when it sinks abruptly behind their dentellate summits, a yellow radiance springs from the motionless axis that our errant world carries through the sky. Its rays break into spangles, are rounded out into domes, are draped in curtains, crackling and inflamed, and the long night of the pole is nothing but a firework display with rutilant rockets.

Then the sun seemed motionless, crazy cascades leapt over the rocks, and the window-frames were opened in the immense greenhouses where orange-trees flourished.

The fays uttered cries of joy, and the sylphs glad to find the flowers of distant lands, said: "Next winter, instead of going so far, we'll come back here."

Perce-Neige was waiting for her guests under the porch of the palace.

"Be welcome," she said, "dreamy sylphs and laughing fays. Be welcome, heroes of the North. You, my sisters, kiss me, and you, Grésil, go and put on an ermine doublet in order not to freeze us.

The table was laid under the crystal cupola starred with gold, in an immense hall draped with bearskins, the parquet of which allowed the sea-bed to be seen, where jellyfish as blue as periwinkles were swimming among pink daisies and seaweed the color of blood.

The table was immense, but the guests were so numerous that everyone could speak to the ears of two neighbors. The Aesir had come with their tall companions with bright eyes and fine hair, The giant with the white beard clinked his cup with Odin's, and the vague gods of the first days, forgetting their defeat among the brave men of today and the heroes of yesterday, believed as they gazed at the brides in their golden diadems, that they were seeing the twin sisters who sowed the still-warm earth with lilies-of-the-valley in the dawn.

The dreamy sylphs and the laughing fays were, at that table, like flowers in a forest, and the daughter of the waves with ivory shoulders, among those brown breastplates and golden shields, seemed like a pearl on the pommel of a sword.

The queen had only one ruby on her white dress and a single snow-rose in her black hair, but her eyes were so brilliant and her cheeks so fresh that Balder the poet, sitting opposite her, said, smiling: "If I were a blue butterfly, I would burn my wings on her curved eyelashes; If I were a gray squirrel, I would surely steal two vermilion apples."

287

Under the crystal floor, great whales passed with velvet sparkles, and playful seals performed mad round dances.

The midnight sun put sprays on the summits, diamonds on wings rubies on cups and coral on lips; it was a fine feast.

Then Balder, the immortal poet, took up his tortoiseshell harp, and the quivering strings sang under his fingers like fir-trees in spring, like a cliff in autumn, like the ripening wheat and like the fading hay. At those chords, falling like fresh dew and rising in ardent flames, veins swelled, and Odin the wise said to Noël's beloved:

"You will always be the firefly of the gardens of the Orient, the ermine of the polar snows; you will be Norway, the embalmed rose of the North. You will always be the beloved, the one who will never be forgotten, the mother of handsome reapers with sonorous scythes."

Then, the undine with ivory shoulders having got up, Thor of the heavy hand said: "Among us, you are like the narcissus between tall reeds; it is necessary that you we can see you." And he placed her on his golden shield.

On the golden shield sustained by the Aes, her arms outstretched, the daughter of the waves sang:

"I shall push their foamy boats, between the reefs I shall guide them, and in the days of winter and the nights of summer I shall sing, Norway, your immortal youth, your radiant beauty.

"The sea will be for them the ever-fertile field, the ever-tuned harp, the ever-open book, the ever-laden tablecloth."

"Climb up next to her," said Thor to Noël's beloved.

The woman who had been merely a fay only yesterday climbed up on to the golden shield.

"Hurrah for Norway!" cried the Aesir, the sylphs, the fays, Otto's companions with the unchipped swords, the virgins with heavy tresses and the Viking with white arms.

"For me, you will always be Argentine" said Perce-Neige.

"And for me, always my godmother," added Noël, smiling.

LEMMI KAINEN, THE JOYOUS HUNTER
A Finnish Tale

Part One

I

Lemmi Kainen,[24] the joyous hunter, in harnessing his sleigh; he is going to Lapland to the icy land of darkened. For a long time he has been thinking about that voyage; in spring he shod his horse; having forged the shoes during the winter. "Why," his mother says to him, "are you going to that accursed country which devours men."

"Oh, my dear mother, out there, in the home of an aged hostess, there is a virgin who is the honor of the land and the glory of the waves; the whiteness of her bones shines through the transparency of her flesh, and the ivory of her bones is so clear that one can see their marrow flowing.

"When she wears her gold necklace and her sparkling brooch, she scintillates like a rainbow over a waterfall, she is as radiant as he midnight glow on the snow.

---

[24] This character is a variant of Lemminkaïnen, one of the heroes of Lonnrot's *Kalevala*, in which he appears to be a composite drawn from several folktales. The early chapters of L'Estoille's story are adapted relatively straightforwardly from several of the *runots* of the *Kalevala*, as rendered into French by Louis Léouzon Le Duc, where the hero's name is rendered Lemmikainen; the story also varies other names, so that Ukko becomes Oukko, Ulappala becomes Ulappola, etc. The last section, however, is adapted more freely in order to provide a conclusion that the original does not.

"When she turns the wheel of the mill, one believes one is seeing a service tree with red fruits leaning over the white flour; when her fingers knead the white flower, one might think her a currant bush shedding its rosy pearls.

"When she goes to wash her linen chemises under the birch-trees, the salmon stops in its course; When she hangs the cloth over the elder bush, the swan stops in its fight; and the rushes of the bank say to the salmon: 'Her teeth shine more brightly than your scales; and the passing cloud says to the soaring swans: 'You're jealous.'"

"You're forgetting, my son, that around the honeycomb there are the stings of the bees; those accursed Lapps know all enchantments; with a word they can send you into a miry marsh; with a word they can force your arm to stretch out over coals and your fist to plunge into the hot ashes."

"If the witches want to contend with me," replies the joyous hunter, "they'll repent of it; while following my dogs over the heather, I've found many secrets under the hare's feet; while spying on the squirrel I've read many things on the rugged bark of the gray pines."

"Don't go, my son," says the trembling mother, "to ask for the virgin of the cold dwellings; you can't speak the language of the Northern lands."

"Oh, my mother, what I shall have to say the virgin will understand; I've asked it of the grouse when the raspberries are in flower, of the quail when the barley rises, and the deer have said it to me when the they emerge bloody from the thickets, and the bear when it stops, joyfully, swinging its velvet paws."

He passes a comb through his hair, he shakes it over the hearth and he says, as he places it in the beam: "Misfortune will attain Lemmi Kainen when blood flows from the teeth of this comb."

He mounts his sleigh, he shakes the silver reins and the whip garnished with pearls, and in spite of his weeping mother he sets forth joyously for the lands of the North.

II

The sleigh slides on its maple-wood runners, the horse sounds its little bells gaily and the cuckoo that opens its wings on the crest of the hill seems to be flying in the mist that rises from its curly mane. The blue dogs follow, their rosy tongues dangling.

The sleigh glides for one day, two days, perhaps three days; it has crossed the frontier of the icy regions; the joyous hunter enters a village.

"Is there someone in this dwelling who can take the collar from my horse?" he shouts, at the threshold of the first house.

"There's no one here to receive you," replies a child sitting on the step.

The insouciant Lemmi Kainen shrugs his shoulders and goes further on.

At the second house he asks again, and an old woman chatting by the fireside replies to him: "Turn behind the hedge; you'll find the chicken run; there's a place next to the cock in the henhouse."

If I had time to waste, thinks Lemmi Kainen, *I'd take pleasure in breaking an egg on the nose of that chatterbox.*

At the third house he enters the courtyard noisily, strikes the ground with his whip and shouts: "Hola, someone!"

A young boy appears. "Put my horse under shelter," he says, cracking the heavy whip.

The boy hastens to remove the collar and raise the shafts.

"I know how to talk to them now," murmurs Lemi Kainen gaily, and he heads toward the house, the door of which is closed.

Through the mossy walls he can hear a chorus of witches chanting the praises of Hiisi, the somber giant of the icy Hel, but he enters without hesitation.

He pushes the door so gently that the dog does not hear him come in.

291

"What do you want?" growls the hostess. "A man does not sit down at the table here without being invited."

"A paltry man, venerable hostess," replies Lemmi Kainen, leaning n his heavy sword, "But a brave one sits down anywhere; he has an invitation engraved on the blue point of his sword."

Then, standing in the middle of the assembly, whose members roll their eyes and grind their teeth, he sings the magic words that all obey on land and on the water, in the brightness of the sky and the darkness of Hell.

Immediately, stone gloves encase the fingers of the witches and stone hats curb their necks, and millstones weigh on their shoulders, and the hostess is dragged by a colorless cat in a sleigh without cushions.

"Oh!" she cries, putting her fleshless hands on her flesh-less back. "Stop this enraged cat." Her ankles surpass the traverses of the sleigh by a handspan. "Stop this diabolical cat and I'll broach a barrel."

"Oh," cry the witches, "we ask for mercy."

He laughed, the joyous hunter, but he only wanted to drink a glass of beer; he was in haste to arrive where the rose of the North flowered; he pronounces the words that reattach what other words have loosened, and the hostess no longer feels the tips of her ankles, and the witches no longer feel the weight of the millstones.

"You're a cheerful companion," said the hostess. "Drink to your thirst."

"Why, joyous traveler," said an old blind man then, "did you make mock of the others without making mock of me?"

"Because you're venomous," replied Lemmi Kainen. "If I had caused you to mount the sleigh of Hiisi, your drool would have soiled the roads over which I must pass in order to go and pluck the rose of the North."

The aged Ulappola went out without responding.

"You're a joyous companion," said the hostess, "but the man who wants to return to his lodgings ought not to spread brambles over the route where he will pass again."

She was thinking about the old blind man, who had left with anger in his heart. Lemmi Kainen had forgotten him; he had found the beer good, he had laughed at the witches. He departed, cracking his whip garnished with pearls.

III

He travels for one day, two days, perhaps three days, and, not far from the limits of Hiisi's icy domain, near the River Tuani, he arrives at the rugged house that hides the virgin, as a mussel hides a pearl.

"Venerable hostess," he says, "give me your daughter for a wife; I shall treat her well. When I eat, she will lean on my breast; when I march, I shall carry her in my arms; when I stop, she will fold her arms over my shoulder; when I sleep, she will place her head over my heart."

The hostess responds: "I'll give you my daughter when you've traversed the domain of Hiisi and caught his blue reindeer.

The joyous hunter immediately puts on snowshoes lined with wolfskin, and then tips two long staffs with iron.

While he is lining his snowshoes and fitting iron tips to his staffs he sings like the quail when the barley grows like the grouse when the raspberry-bushes flower, and the virgin of the cold dwellings thinks she feels the breath of spring on her cheeks.

But while he sang, the dark god of Hell had heard the old woman's words and he created a blue reindeer. Its head was made of turf, its hooves of willow, its legs of the stakes of a hedge, its back of long poles, its ears of water-lily leaves, its skin of fir-bark, its flesh of rotten roots and its eyes of pearl-shells.

And the reindeer started running, and climbed to the fields of the Lapps.

Then Lemmi Kainen departed, his snowshoes on his feet and his staffs in his hands. He took a step and was no longer seen; he took another and was no longer heard; he took a third step and he seized the reindeer.

As he was weary from having run so rapidly, he wove a rope of birch in order to hobble it, planted a hedge of oak-branches to prevent it from running away and went to sleep for a moment.

In the meantime, Ulappola, the old blind man, saw him; he could have strangled him in his sleep with a snake, but he said to himself: *It's necessary to strike an enemy when he's joyful, in order that death will be bitter to him...*

"Venerable hostess," said the joyous Lemmi Kainen, "here is Hiisi's reindeer; give me your daughter in order that she might drink from my cup and sleep beside me."

She replied: "I'll give you my daughter if you can put a bit on Hiisi's black horse, if you can bridle the foamy horse, which has bronze hooves and an iron mane."

The joyous hunter immediately buckled his silver bridle with a steel bit.

While he was buckling the reins and polishing the bit he sang what the red deer bell when they emerge bloodied from the thickets and what the bears growl when they waddle, rubbing their hairy paws gaily, and the virgin of the North thought that she felt the breath of spring passing through her heart.

Then he departs joyously, the bridle over his shoulder and the bit in his hand.

He marches for one day, two days, and he arrives in the prairie where the proud stallion is playing with the foals. Fire is crackling in his coat, smoke is rising from his mane.

"That's a fine horse," he said, "the finest of horses; I'll have please in bridling it, but to catch it I'll need help."

And he invoked the god of the sky.

"Oukko," he said, "you who sit on the axis of the world, open the granary of the heavens, untie the sack of white flour and make the snow fall. Let it fall to the height of a staff, let it rise as far as the mane of the great horse, all the way to its nostrils."

Oukko heard the man to whom he had never refused any-thing; he sent the new snow and it rose to a height of three aunes around the flanks of the great horse.

Then Lemmi Kainen advanced quietly, talked to the great horse quietly, and quietly passed his hand over its back. The snow rose all the way to its nostrils, and he bridled it.

Then the wind swept the snow away, but the joyous hunter was holding the bridle with a firm hand; he cracked his whip and departed, as rapid as lightning.

In the meantime, Ulappola, the old blind man was watch-ing; he could have broken the ice of the lake under the horse's feet, but he said to himself:

When one is sure of avenging oneself, one can wait, waiting is pleasant; when beer is good one drinks it in small sips, when bread is white one eats it in small fragments.

IV

"Venerable hostess," said Lemmi Kainen, "here is Hiisi's horse; give me the dove, that I might make her a nest."

"I'll give her to you gladly," the old woman replied. "The reindeer is in the cowshed, the horse is under the hangar, you have paid her price; but if you want to make her the dove of your nest, your immortal companion, it's necessary that she allows her wings to be bound, that she puts her had in yours of her own accord."

And she went to find her daughter, her golden apple and her flowery staff.

"Oh my daughter," she said to her, "my beautiful poem, my cheerful song, don't forget that she who departs for one night must depart forever. If you make a bad choice, you will weep all your life, you will groan every year for having quit your mother's house, the land of your childhood, the hearth of your nurse."

"Stranger," said the virgin, "How did you know that there was a daughter to marry in this house?"

"I was going forth without thinking of anything," the hunter relied, gaily, "when I saw starlings flying in the garden and I said to myself: *There's a daughter to marry in that house*, but as I wasn't in search of a wife, I went to sleep under the elder in the hedge."

"And what did you see in a dream?"

"I saw the stars combing their golden hair and the daughters of the sea braiding their silver hair, but when I awoke at dawn, I saw the smoke rising thickly from the roof and I said to myself: *There's a good housekeeper in that house, who'll wake with the cock every morning.*

"As I had a cousin who wanted to enter a household, I climbed on to the house, I looked through the hole in the roof and I saw a shuttle running over a loom like an ermine between stones, and heard the spindle rattling like a woodpecker between the branches of a beech, and saw the roller spinning as rapidly as a squirrel around a pine. And I said to myself: *There's a skillful weaver in there*."

"And then," said the young woman, "you said to yourself: *I'm looking for a good maidservant...*"

"Then," replied the joyous hunter, "I parted the smoke with my hands and I leaned over in order to see better. I have no need of anyone to light my fire at dawn; I sleep under the snow and I warm my feet in the moonlight. I have no need for anyone to weave me a cloak; the bear is my weaver, the marten my tailor; I have my arrow for a needle and my danger for scissors; but I'm seeking a rose to flower my mouth, and I can see a white rose leaning over the loom..

"Then I said to myself: *For that white rose I shall dig a garden turned toward the sun; around that garden I shall make a hedge of my veins; in that garden I shall hollow out a spring that will never dry up; she will never be cold, she will never be afraid, she will never be thirsty.*"

"Since you only want a wild rose," replied the smiling virgin, "you may pluck her."

Meanwhile, Ulappola, the old blind man, was listening behind the door.

"It's time to brew the barley," he said, "I'm beginning to be thirsty." And, nodding his head, he went to the ford of the river over which it is necessary to pass to return to Kalewala, to the ford of the river Tuoni.

V

The barrel of beer is empty, the fat pig has been eaten, the sated guests are leaving; Lemmi Kainen presses to his breast the white rose of the snows, the gentle teal of the Northern lands. He wants to carry her away; his sleigh is at the door, his horse is shaking the little bells on its collar gaily.

"O my brother, my little brother," says the old hostess, "you have already waited for a long time; wait a little longer. Your beloved is not yet ready, the love of your life is not yet ready to depart; she has only put on one sleeve of her pelisse, it's necessary for her to put on the other."

She kisses her eyelids, and passes a hand over her tresses.

"O my brother, my little brother, you've waited for a long time, wait a little longer; she has only put on one shoe, it's necessary for her to put on the other; she has only put on one glove, it's necessary for her to put on the other."

The joyous hunter smiles, and the virgin hastens to lace her shoe and put on her glove. She still has one foot on the threshold, but she already has one on the sleigh.

"O spouse, my poem, my green stem, adieu!" says the old hostess. "If misfortune touches you, weep into your hand, and when your hand is full, come to weep in your mother's heart. When you come to visit us, our house will be larger than a step, its threshold higher than a beam."

Then the bride lets tears fall into her hand; she sighs:

"Yes, I believed that one was not a woman as long as a mother cared for you, as long as one slept of the bosom of her nurse. I believed that I would be a head taller, and surpass others by an ear when I only had one foot on the paternal threshold and the other in my husband's sleigh. I sighed after that day as after a fecund year, but that days has come and I am weeping."

Then, to console her, the mother says to her: "Don't weep, child; you're not being taken into the mire of a marsh, into the mud of a stream. Your husband is nourished on white bread, and you will eat bread that is whiter still; the dogs do not sleep in his house, he does not lie down on straw; there is an elder wood where he hides his granary, an orchard where his wheat ripens, and when he wants gold he goes into the forest to seek it between the claws of the bear and on the horns of the elk."

She is already sitting in the sleigh; the mother puts her hand on the bridle and says: "Oh, my daughter, listen to my last advice. In your husband's house, let your ear be as fine as that of the mouse, let your feet be as light as those of the hare, let your heart be a flowering plum-tree, let your lips be a honeycomb. Make your pelisse of a single wisp of wool, make beer with a single grain of barley and do the cooking with two sticks of wood.

"And you, my son do not indicate with the whip the route that she ought to follow. She is still only a child, instruct her in your house with the doors closed, and in order to chastise her have nothing but a rush clad in wool.

"Depart with good fortune and come back with peace."

The joyous Lemmi Kainen cracks his whip, and the white horse sets forth.

"I thank you, all of you who live under this roof," the Northern virgin cries again blowing a kiss. "Remain green, moss roof; it will be good to see you again..."

The sleigh disappears in the dust of the road.

VI

They pass in the maple-wood sleigh over snow already softened by the first kiss of spring, between the fir-trees whose branches are blackening, beneath the birches whose buds are swelling.

"You whom I have had so much difficulty in obtaining," says the joyous hunter, "Will be received in my house like the swallow in the months of May; you are awaited there, you will be the robin of the roof, the sparrow of the service tree, the warbler of the hedge."

"Oh, my master, my sweet master," responds the hostess with the dark eyes, "before entering the land where the apples ripen, the plums are velvety and the wheat is maturing, let me bid adieu to the great river that is singing in the desiccated rushes.

"I went to listen to it when I was a girl, when the unknown spoke in my heart; I'd like to know whether its plaint was the echo of amour.

"Oh, my master, my sweet master, let me bid adieu to the swans that ripple it, the beautiful swans of the North, which, wings outspread, resemble white boats on sapphire waves.

"I went to ask them, when I was a girl, for the word that enables amour; today I want to tell them the name that I was seeking."

Under the breath of amour, the joyous hunter was like a cloud under the breath of the wind; before passing over the ford, he stopped his sleigh.

"Hear, my beloved, hear the rushes sing! See, my beloved, see the swans swimming," said the brunette hostess.

"Where you are, I only see you," replied Lemmi Kainen, when he sensed a burn in his heart...

Old Ulappola, the old man with the closed eyes, was waiting by the river, on watch near the ford. Like an arrow he had launched a serpent at Lemmi Kainen's heart. He fell from the sleigh, dead, and the old man pushed him into the river.

Then, the woman who loved started moaning: "River, take me where you are taking him."

And the swan, the beautiful silver swan, said to her: "The great river cradles like a nurse."

"I don't want your body to touch his," said the accursed sorcerer when the Northern virgin plunged like a white gull into the green waves; the weight of his sword will anchor him to the mud of the gulf, while you shall be the foam driven by the wind."

He pronounced the words that he had read by night under the belly of snakes and on the back of toads, and the rose of the North became a wisp of foam over the bottomless gulf.

Part Two

I

Lemmi Kainen's mother is weeping; day and night she repeats:

"He's taking a long time with his request for marriage! Misfortune has overtaken my poor child!"

One evening, on raising her eyes toward the beam, she saw blood dripping from the teeth of the comb and she cried: "Alas, unfortunate mother, alas! Your son is under the weight of misfortune. Is he wandering between the pines of the hill, in the heather of the dunes? Is he on the boundless lakes, in the bottomless marshes? Woe betide the woman who no longer knows where her blood flows, where her flesh stirs!"

She sets forth. Night and day she searches for her lost son; in winter and summer she calls to him. In winter she travels on snowshoes; in summer she sails in her boat. She runs like a wolf in the great woods, like an otter in the deep water, like a squirrel in the branches of pines, like a weasel in heaps of stones. She searches the branches, she rummage in the grass, she digs down to the roots of the heather.

A road opens before her; she greets it and says to it: "O road created by God, have you seen my son?"

The road responds to her in a shrill voice: "I haven't seen your son, I haven't heard the sound of his footsteps. Perhaps the poor fellow has been trapped by a spell in the fiery plans of Hiisi."

The disconsolate mother rummages in the grass, digs down to the roots of the heather and parts the stubble, but she does not find her son.

Ahead of her the moon rises; she greets it and says to it: "O moon created by God, have you seen my son?"

The moon replies, sagely: "I haven't seen your son, I haven't heard the sound of his footsteps. Perhaps the poor fellow is buried under a block of ice, under a shroud of snow."

The disconsolate mother digs down to the roots of the heather, parts the stubble and tears up the moss, but she does not find her son.

Ahead of her, the sun rises; she greets it and says to it: "O sun created by God, have you seen my son?"

The sun replies to her in a soft voice: "Your unfortunate son is in the black river Tuoni, in the abyss of death. Death had struck him with her sword; she has made a clod of turf with his head, the branches of a willow with his feet, a putrid root with his flesh, a water-lentil with his eyes and a bundle of straw with his hair."

Then Lemmi Kainen's mother goes to the smithy.

"O my brother laborer," she says to him, "forge me a rake with teeth a hundred aunes long and a haft two hundred aunes long."

When Lemmi Kainen had felt his body falling to pieces in the abyss, he said to himself:

"Since the evil is without remedy, it's necessary to reconcile oneself; I had engraved on my breastplate the word that softens the claws of bears and the word that breaks the tips of arrows, I didn't engrave the one that stops snakes, because I thought I'd always be able to crush them under my heel. Lemmi Kainen, you're no longer the joyous hunter, what will you be tomorrow?

"Adieu, my body, you were a worthy servant, ever ready to march; you weren't demanding either for drink or nourishment; I'd like to find your peer where I'm going.

"You're already no more than a clod of turf bearing a mallard's clutch; you're no longer anything but a willow branch balancing a nightingale's nest; you're no longer anything but a rotten root shining in the night to illuminate the hunter's path; you're no longer anything but a water-lentil, marking the place where a sing wells up in the marsh; you're no longer anything but a bundle of straw, rendering strength to an unharnessed horse.

"Adieu, my body; it's too cold in this green water."

His soul was about to depart for the land where the sun never sets when he saw a white gull plunge into the waves.

"Your body will repose next to mine," he said then, "dear friend of my dead youth, and our two souls will go together into the flowery wood where the roses are eternal. Close your eyes quickly, in order that your soul can open its wings; stop the beating of your heart quickly, in order that it can escape its cage."

But he no longer saw anything but a wisp of foam floating on the eddies of the gulf; the sorcerer pronounced the accursed words; the rose of the North, the rose of the snows, was no longer anything but a mirror for dragonflies, a sleigh for mosquitoes.

"I don't want," he said, "to leave you alone in that green water; I want to dwell there with you."

He was seeking a means of not quitting the wisp of foam, the iridescent bubble, when he saw a salmon passing by.

"Where are you going?" he said to it.

"I'm going to the sea," replied the salmon. "When I've gone there, I'll come back, in order to return tomorrow. I come and go without ever stopping."

"Great salmon," he said, "will you give me a little place in your gill; I know beautiful songs and I'll sing them in your ear."

"Gladly," replied the salmon. "I'm still deafened by the din of the waterfalls when I hear the waves roar; you can put the wax of your song into my ear."

He is in the gill of the salmon, but while singing he leans out, he leans on a fin and, instead of going straight ahead, the great fish circles, without being able to quit the whirlpool in which the iridescent bubble is floating.

"I'm thirsty for salt water," cries the great fish. "Go away, accursed singer."

"It's not for you that I'm singing," he replies, it's for the one who was a white rose, for the iridescent bubble shining like a spark."

II

As soon as the laborer had forged the rake, the disconsolate mother borrowed the plumage of the jay and the wings of the skylark, and flew without stopping to the river of Tuoni, to the gulf of death.

There she went into the water ankle-deep and dragged her rake three times in the abyss; the third time, she drew out a bundle of straw.

"This, then," she said, "is the hair that I combed, the blonde curls that I loved to roll beneath my fingers."

But there were water-lentils on the haft.

"I recognize my child's eyes," she said, "his beautiful green eyes, his beautiful bright eyes, which had the color of the wave when it rolls over a beach of golden sand."

She went into the water knee-deep and dragged her rake three times in the abyss; the third time, she drew out a clump of roots.

"This, then," she said, "is the flesh of my flesh, which my milk made as firm as a beet, as pink as an apple."

But the clump was bound by a willow branch, on which two leaves had sprouted.

"I recognize my child's feet," she said, "The two feet that I warmed in my hands when he was asleep in his cradle, the two little feet that resembled two flowers of a plum-tree."

She went into the water waist-deep and ragged her rake in the abyss three times; the third time, she drew out a clod of turf.

"This, then," she said, is the head that laughed at me, there are the lips that dried up my tears."

She gathered together everything she had drawn out of the abyss and remade the body of the child she had laid upon her knees.

"Mother," the crow said to her, "You cannot make a man out of a drowned body. A dead hero is only rotting flesh; throw it in the river."

"What I have done once, can I not do again?" replied the disconsolate woman. And she warmed the cold flesh on her bosom, and closed the wounds with her lips, and opened a vein in order to give blood back to the empty veins.

She saw the veins turn blue, saw the skin grow back over the wounds, felt the body warm up, and she cried: "Ah! If I could only find my child's soul! If I could only recover the butterfly that the flower of a kiss had settled on my heart, I could remake something from nothing. I would have done again what I have done before."

She went into the water shoulder-deep and dragged her rake three times in the abyss; the third time, she brought out a salmon. The soul hidden in the gill escaped and entered into the body from which death had expelled it.

"O my mother, my dear mother," said the joyous Lemmi Kainen, "my body was asleep in that green water, but my soul was dreaming there. While drawing your rake in the abyss, did you see a wisp of foam on the whirlpool?"

"Yes, my son, my handsome child, I saw an iridescent bubble on the whirlpool; the haft of my rake pushed it, and it departed on the stream for the ocean."

"My tender mother, my dear mother, it would perhaps have been better for me if you had left me in the green water," replied the joyous hunter.

III

One morning, Lemmi Kainen said: "Mother, give me my breastplate and my weapons."

"What are you going to do, my son. You were laboring this morning and you've stopped in mid-furrow; the sun has not yet risen and the blood-thirst has gripped you; what's the matter, my son?"

"I want to return to Lapland; their beer was good, I want to drink some more."

"One is often poorly received, my son, when one is not invited.

"The dog goes where it is summoned, but a man marches and goes forth. Give me my weapons, Mother; the invitation is written on the tip of my sword.

The poisoned arrow of the accursed sorcerer, thought the anxious mother, *has bitten my son in the heart, and the venom has remained in the wound. There are no longer any fresh lips to suck that dolorous wound; that is why my poor child is sad. A venomous bramble is growing in his heart as if in a hedge; beside the embalmed thorn there is a poison that can kill.*

Lemmi Kainen has not heeded his mother; he has marched by day and by night; he is on the threshold of the festival hall.

"The noble guests have been invited," he said, "but the noblest has not been invited."

"Lemmi Kainen," replied the host, "the table is full; another guest would inconvenience the rest."

"Then it's necessary to make room," said the joyous hunter, drawing his sword. Let's measure our blades, and the one whose sword is the longest will strike the first blow."

The swords were measured; the host's was the longer by the thickness of a grain of barley, the thickness of the black stripe under a fingernail.

"Strike first," said the joyous Lemmi Kainen

The host lifted his sword, but it collided with the beam.

"Let's go outside," said Lemmi Kainen. "Blood stains the floor and soils the benches; on the snow, red blood is no longer red."

They went out; the host struck once, twice, three times; he did not even brush the skin of Lemmi Kainen. Then the hero raised his sword and at the first stroke he severed the head of the Lapp.

In the courtyard there were stakes surmounted with human heads; only one had no head. Lemmi Kainen fixed to it the one he had just cut off.

In the meantime, however, the guests had drawn their swords and they rushed upon him.

"This is what I wanted," said the joyous hunter; "I have a fire burning in my heart, it's necessary that I put it out; I have a wound in my heart that rosy lips cannot suck; it's necessary that the blue lip of the sword sucks the poisoned wound."

The combat lasted until the end of the day, and not one sword was able to bite Lemmi Kainen.

He returned, head bowed, to his mother's house.

"My nurse, my good mother," he said, "put butter, flour and pork in a sack; I'm going to go far away; I want to flee myself. Where is it necessary to go, dear mother, to hide my crime? I have killed my host with a sword."

"I don't know where to tell you to go, my son," replied the sage hostess. "In order to forget, it would be necessary to go where your shadow cannot follow you; that would be too far. It's necessary to put between it and you a leafy jumper bush and a service tree laden with fruit, and yesterday's sun will no longer cast its shadow on tomorrow's path. I know a young woman as supple as a juniper, her lips shine like sorbs, which become soft when one keeps them on the beam, or on the tablet of the hearth."

"No, my mother, no; there was nothing in my heart but a little clod of earth, exactly enough to plant a rose-bush; death has torn away the rose-bush, and the entire earth has remained attached to the roots. Adieu, Mother; I'm going wherever my boat takes me."

His boat took him into an azure grotto where the daughters of the sea were dancing in the sand. Perhaps there were two hundred, and every time they laughed, pearls fell from their lips and rolled over their ivory breasts like dewdrops.

"There you are, Lemmi Kainen the handsome hunter," they said. "Come, you'll forget your troubles." And they extended their arms toward him, their white arms circled with amethyst.

"Come," they said, "We have houses of crystal and amber, in which the beams are coral, where hydromel foams in nacreous shells; come, our tresses are harps that sing songs of amour."

"Have you, beauties," relied Lemmi Kainen, "seen a wisp of foam floating over the waves?"

"Perhaps we've seen it, we've often seen it, that crazy foam pushed by the wind," said the daughters of the sea, knotting their round dance again.

"In my maple-wood sleigh," replied Lemmi Kainen, "she was, beauties, more beautiful than you, that iridescent foam that rotated over the gulf where my soul sang. I left my gaiety in a curl of her hair. On my boat pushed by the wind I am not like seaweed floating without roots, like a broken pine-cone tossed by the waves.

"Man is born for dolor; I, to whom my mother has twice given life, am twice as unfortunate as other men."

"With us, you'll forget your trouble," said the daughters of the waves. "Our arms are whiter than moonbeams, softer than the necks of swans; our lips are fresher than woodland strawberries, redder than service-tree berries."

There was only one radiance in my heart, just warm enough to enable a rose to blossom; the rose opened; the rose faded, and now my heart is frozen. Adieu, daughters of the waves."

IV

Floating at hazard, the boat groaned; "What am I good for? Why have I been nailed?"

"Don't weep without reason," said Lemmi Kainen. "I know why I weep, and yet I'm wrong to weep; every evil has its remedy. The remedy for sadness is the song of swords; when their blue tongues lash out, one no longer hears the heart speak. I shall go in search of another man, a man who wants to be the companion of Lemmi Kainen, and when you return to port you will be red, gray boat."

He takes the tiller and steers the boat to where Tiera, the companion of his childhood, is fishing.

Tiera's father is outside the door, carving the handle of an ax; his mother is on the threshold, turning a churn; his brothers are in the courtyard, repairing a sleigh; his sisters are at the river, washing the linen. They all say to him: "Tiera does not have time to go to war; he got married this morning."

But Tiera was in the house; he has overheard. Without speaking, he picks up his spear, goes out by the back door and comes to sit down in Lemmi Kainen's boat.

The boat flies over the crests of the waves; like two falcons, they hunt along the coasts of Lapland, in the mouths of the rivers that carry polar icebergs. Their claws are sharp; there are silver necklaces and golden rings in the boat; their swords have no slept in their scabbards; the boat, gray yesterday, is red today.

"Let's return to port," says Tiera. "Winter is imminent and our hands are full."

"I'll give you my share," Lemmi Kainen responds. "What do you expect me to do with it? No one is waiting for me. I'll only keep one ring, the most beautiful, for my old mother who is spinning with her distaff, alone by the fireside. The poor old woman had put her youth into songs to lull her grandchildren; leaning over a cradle, she will not see the days of her youth again; the cradle will always be empty in the hearth of Lemmi Kainen.

"You've left a wife of the morning back there; the winter is here, she'll be cold by night; adieu Tiera, my companion. For myself, I'm awaiting the winter as the bush awaits the spring; perhaps the snow will extinguish the fire that is burning me, and perhaps the frost will put flowers on the desiccated bush that pricks me today in the place of the heart.

"Here is the winter; it imprisons the cauldron on the hearth, the bucket in the well, the hands of young women in the dough. Here is the evil bird with steel claws; it shakes the feathers of its wings and white down covers the roads; it shakes the feathers of its tail, and gray down hides the stray smoke of the roof."

Lemmi Kainen is alone in his boat; the hard waves squeeze it; it groans:

"I had feet like a duck, beautiful yellow feet, which beat the water in cadence; now they're trapped by the ice."

"Boat," Lemmi Kainen replies, "Don't weep without reason; I'll trim your feet and you'll run faster."

He detaches the boat from the claw of the cold and sets it upright on its keel; he makes four stays from two oars, orientates the sail, and the boat becomes a sleigh to which the wind is harnessed.

Now it glides around gulfs and along straits, and Lemmi Kainen, in order to pass the time, makes a harp of his dolor.

V

I'm beaten on land, I'm beaten on the water, Lemmi Kainen said to himself when the thaw came, *and tomorrow no one will know my name. When this ring is worn away, who will know that I took it at sword-point? When the head of the host has rotted away, who will know that I cut it off?*

Then he saw Wainamoinen,[25] who extracted the world from an eagle's egg, coming toward him in an antique boat, and his brother Ilmarinnen, who forged the lid of the sky, in which the marks made by the hammer and the bite of the pincers cannot be seen.

"Joyous hunter," the god without malice said to him. "We're going to Lapland to recover the mill that Ilmarinnen forged at the time of his betrothal, the mill that can grind everything that has been created, and which separates the flour from the bran of everything; do you want to come with us?"

---

[25] This is the manner in which the name more usually rendered as Vainamoinen is given by Léouzon Le Duc.

By doing that, thought Lemmi Kainen, *I'd engrave my name alongside those of the gods, on a stone that time won't erode.*

And he allowed the waves to carry away his boat and sat down on the rowers' bench in Wainamoinen's boat.

They were going Northwards when the boat suddenly stopped on the back of a pike. Lemmi Kainen plunged his sword into the water and agitated it under the keel, but the sword broke and the boat was not disengaged. Ilmarinnen tried and was no more fortunate; then Wainamoinen cut the pike in two with a single thrust and threw the head into the boat.

"A pike's head is good for nothing," said Lemmi Kainen.

The god without malice smiled; from the bottom of the boat he took a log of plum-wood and a fir-wood plank; he hollowed out the log with his sword, thinned down the plank, and fixed them together with the pike's teeth.

"What's that?" said Lemmi Kainen. "If it's a churn, why have you given it such a long handle?"

The god without malice smiled. He plunged the largest of the pike's teeth into the case, and five others into the shaft, and he stretched five of his hairs over the ivory pegs.

"What's that?" said Lemmi Kainen, passing his fingers through his hair. "What's that? One might think one were about to hear doors grating whose hinges hadn't been oiled."

Then the great and ancient Wainamoinen leaned the kantele on his breast and made the strings resonate.[26]

At those chords, the wolf quit the marsh and the bear the cavern, the eagle descended from the cloud, the seagull rose from the wave, and the warblers and the finches came to settle on the divine singer's shoulders.

And all the eyes that were gazing wept soft tears; and the strings quivered so sweetly under his fingers that the divine singer started to weep, like those who were listening. Over his white beard, over his broad breast, the tears slid, more numer-

---

[26] The traditional Finnish kantele is a kind of "box zither" related to the Russian gusli.

311

ous than the berries of myrtles on a hill, than the heads of swallows around a fir-tree, than the eggs of grouse on a heath; they rolled all the way to the ground, made a river at his feet, and changed into pearls when they fell into the sea.

"On the land and on the water, in Heaven and in Hell," said Lemmi Kainen, "all angers must be calmed, all chagrins forgotten, all flames extinguished; my heart is turning green like the grass, flowering like the plum-tree."

VI

Lemmi Kainen has torn up the rock in which the mill was sealed which separated what is good from what is bad, and the ancient Wainamoinen, to pay him for his trouble, had given him the kantele.

But will he be able to draw the sounds from it that the divine singer drew?

The case is plum-wood, thinks Lemmi Kainen, *the table is fir-wood, why would the case have forgotten the song of warblers? Why should the table not remember the twittering of sparrows?*

"The pegs are made of pike's teeth, thinks Lemmi Kainen, *the strings are five of the Creator's hairs. Why would the pegs have forgotten the murmur of the waves? why should the strings not remember what the stars sad when they called to one another in the silence of the heavens?*

He sat down on a rock overlooking the sea under a pine tree sheared by the wind, he took the kantele on his knees and he said to it:

"I'm only a soldier, I'd redden your strings if I touched them; if I tried to turn your pegs I'd break them; they're not as hard as the ribs of a bear; if I supported the table against my breast I'd blacken; my heart is no longer anything but charcoal; if I played with your case, I'd spoil it, I'm still only a child. Vibrate alone, then, in the breath or the orchard, the breath of the hill, the salty breath of the waves, the fiery breath of the skies."

312

And the kantele resonated on the polished rock, under the topless pine, and the fisherman stopped his boat, and the laborer stopped his low, and the young woman thought she could hear the first beat of her heart, and the young mother thought she saw her nursling's first smile.

It sang the beauties of blonde Finland, the sinuous straits, the great tranquil lakes from which the waterfalls leap recklessly, and the fir-woods that flow over the hills like green rivers, and the silver birches that resemble their foam, and the shiny elders that resemble their rocks.

And blonde Finland, like a white hind, gests up smiling from her bed of arbutus. Her eyes are as bright as the wave, as brilliant as the spray; her breath has the perfume of honey and her voice the rustle of the wings of blue butterflies.

What my mother has done, why should I not do? thought Lemmi Kainen; *while the words fell from her lips, while the strings sang under her fingers, my body was in pieces in the depths of the abyss; with her love she reconnected the scattered fragments; why, with my amour, should I not render life to the one that death has taken from me?*

She was half of my soul, half of my heart; if I remade her severed wing with my soul, if I remade her severed head with my heart, I would have remade what death has taken from me, I would have rendered life to my beloved.

And he sang until sunset, until moonrise; and the valleys rose up and the hills were lowered, and the mountains trembled, and the rocks began to vibrate. The pines shivered with joy on the heath and the shingle danced on the beach.

Then the one who had got up, like a white hind, from her bed of arbutus, leaned toward the inspired bard, smiling.

"I was nothing but foam on the shore," she said; "do you recognize me, Lemmi Kainen?"

VII

Before her hearth, beside the cradle always empty, the venerable hostess moans: "The village awaits the new moon, the people await the sunrise, the children await the strawberries, but I am only waiting for my son."

She has been waiting for him through winters and summers, since the day when he mounted his boat.

"I was waiting yesterday," she sighs, "I am waiting today, perhaps tomorrow I shall no longer be waiting; is there a tomorrow for heads that are tottering? Mirror of my youth, where are you? You to whom I have twice given life, where are you?

"By your fire, I am no longer anything but a brand about to be extinguished; under your roof, I am no longer anything but a beam that is about to break; when you return you will find a fox lying in the embers, an owl nesting under the roof."

She hears the sound of a sleigh on the paved road; by leaning on the walls she goes as far as the door.

"It's him!" she cries, and her hands tremble like dry leaves. "It's him! Rejoice, windows, you are about to see him; bow down, threshold, he's about to enter; foam, beer, he's about to drink you.

"Oh, my son, my beautiful child, you have finally come back from the cold country; the apple-trees are in flower in the orchard, and you have snow on your beard."

"My good mother, my dear little mother, this is not snow that is whitening my beard; since I quit you I have been wandering for ten years on the waves, I have been dreaming for ten years on a rock; I spent ten years going, and ten years coming back."

Then the poor old woman starts moaning:

"Twice you have dried up my teats, twice you have drunk my blood, and you will not give me a nursling to rock, and you will not give me pretty red lips to refresh my desiccated lips."

"Poor dear mother, weep no more; I have found my bride again; she will sit down beside you on the bench of the hearth, under the linden of the door."

"Pantry, open up." says the mother, "the mistress is coming; cowshed, open up, the mistress is coming. Can you hear the cattle bellowing, and the ewes bleating."

"Yes, Mother," replies the joyous Lemmi Kainen, "I can hear the ewes bleating, they know her; I can hear the cattle bellowing, they love her already.

"Sit down, Mother, bear the bark cradle; I will show you my dove, my eternal companion."

Then the bard sits down by the fireside. He makes the kantele sing. And the old mother thinks that she can see the one who stood up like white hand come in smiling; he sings again, and the aged mother thinks she can see a child in the bark cradle.

For winters and summers, at all hearths, Lemmi Kainen has been singing to his blonde bride, and while he sings, the young and the old think they can see Finland, like a white hind, get up smiling from her bed of arbutus.

Amour has made of the joyous hunter an inspired bard.

315